C000016970

H L DANIEL

PASSAGE *of* LOVE

WHEN THE PATH TO HAPPINESS MEANS
CONQUERING A HAUNTED PAST

H L DANIEL

PASSAGE *of* LOVE

WHEN THE PATH TO HAPPINESS MEANS
CONQUERING A HAUNTED PAST

MEREO
Cirencester

Published by Mereo

1A The Market Place Cirencester Gloucestershire GL7 2PR
info@memoirsbooks.co.uk | www.memoirspublishing.com

PASSAGE OF LOVE

All Rights Reserved. Copyright ©H L Daniel

No part of this book may be reproduced or transmitted in any form or
by any means, graphic, electronic, or mechanical, including
photocopying, recording, taping or by any information storage or
retrieval system, without the permission in writing from the copyright
holder. The right of H L Daniel to be identified as the author of this
work has been asserted in accordance with the Copyright, Designs
and Patents Act 1988 sections 77 and 78.

The views expressed in this work are solely those of the author and do
not necessarily reflect the views of the publisher, and the publisher
hereby disclaims any responsibility for them.

ISBN: 978-1-86151-136-2

For KD
Unfazed by the craziness, you continue to be my love,
my rock and my life's partner.

CHAPTER ONE

In the land of plains and low plateaus covered by rain forests in the west and Lake Volta in the east, Ghana, formerly known as the Gold Coast, was thriving, thanks to its natural resources, including gold, bauxite, aluminium, timber, cocoa and oil.

It was July 1974. Brilliant sunshine and the refreshing sea breeze made the weather pleasantly warm. Workers hurried along the busy streets of Accra while tourists lay lazily on the beaches tanning their skin. Children run around merrily building sandcastles and playing on the canoes.

Kamil had been in the office since 6 am. As one of the country's top barristers and an adviser to the president his workload had increased drastically, but he loved serving his motherland and carried on diligently. The long hours and assignments around the world at very short notice were irritating his wife, Araba. Even his daughter, Zhara, had started complaining that he was always working. He loved them dearly but he was passionate about his work and hoped to make it up to them.

As exactly 6 pm Kamil left the office and made his way home. It was much earlier than usual but he'd vowed to have dinner with his daughter while her mother was away on business, and he was determined to keep that promise.

Kamil was reading the *Ghanaian Times* when Zhara came down the spiral staircase. She looked adorable in a frilly white nightgown, with dark curly hair all over her cute little face. She'd left after dinner to finish her latest book, Chinua Achebe's *Things Fall Apart*, and he assumed she had fallen asleep.

"Daddy, I forgot to give you this." She handed him a letter.

He kissed her. "Good night princess, sweet dreams."

She rubbed her sleepy eyes. "Good night, daddy."

Kamil opened the letter, read it and decided to call Araba. It was 9:15 pm in Accra and around 4:15 pm in New York.

"Room 137, please" he said when the receptionist answered the phone.

"One moment, sir."

"Hello?"

"Hi darling, it's so good to hear your voice."

"Yes honey. I'm so glad you answered. I thought you might still be at the conference."

"We wrapped up at 3 pm. Is everything OK?"

"Oh yes! Zhara has done it again. She has been promoted from Class 5 to Upper 6, but that is not all. She has been awarded a prize for gaining top marks in English Language, European and African History and English Literature."

"Really! Is she there?"

"No honey, she's gone to bed."

"Aaaahhhh! How has she been?"

"Fine, but I can tell she is missing you."

"I miss her too. When will she receive the prize?"

"Hold on, let me check. The prize-giving ceremony is on Friday. Can you make it?"

"I wouldn't miss it for the world. We're nearly done here. I'll book the night flight home. I miss you so much."

"Me too, my dear."

"I love you."

"I love you more!"

Kamil hung up the phone. He was delighted that Araba would be home in four days.

CHAPTER TWO

Kamil left home at 6:30 am on Thursday morning. He was in high spirits and couldn't wait to pick up Araba from the airport that evening.

He had just returned to the office from the High Court when his assistant put the call through to him.

"Sir, the operator is on the line. You have a call from London."

"Hello?"

"I have your wife on the line."

"Thank you. Put her through."

"Darling..."

"Hi honey, are you all right?"

"Can you believe it? The flight from New York was delayed by two hours and by the time I reached here it was too late to make the connecting flight to Accra. Damn!"

"It is frustrating, but it's not the end of the world. When's the next flight?"

"Tomorrow morning. But it means I will be stuck here for 24 hours when I could have been home with you. Most importantly, I will miss my baby's prize-giving ceremony. Oh no!" she cried. "I really, really, really wanted to be there!"

"Don't worry my dear, I'll be here and she will

understand that it could not be helped. Take a deep breath and hit the shops. I am sure the retail therapy will do you lots of good. We shall tell you all about the ceremony when we pick you up on Saturday. I miss you honey."

"I miss you too, terribly."

"See you soon." He hung up the phone and stared blankly at the wall.

Kamil put the papers he'd been working on in his briefcase. It was just after six o'clock in the evening. He was about to shut the door behind him when he heard the phone. Wondering who might be calling, he turned around and went back in.

"Hello?" He said.

"Good evening sir."

He recognized the high-pitched, authoritative voice instantly. It was none other than the president's private secretary.

"Good evening, Winifred. How are you?" he said, hoping she would be quick.

"I am very well, sir. A United Nations delegation has just arrived from Geneva and all senior members of the cabinet are to attend a briefing with the President tomorrow morning at 8 am prompt. A meeting with the delegates is scheduled for 10 am at Osu Castle. This will be followed by a press conference at noon and lunch at the Ambassador Hotel. I hope you can make it." It was an order, not a question. She paused for a response.

"Of course, Winifred, I will be there."

He hung up the phone and hurried out of the building. How could he be in two places at the same time, he thought. He could not afford to miss any of the meetings but then Zhara's prize giving ceremony was equally important.

That night, after much tossing and turning, Kamil came up with a plan which he hoped would solve his dilemma.

CHAPTER THREE

Zhara stood behind the stage, waiting to be called. She was a pretty girl with big brown eyes. She looked immaculate in a green pinafore and white shirt with dainty white socks peeping out of her black leather shoes.

From the corner of her eyes she saw Sister Mary Lorraine, the head teacher, moving swiftly towards her. Even though she was not slouching, she did not wish to face the nun's wrath, so she stood upright, nose pointed upwards, chest out, and tummy and bottom tucked in.

"Zhara, your father just called" the nun said hurriedly. Her cheeks appeared flushed, possibly due to rushing around or the hot weather. "He hopes to be here soon." She paused to catch her breath. "Oh yes, he said the traffic is dreadful. I wouldn't hold my breath if I were you".

"Thank you, Sister," Zhara said, grinning politely.

Suddenly she heard her name. She climbed the stage and was greeted with raucous applause.

The headmistress, Sister Lucinda, gave Zhara a dazzling smile and presented her with the three medals for gaining the highest mark in three subjects.

Zhara curtsied and smiled delightfully. She scanned the audience for her father but could not find him.

Suddenly she saw Kukuwa, her best friend, grinning like a Cheshire cat with her chest purposefully puffed out. Seeing her clapping with all her strength made Zhara glow with affection.

Kukuwa continued clapping even after Zhara had left the stage. A deadly glare from Sister Mary Lorraine sent Kukuwa's arms crashing to her side.

Zhara walked briskly to her classroom, long braids swaying from the place on her neck where the smooth chocolate flesh met the starched white collar of her shirt.

Now nine, she had begun kindergarten at the Catholic school a week after her fourth birthday. She'd had a traumatic experience at her previous school when the headmaster had shaved off her hair after a sudden bout of insanity. The incident had made her very introverted and weary of people.

The mixed Catholic primary school was much larger than her previous school, but with the care and kindness of her class teacher, Mrs Crentsil, she was able to settle in. Most of the teachers grew fond of her because she looked smart, was attentive in class and had impeccable manners. Her shyness and reluctance to mix with other kids concerned the teachers, but they hoped she would grow out of it.

At break time she would rush to the library in search of books to read. Her favourite authors were Maya Angelou, Shakespeare, Barbara Cartland and Chinua Achebe. By the age of nine she'd read Jane Eyre, Black Beauty, Alice in Wonderland, Oliver Twist and nearly all the Kweku Anansi stories. Through reading she could escape into a different world and leave her fears behind.

Kukuwa had been looking for Zhara. "There you are!" She cried, delighted to have finally found her. "Your driver is waiting for you. Are you coming?"

Zhara nodded.

Kukuwa noticed the tears. "Are you OK?"

Zhara inhaled deeply, then she pouted. "My daddy isn't here. He promised. He said he would come!" She sniffed loudly.

Kukuwa put her arm around Zhara. "Don't cry" she said, as they walked towards the car park. "Today should be your happiest day, you've done so well. Don't be sad, I am sure there is a good reason why your father is not here."

The girls had been friends since their second term in kindergarten. Before that they had barely known each other. It had been just after eleven in the morning. The girls were both four, about the same weight and height and almost identical. Sister Margaret, the maths teacher, had seen Kukuwa under the cocoa tree. Assuming she was Zhara, the nun bounded out of the classroom and yelled, "Zhaaa-raa! Come here immediately! You should be on the playground with your mates, not all alone under the tree!"

Kukuwa had heard Sister Margaret, but hadn't realised she was talking to her, so she watched the nun lunging towards her with a cane. Sweat poured from the nun's brow onto her reddened cheeks as she huffed and puffed. A few steps away from Kukuwa, Sister Margaret had seen another child coming towards her. "Please Lord, it cannot be!'" she had screamed. Convinced she was seeing the same child twice, she had dropped the cane and run to her classroom.

Kukuwa had been puzzled by the teacher's peculiar behaviour and began laughing lightly. Zhara joined the infectious laugh. Unable to stop themselves, the girls had laughed so much that their bellies hurt. Together they sprinted to the playground, jumped on the swings and aimed for the skies. A strong bond had begun between the four year old girls who never spoke unless spoken to.

Zhara was still moping when the driver pulled into her house. Swinging out of the back seat, she slammed the door and strode towards the front door. Just as she turned the knob she heard a voice behind her. She whirled around and screamed, "Daddy, Daddy, Daddy!" Charging towards him, she leapt into his arms, holding on tightly to the medals.

Kamil kissed her cheeks and put her back on her feet. "Ah, what have we here?" he said, pointing at the three medals.

"Daddy," she said excitedly, "this is for gaining the highest marks in English Literature, this is for African and European History and this is for English Language."

"They are beautiful!" said Kamil. He was running his fingers along the centre of the medals, where her name had been engraved, when she remembered that she was supposed to be angry with him.

"Daddy, why didn't you come? You promised!" she scowled.

"I am so sorry, my princess. I left the hotel at 1 pm, hoping an hour would be plenty of time to get to your school. If I'd known how bad the traffic was, I would have left earlier. It usually takes about 30 minutes to get to your school from Osu but it took two and a half hours today. Can you believe it? I was stuck at Kwame Nkrumah Circle for two hours."

"Sister Mary Lorraine said you were stuck in traffic but I lost hope when she said she wouldn't hold her breath, if she was me. Daddy, you should have been there! It was not the same without you and mummy."

"I know darling, we both wanted to be with you today." He opened the door and walked with her to the living room. He put his briefcase on the floor, sat down and sat her on his lap. What I want you to learn is that we don't always get what we want in life, but we should always give thanks to the Almighty, and be grateful for what we have." He took her hand in his. "You must never forget that your mother and I love you very very much. We thank God that he has given us an exemplary daughter who is healthy, smart, beautiful and excels at everything she puts her mind to. Princess, we are very proud of you. Are we forgiven?"

Zhara put her hand on her hip. "Yes, Daddy." Then she grinned cheekily. "Can we go to the zoo?"

"Certainly. We could even pass by the bumper cars. Would you like that?"

"Yes Daddy, I would love that very much." She giggled.

He kissed her forehead. "Then we could stop by Mandarin for dinner."

The mention of her favourite Chinese restaurant made Zhara's eyes sparkle. She threw her arms around her father. "I love you Daddy. You are the best!"

CHAPTER FOUR

Armed with presents, guests started arriving at 2 pm on the beautiful August day. By 3 pm the house was packed with friends, relations and well-wishers. They had come to celebrate Zhara's eleventh birthday and the completion of her parent's new house.

Girls in pretty dresses and smartly dressed boys danced, played and enjoyed an assortment of refreshments whilst their parents and other adults ate, drunk and chatted.

At 7 pm everyone gathered in the front porch and sang Happy Birthday to Zhara. She blew the candles and cut a piece of the gateau for each of her guests. An hour later, as more adults were arriving the children departed with their goody bags.

At 9 pm, Zhara kissed her parents and dashed to her room to open her presents. She tried to sleep at 10 pm, but the excitement made it impossible. After hours of tossing and turning she lay on her back and stared at the ceiling. The sound of loud music, laughter and chattering brought a smile to her lips. She'd noticed her parents cuddling at the party. They seemed more in love than ever, and had been jubilantly counting down the days to the move to their dream home. She could not believe how quickly the massive concrete structure surrounded by scaffolding and building materials had been transformed into a luxurious six-bedroom oceanfront mansion. And in exactly six days she would be off to boarding school and bidding farewell to the three-bedroom bungalow she'd called home for most of her life.

Zhara looked forward to moving into the new house, but she knew she would miss the vibrant community with its market complex, the Presbyterian Church, the best kelewele (small slices of fried plantain) at the stall near Mother's Inn, and the friends she had grown up with, especially her pal, Tamali, and her first ever crush, Anokye.

As she gazed at the dark shadows around her tiny bedroom she flashed back to when Tamali and her family moved into the large storey building opposite her house. Before their arrival there had been a lot of talk about the five-foot businessman and his seven-foot wife who were returning from Germany with their son and daughter. Unlike her older brother who kept to himself, seven-year-old Tamali was a handful. Ebony-coloured and lanky with beautiful green eyes, she enjoyed playing with the area boys. They would climb trees, ride their bikes frighteningly fast and fight each other. Tamali was rumoured to floor most of the boys and wasn't to be toyed with.

She'd been living opposite Zhara for about a month when she decided to get acquainted with her six-year-old neighbour who never came out to play. Wearing her brother's T-shirt and shorts, Tamali had climbed Zhara's wall and peered into the house. Zhara was playing contentedly with her dolls under the mango tree. Glaring at the prim-and-proper girlie girl in a lemon frilly dress with yellow, green and white ribbons in her long twisted curls, Tamali yelled.

"Hi! Can I play with you?"

Zhara looked suspiciously at the tomboy with a short afro hairstyle, but said nothing.

"My name is Tamali. Can I play with you?" She persisted.

Zhara shrugged, "OK."

With a broad toothy grin Tamali jumped down and scuttled across the lawn towards Zhara.

"Hi," Zhara said quietly. "Sasha, say hello to Tamali" she whispered, lifting the cappuccino-coloured doll with red lips, huge brown eyes, long lashes and thick curly hair. Then she raised the slender porcelain doll with long blond hair and baby blue eyes "Barbie, say hello to Tamali."

Tamali sat beside Zhara.

"Who would you like to play with?" asked Zhara.

Tamali hadn't been keen on either of the dolls, but she'd found Sasha's bright orange hot pants rather amusing, so she took her. Within a few minutes Tamali had abandoned Sasha and was up the mango tree shaking down the fruits. She jumped down, gave half the fruits to Zhara and devoured the rest. Zhara had been amazed at how quickly Tamali scoffed down the fruits. They played hide and seek, bottle-tops, ampe (a girls' game with jumping and clapping). Though complete opposites, they seemed to enjoy each other's company and became firm friends.

The quest for adventure, which was usually instigated by Tamali, grew as the girls got older. Zhara's love for fruits and Tamali's passion for danger led them to a farm many miles away from home during the Easter holiday. Zhara was nine and Tamali ten at the time. They had not intended to ride their bikes that far but were blown over by the abundance of fruit on the farm. There were guava trees, papaya trees, banana trees, coconut trees and yoyi (velvet tamarind) trees. Also on the farm were geckos, lizards, snakes, scorpions and giant ants. Tamali was undeterred by the creepy crawlies but Zhara was petrified even though she yearned for some of the yoyi, the tastiest fruit she'd ever eaten. While Zhara remained on her bike at the edge of the farm, a good distance away from any danger, Tamali took off her T-shirt, grabbed a long stick and run around the farm plucking as much fruit as she could carry.

Zhara smiled when she remembered their silly spitting contests. When no cars were coming they would stand on one side of the road and spit, aiming it to go beyond the road to the pavement on the other side of the road. Zhara had never managed to make it all the way, but Tamali rarely missed. She is truly unique, Zhara thought. She laughed out loud when she remembered Tamali's mum's moan that she wished her daughter would behave like a girl and stop wearing her brother's clothes.

The clock read 3:15 am, yet the party was still going on. Zhara was feeling thirsty, so she nipped into the kitchen for a drink. She ended up with a bottle of muscatella and a thick slice of cake. A sip of the refreshingly chilled, sweet fruit-flavoured drink brought back memories of her first-ever crush, Anokye. She'd gone to the supermarket with Tamali to get a bottle of muscatella when she saw the eleven-year-old dark coffee hunk smiling at her with pure white teeth and eyelashes that went on forever. He walked over to Tamali and whispered something in her ear before leaving. When Tamali told Zhara that he was a year above her in school and he wanted Zhara to be his girlfriend, she'd glowed from head to toe. Anokye developed a habit of riding his bicycle incessantly in front of Zhara's house. When they saw each other he would grind to a halt and give her the cutest smile. Their puppy love culminated in gazing sheepishly into each other's eyes. Sadly it never quite got to the dizzy heights of holding hands and without knowing if they would ever meet again, it seemed like it was almost at an end.

She thought back to the not-so-pleasant incidents, one of which was her first fight. She'd been on the way home from school, day-dreaming about the upcoming camping trip with the Brownies. As she turned the corner from the Kaneshie Polyclinic she'd heard footsteps behind her. She turned quickly and came face-to-face with Dorinda, a nine-year-old going on 30. Judging by the look on Dorinda's face it was obvious she was looking for trouble. Zhara had heard about Dorinda and her bullying antics, so instinctively she scarpered, but she wasn't quick enough. Dorinda and her cohorts, a gang of six cornered Zhara, intending to beat the living daylights out of her. Why me, she thought at the time. She'd done nothing wrong to any of them.

Outwardly Zhara appeared brave, but she was crumbling inside. Dorinda stepped forward, hands akimbo. "We've been looking for some action with a pampered daddy's girl and look what we've found," she'd said, laughing her head off. "Now, Oh pretty one, can you give me a good reason why I shouldn't kick your fat ass all the way home to your mummy and daddy?" She sneered.

Zhara tried to think of an answer, but just as she opened her mouth, Dorinda shoved her, with such force that Zhara's school bag flew off her shoulder and landed on the dusty pathway. What happened next was as much a mystery to Zhara as it was to the girls. One minute Dorinda was in Zhara's face, shouting and gesticulating, the next moment Zhara had miraculously slapped Dorinda so hard she'd fallen on the ground and was whimpering like a baby. Zhara had glanced at the floored bully, brushed the dirt off her uniform, picked her bag from the pathway and headed home. Oddly enough, instead of going to the aid of Dorinda, her friends left her and trailed behind Zhara as if she was a heroine. As Zhara quickly made her way home the girls circled around her, telling her they had always liked her and had pleaded with Dorinda not to fight her. Though surrounded by people in a busy street, Zhara had felt incredibly alone. She regretted hurting Dorinda and wished she hadn't told her parents that she would like to walk home from school. Overcome by emotion she left the girls and ran home.

Suddenly, other memories began to surface, memories she chose not to remember. It was nearly 4 am and the party had finally died down. Closing her eyes firmly she repeated the Lord's Prayer until she fell asleep.

CHAPTER FIVE

In the small coastal town of Saltpond in the Central Region of Ghana, the Ayerye Festival was being celebrated with the beating of traditional drums, an integral part of the cultural heritage of the Fante people. Masquerades paraded before the durbar of chiefs in colourful costumes. The traditional warriors, known as Asafo danced as if possessed. About a mile away, girls were arriving at the only secondary school in the area, one of the main attractions of the town.

Formerly known as Saltpond Girls, the school was founded by Dr Kwame Nkrumah, the first president of the Republic of Ghana, as a special gesture of appreciation for the part played by the people of Saltpond in the political history of the country. His aim was to empower the young girls in the community to strive for education and excellence. Zhara had chosen to study at the Methodist Girls' school because it was a short distance from her grandmother's home. She and Kukuwa had planned to study there together, but it was not to be. It was the norm for all students to keep their hair very short. While this did not bother a majority of girls, their mothers wouldn't hear of it. Zhara's mum had cut her daughter's hair reluctantly, but Kukuwa's mum was not willing to give up the long thick curls she loved to comb, plait, braid, stretch and cornrow. To retain every inch of her daughter's hair, Kukuwa's mum sent her to a boarding school in Europe. Thus, with heavy hearts, the girls went to different schools.

The school was massive, a huge stretch of land and buildings surrounded by a dense forest with gigantic trees. As she drove with her parents from the main reception to her dormitory Zhara felt a wave of panic. Chinery House was a huge two-storey building with several dormitories, shower rooms and toilets and a large storeroom. The housemistress lived a few yards away and the house prefect was in one of the special rooms reserved for sixth-formers. Zhara was shown to her room. It was towards the end of the ground floor and had two rows of bunk beds with a small locker at the head of each bed. On learning that the corner beds were reserved for senior girls Zhara plumped for a lower-bunk away from the door.

Fighting back their trepidation, Kamil and Araba wondered how they would get by without the warmth of Zhara's smile. They wished they could take her back home with them, but knew her education and independence were vital for her future development.

Holding back the tears, Zhara waved her parents goodbye. Being away from them was much harder than she'd anticipated. She cried herself to sleep and woke up disorientated. It was the middle of the night. The sound of crickets, hooting owls and loud breathing all around her was as alien as the simmering heat and pungent smell. Looking around in a daze, she opened her locker and took out a bottle of water. With trembling hands she took a sip and didn't stop until the bottle was empty. She tried to fall sleep but couldn't. As she yawned and stretched she felt an overwhelming urge to use the bathroom. Scurrying to the door she unlocked it and raced from the corridor to the dimly lit bathroom. She hurried back to the dormitory, locked the door and slid under the covers, praying for the term to end quickly so she could return home to her parents.

Zhara's second day commenced with clanging bells, loud voices and banging lockers. The atmosphere seemed tinged with frustration as senior girls of all shapes, shades and sizes rushed around with their buckets.

The toffee-coloured girl on the bed next to Zhara was called Nadia. She was in the third year and was from Ouagadougou. Nadia helped Zhara tidy up for the weekly Saturday morning inspection. After a tutorial on house rules Zhara left for the canteen with Nadia for breakfast.

Later that afternoon, while engrossed in a Mills & Boons novel, Zhara heard the bell ring for lunch. She put the book under her pillow and made her way to the canteen. The long queues and cheerful faces indicated that the menu was well liked. A whiff of the spicy aroma of fried plantain and black eye beans warmed Zhara's heart. Grabbing a plate, she served herself and sprinkled a spoonful of palm-nut flavoured gari (dried, grated cassava) on the beans. It was whist she was making her way to one of the empty tables that Zhara noticed a girl smiling at her. When Zhara returned the smile the girl's face lit up like the morning star. With a few quick strides she arrived at Zhara's table.

"Hi, I'm Juliana." She said with a heartwarming smile. "Can I sit with you?"

"Of course," said Zhara.

Juliana sat opposite Zhara. Her plate was heaped up with food. She looked painfully thin and her pleated uniform was begging to be ironed.

"You looked so miserable after your parents left," she said. "How are you feeling today?"

"OK, I guess," said Zhara, wondering how she knew.

"I had wanted to talk to you then, but I changed my mind."

"Really?" Zhara took a forkful of fried plantain and chewed thoughtfully. "Why did you change your mind?"

Julie spoke with a full mouth. "You looked like a typical daddy's girl. You know, arrogant, aloof, head in the clouds, spoilt, no manners..."

"Actually, I don't know," said Zhara, rising and reaching for her tray.

"Please don't go," Juliana smiled sweetly. 'I did not finish what I was saying. I said, you looked like, not look like. That was what I thought when I saw you yesterday, but I know now that I was wrong.

Zhara sat down. "What made you change your mind?" She asked, frowning.

"Your eyes, I mean the sincerity in your eyes. That is

what made me realise that you are genuine, and not spoilt and pretentious, despite your father's position in the government."

"And how did you know that?" Zhara asked.

"News travels fast around here. One of the senior girls remembered seeing him in the newspapers. She told a friend, who told a friend, etcetera, etcetera. But don't worry, your secret is safe with me. So you are not angry with me, she said, cautiously."

"Of course not."

The conversation moved on to illicit activities of senior students. Juliana seemed to know quite a lot for someone who'd only been at the school for a day. She talked animatedly and shoved down her food as if her life depended on it. It was remarkable. Zhara wondered how anyone could eat so much and yet remain so thin.

It was while Juliana was picking the last crumb from her plate that Zhara noticed that her hands were severely chapped. She also had a blister on her right arm, which looked very sore, and a scar just below her neck.

"How did you get the scar on your neck?" Zhara asked, looking very troubled.

"I will tell you, but not here." Juliana said quietly. "Would you like a tour of the school?"

"OK." Zhara nodded enthusiastically.

The girls put their trays away and stepped into the fresh air. As they strolled along the tree-lined avenue a vulture hovered above them. Shifting her eyes upwards, Juliana looked fixedly at the large bird.

"That looks very much like a witch" she said.

"Really?" Zhara looked bemused.

"It's easy to tell, even when they're disguised as one creature or another. Witches have markings on their body, like a teat, mole or raised pustule."

"And how do you know such things?"

"My stepmother is a witch. She stole my father from my mother. When he came to his senses and returned home to us, she used evil potions to make him return to her. To ensure my father remained under her spell, she killed my mother."

"That must have been awful. I'm so sorry."

"It was, and still is, but such is life. My father may be with her, but he will never love her, not like how he loved my mother. The evil witch has the devil's mark, a large ugly mole right under her nose, with hair sticking out of it. It serves her right! I wish she would fly away on her broom and never come back. Do you know that a witch cannot say the Lord's Prayer without stumbling over the words?"

Zhara's jaw dropped. "I had no idea!" she said with a look of bewilderment.

"Well now you do" replied Juliana. She was hopping along the street from one leg to another. "My stepmother never prays and she doesn't go to church either. If she were to fall into the sea her body would float to the surface, because the ocean, wide as it is, would not be able to contain her pollution."

"You sound like you really know a lot about witches."

"Yes, I do." she said confidently. "I've read a lot about

them. When my father gets upset with my stepmother he calls her a witch. Would you like to know what he says about women?"

Zhara wasn't sure if she wanted to hear any more of her stories. "Well, OK then," she relented.

"Hmm…" Juliana rolled her eyes. "He said where there are women, there is bound to be trouble and confusion. He thinks women are devious and evil. He believes they hate each other, and" - she rolled her eyes again but this time only the whites were showing - "those who wish evil on others can never have what they wish for in life. That is why my stepmother can never have children. Much as I love my father and my younger brother and sister, I just couldn't wait to leave home. I studied really hard so that I could get into secondary school. It had to be a boarding school and as far away as possible from the evil witch who makes me sweep the compound, scrub the floor, wash her clothes, iron them, go to the market, and cook and clean from dawn to dusk. My home was like a prison and the only free time I had was when I was at school. After doing all the endless chores I was rewarded with a tiny plate of leftover food. And if I don't do everything exactly as she wants it, I get whipped, kicked, slapped, punched, pushed around and called vile names. A few months ago I took too long to iron her dress. She got mad and shoved the hot iron in my face. I ducked and the iron caught me right beneath my neck. Then there was the time when she found me in bed at 7am on a Sunday morning. I was supposed to be up by 6am but I overslept because I worked till midnight the night before. Can you believe that the evil woman poured a bucket of freezing cold water on me, while I was sleeping?" she said gloomily. "So there," she said stamping her feet on a tiny twig until it was crushed to bits, "now you know why I have so many bruises and look as thin as a scarecrow."

"Does your father know how your stepmother treats you?"

"He didn't at first because he came home late every day. One day he came home early, which surprised us all. I stopped ironing her clothes and threw my arms around him. He held me for a long time. Then he stood back and took a good look at me. I think he must have felt my bones. It was the first time I saw him cry. With tears running down his cheeks, he examined each of my bruises. It was as if he knew everything, but couldn't stand up to her. Later that night I heard the arguing. My dad was trying to make a point in a gentle yet determined voice, telling her that I had to be treated with love and kindness and more importantly she had to feed me properly with the money he provides."

"What did she say?" Zhara asked wearily.

She kept hollering like a fishwife. "I always treat her with kindness. That girl knows how to wind you up, and you always take her side. This is my house too and as long as she lives under my roof she will do as I say!"

"Did your stepmum change her attitude towards you after that?"

"No. But I am glad that she is nice to my brother and

sister. You see, my sister is very pretty, unlike me, so she can pass her off as her own, since she can't have children. As for my brother, he is such a gentleman and looks just like my father, so she adores him. So it is just me; the ugly duckling, that she despises. She said I remind her of my mother. I am sure her hatred for me stems from her guilty conscience, but I really don't care, I'm just glad to be here, out of reach from her devilish claws. Do you know why there are many broken homes?"

Zhara shook her head.

"Well, it is due to drunkards and harlots." As they approached Butler House she preened her neck to ensure no one was listening because she was prone to expand on the truth, to add piquancy to her stories. "Shh!" she put her index finder in her lips, "a harlot is a kind of woman."

"What kind?" asked Zhara.

"The worst kind, the kind who go with men for money - whores, sluts, slags and prostitutes. They can be found in bars and street corners, wearing next to nothing, lips painted red and drenched in cheap perfume. These shameless tarts set out to trap all sorts of men - married, single, rich, poor, smelly, fat, thin, short or tall. Anything goes, so long as they are paid. They take control of their victim's mind and make them tsitsinto or mumu [idiots] and the married ones abandon their wives and children. The heartless sinners who break homes will burn in hell! Do you know the seven deadly sins?"

Zhara shook her head again.

"They are greed, laziness, gluttony, wrath, envy, pride and for-ni-ca-tion."

"Forni... what?" Zhara looked confused.

Juliana rolled her eyes indignantly. "Don't you know anything? Fornication is ..." She formed a circle with one hand and plunged a finger from the other hand slowly back and forth through the circle."

A crease formed between Zhara's brows. Thrown into a world she knew very little about, she looked to the skies and sighed loudly, longing to be home with her parents.

CHAPTER SIX

The bell tolled just at sunrise. Zhara rubbed her eyes, yawned and stretched. Then she threw off her sheets, dragged herself from the bed and went to the bathroom.

Feeling refreshed she dragged out her trunk from underneath the bed and picked out each of her four sets of cloth, wondering which one to wear to church. The green cloth with gold alphabets caught her eye. She also had an orange batik with blue petals, a purple patterned wax print and a blue cloth. Settling for the green cloth she got dressed, tidied her bed and followed her roommates to the canteen.

Juliana waved frantically when she saw Zhara.

"You look stunning!" she whispered when Zhara reached her. "Your top is so nice, I have to draw a sketch and ask my seamstress to make me one, just like that."

"Thank you. You look different too." Zhara said thoughtfully, "mature, slightly curvier and radiant."

"That's what everyone says. Wearing cloth covers me up and makes me look slightly bigger, but the thought of worshiping my Lord ignites the happiness buried deep within my soul."

Zhara tucked into rice pudding and a slice of buttered bread whilst Juliana devoured a huge bowl of porridge and a chunky piece of sugared bread layered with butter. The girls then decided to head to church even before the bell had rung.

As they neared the oblong shaped building a heavenly melody of Amazing Grace filled the air. Enchanted by the choir and masterful notes coming from the keyboard the girls quickly slid onto a pew at the front of the church and hummed.

"I would love to play the piano like that," said Zhara.

"Me too" said Juliana. The man playing the piano is Mr Thompson. He teaches first year students and I hear he is very strict."

"That does not bother me at all. I would love to be his pupil and maybe someday I can also play the piano like that."

After the service the girls changed into their casual uniforms and went to the library.

They were heading back to Zhara's dormitory at 11:30am when two girls approached them. Their uniforms indicated that they were in the third year. One was short and stout, with a face full of zits. Her companion was slightly taller and prettier.

"Hey! You! Come here!" Shouted the taller of the two girls, deep-set eyes glaring at Zhara. "What is your name?"

Just as Zhara was about to answer the other girl shouted in a high-pitched piercing voice. "Are you deaf, dumb or stupid?" The contempt in her voice was alarming.

Deciding their uproar was totally unnecessary, Zhara walked past them. Juliana followed.

"Come back here!" Yelled the stout girl, eyes burning with rage.

Zhara and Juliana turned around but maintained the distance between them and the senior girls.

"Look at these homos [first year students]!" Ooh, when I am talking, they have the audacity to walk away. You haven't heard of me eh? Make sure you ask your ignorant mates about me, Felicity, and you will get the shock of your life. We rule this school, not the stuck-up prefects. I said, what is your name?" she roared at Zhara.

The words spilled out of her mouth. "My name is Zhara."

"Ooh!" Felicity tittered, "so you can actually speak! Kneel down, before I brush your face."

Zhara did as she was told.

The other girl took a few steps towards Zhara and stared at her. "My trunk is at the admin block" she said in a very bossy tone. "It has my name, Atwee Obilitekomey, clearly marked on it. You better not get the wrong trunk OK? Otherwise, you will regret the day you were born! You will carry the trunk, on your knees, from the admin block to my House. Got that?"

Zhara nodded.

"Good" she said with a condescending smile. She wagged her finger in Zhara's face, "on your knees, not your legs, with my trunk on your head, from the admin block to room 16, the last room on the first floor at Scotland House. If you play any tricks with me, you will regret the day you were born."

The girls turned their attention to Juliana. After scrutinising her from head to toe, they fell about laughing.

"And who is this ugly duckling?" mocked Felicity.

Atwee laughed her head off. "She must be from the concentration camp."

Felicity screwed her face up scornfully "did they not feed you there?"

Juliana bit her nails nervously whilst the girls laid into her.

Juliana came up with a plan as soon as the girls left. She could tell from Zhara's smooth, flawless hands that she wasn't used to hard labour, and as it was approaching lunchtime she figured it would be the best time to carry out what she had in mind. Even though it involved skipping lunch, she was sure it would be better than facing the wrath of the bullies.

"Zhara, I have an idea" she said with an angelic smile.

"What is it?"

"When the bell rings for lunch I will ran to the admin block to look for Atwee's trunk and carry it to Scotland House."

"But she said I should do it. I would hate to get you into trouble."

"Don't worry, I know just what to do. I have carried gigantic boxes from my house to the market so many times, this will be a piece of cake. What I will not do, is carry it on my knees. The girl is a sadist! But let's not worry about her now. All you need to do is hide near Scotland House until you see me. You can then carry the trunk a little distance on your knees, in case she sees us and wants to check that you did as instructed."

"OK, but what if they see you carrying the trunk?"

"Don't bother about that. I know a short cut from the admin block. No-one will see me and if they do I will think of a good excuse. Anyway they should be in the canteen. I will hide somewhere just to make sure they are on their way before I make my move. Try not to be spotted and only come out when you see me, or if I call you."

"OK, if you are sure, but be careful."

"I will."

Zhara was hiding behind the science block. It was a few yards away from Scotland House. As soon as she heard heavy footsteps she knew it was Juliana. Moments later she heard Juliana calling her. Emerging from her hiding place she followed the sound of the voice and saw Juliana at the corner of Scotland House. Together they carried the trunk to the top of the stairs. Zhara rolled up the cloth Juliana had used to carry the trunk and placed it on her head. As she dropped to her knees on the chipped concrete floor Juliana carried the trunk and placed it on her head. Then, crawling on her knees as instructed, Zhara moved slowly along the corridor to room 16.

Juliana held the door open for Zhara to get through

and helped her place the trunk in the room. The girls then made a hasty retreat. Just as they neared Zhara's dormitory they saw people coming out of the canteen.

"Thank God!" Juliana said breathlessly. "I am so glad we made it. Your knees are bleeding. Let me see."

Zhara was excited that the ordeal was over and hadn't realised that she was bleeding. "Ouch!" She cried when Juliana tried to wipe away the blood.

"I think we need to go the infirmary. They can dress the wound with gentian violet before it gets worse."

Zhara shook her head. "What I need is a shower. I am sure my knee will get better tomorrow. Why don't you go and have a shower, you are sweating? Then come by for a present."

"What for?"

"For saving my life. Thank you so much. I don't know how I would have managed without you. You are an angel."

"Don't be silly, I did what any friend would do, and you are a lot tougher than you think."

After what seemed like an eternity under the cold shower Zhara returned to her room, got dressed and went to the box room. She opened her chop-box (chest for storing food) and stuffed two corned beef sandwiches, four sardine, a bag of gari, a box of sugar, four cans of milk, two biscuits, two cans of Fanta, two cans of Pepsi and a bottle of shito (spicy shrimp sauce) in a carrier bag. The bleeding on her knee had receded, but the pain was excruciating.

Juliana returned to Zhara's room just after 4 pm. She was overwhelmed when Zhara gave her the provisions she'd retrieved from her chop box.

"Are these really for me?" She asked, overcome with emotion.

"Yes, and there is more where that came from. You skipped lunch just to help me, I will never forget that."

"Thank you. You are very kind."

"Thank you" Zhara said gratefully.

CHAPTER SEVEN

As the whispering canoes broke the waves on the Atlantic Ocean, the words from Zhara's dreams dripped silently from her quivering lips: "Mummy, Daddy, please help me. Help me, help me..."

It was 6:15 am on Monday. Nadia had just woken up when she saw Zhara shaking on the bed. Nadia tried to wake her but couldn't. She felt her head. It was boiling. She quickly raised the alarm.

The school nurse arrived within a few minutes. Zhara was taken to the infirmary and attended to.

The thought of missing her first lesson upset Zhara so much that she broke down and refused to eat. Juliana and Nadia popped into see Zhara, but it only worsened her misery.

Feeling lonely and miserable, Zhara asked the nurse if she could call her parents. Hearing her mum and dad's voice made her feel better. She told them everything.

At exactly 6pm, Zhara was told she had a visitor. Her heart leapt with joy when she saw her father. Though he appeared calm, she could tell he was fuming. Leaping with excitement, she threw her arms around him and sobbed inconsolably.

A tall, plump, good-looking lady, possibly in her forties, appeared at the door. Zhara recognised her from the previous day's church service. Then she remembered she'd introduced herself as Mrs Asare, the headmistress. Elegantly dressed in a turquoise skirt and rather fetching blouse, Mrs Asare patted her neatly pinned back bun nervously.

"Don't cry, my princess," said Kamil as he tried to console his daughter. He kissed the top of Zhara's head, and tried to remain calm, but his eyes gave him away.

Mrs Asare inched forward. "My dear Zhara," she began. "I am so sorry for what happened to you. I promise it will never happen again. Please don't leave us because of it."

The room was silent, except for the clicking sound of the ceiling fan. Zhara looked into her father's eyes as he sat by her side on the tiny bed. Noticing the anger beneath the smile she took his arm possessively. She had no idea what had ensued between him and Mrs Asare, but she knew it had to be serious if he intended to take her out of the school.

"Please tell me you will stay" Mrs Asare pleaded in a warm soothing voice. "The girls will not get away with that kind of behaviour in my school. Things will change, I promise."

Zhara did not want to leave the school. It wasn't all bad, she thought, she'd met some really nice girls and she was getting used to the bells and strange sounds at night. Zhara smiled at her father and waited for him to respond. His eyes seemed to have softened a bit.

"It's up to you darling" he said firmly. "I will go with whatever you decide."

"Daddy, can I stay?" She asked in a soft voice.

Mrs Asare seemed delighted. "That's my girl!" she exclaimed.

"Yes, my princess. But if this nonsense ever happens again, I will be back, and my decision will be final."

"Mr Al Jamal, nothing will happen to your daughter. Certainly not while I am head of this school. The bullies will be severely punished."

"In that case, she can stay."

"Excellent!" said Mrs Asare. May I ask you and Zhara to join me for dinner?"

"I would love to" said Kamil, "but it's getting late and I have a three hour journey to make. Maybe next time ..."

"I understand" said Mrs Asare. "I hope Zhara can join me? It will give us a chance to get to know each other a little better."

"I will leave that to you two. It appears you have everything under control so I will be on my way." He hugged Zhara. 'Get well soon, my darling, and call if you need anything."

Zhara hugged him back and waved till he disappeared.

Atwee and Felicity were put on detention and had to clean all the toilets in the school for a month.

CHAPTER EIGHT

The talking drums vibrated from the hinterlands. Dawn had just broken on the Atlantic coast. It was a beautiful June day in 1971. The sun was shining, birds were singing and the tropical flowers were blooming. Travellers from all corners of the continent descended on the land of rhythm and Hi-life music. The warm breeze kissed the wide-eyed, expectant faces of the legendary musicians including Tina Turner, James Brown and Fela Kuti as they alighted the Boeing 474, eagerly looking forward to meet their Ghanaian brothers, ET Mensah, Osibisa, CK Mann, Kofi Ghanaba and Blay Ambolay. The capital city, Accra's top hotels, restaurants and dazzling night clubs; Ambassador, Continental and Star hotel, Keteke, Lido, Apollo Theatre, Tip Toe, Casanova and Metropole were keenly awaiting the American and African legends.

Kamil and Araba enthused over the musical extravaganza, but Zhara had other things on her mind. She'd passed her A Level exams and was looking forward to studying estate management and interior design in the UK. Like her fellow Ghanaians, who celebrated every happy occasion with dancing, drumming and singing, she put Michael Jackson's *Off the Wall* on the turntable and moved to the beat. Even death and sadness called for music, to lighten the atmosphere. She'd grown up with the rhythmic pounding of fufu from her grandmother's kitchen, and danced to that as a toddler. She had seen footballers and fans alike wriggling their waists when they scored a goal. Even at church, the angelic voices of the choir moved the rhythm in her soul, and the sound of Muslim prayers, Dua Qunut and Surah Fatiha gave her an overwhelming sense of goodness and tranquillity. So she turned up the music, and danced to her heart's content.

CHAPTER NINE

Zhara returned to Ghana immediately after her graduation and joined her mother's company. She was keen to learn and share her newly acquired skills with the team at the real estate development company in Kimberley Avenue.

She had barely got her feet under the table when Araba promoted her daughter to partner and chief operating officer.

As she grew into the role, Zhara began to notice some serious issues. Her mother's hectic schedule often kept her away from the office. It appeared that, as the saying goes 'when the cat is away, the mice will play'. The playing had got so out of hand that if it wasn't addressed the company could lose its credibility. Zhara's priority was to introduce some guidelines aimed at steering the staff away from their ineffective practices. It was more challenging than she'd anticipated and most of the resistance came from the staff who were related to her. Telling aunts, uncles and cousins in the nicest possible way to change their unproductive conduct was at best, demoralising. In the end, she had to let some of them go. Only those who were willing to work smarter, effectively and pro-actively were retained. A new system was introduced to train and reward staff.

The office gained a positive buzz under Zhara's leadership. Though much younger than her competitors, her inter-personal skills, professionalism and attention to detail brought in so many clients that she had to take on new staff.

She worked diligently, from 7 am to 7 pm, six days a week, to gain the trust and respect of clients, colleagues and associates. But most of all, she made her parents very proud of her achievements in a relatively short time.

With the influx of high-profile clients she made sure her staff were appropriately trained to meet the demands of her clients.

CHAPTER TEN

The heavens opened up in the early hours of the morning, drenching the seventeenth century castles, ocean-front mansions and colonial houses. It then moved inward to the corrugated roofed bungalows, flooded the mud huts in the shanty towns and filled up the open sewers and gigantic potholes. Nothing was spared, not the Korle Lagoon with its distinctive stench, the factories along the industrial area, nor the stalls littered along the market roads.

A flash of lightning illuminated the deep blue sky. Then darkness, complete and utter darkness. Thunder rumbled, shaking the city of Accra.

The sound echoed through Zhara's bedroom. Sitting bolt upright, she rubbed her eyes with the back of her hand. Her bedclothes were soaked in sweat. Flashes of the disturbing nightmare came to her. She'd been in the eye of a storm, running away from something. She couldn't remember who or what it was. The moist ground bounced underneath her bare feet. She'd kept running through a meadow of wildflowers but never seemed to reach her destination. Suddenly the sky darkened. She'd paused to catch her breath but couldn't decide which way to go. A revolting smell lingered in the air. Soaked and trembling she'd tried not to breathe in what could be best described as decomposing flesh. Then she heard the growl. Gathering all her strength and courage she'd run as fast as her legs could carry her. She'd reached the end of the meadow when an image suddenly appeared in front of her, blocking her way. It was hunched over and faceless. Unable to withstand the choking fear that had clawed at her throat she'd screamed so loud that she'd woken herself up.

Zhara switched on her bedside lamp and checked the time. It was 3:55 am. The rain had eased a bit. Just as she switched off the lamp she remembered that something else had happened in the dream. What was it? She asked herself. Lying back on the pillow, she wracked her brain. Just as the images started to appear a sharp pain tore through her head. She quickly went down on her knees and prayed. When she stood up the pain was gone. She got into bed and drifted off to sleep.

Raindrops were pattering softly against the window pane when Zhara woke up. Bright yellow sunshine beamed through the plushly-decorated room. Wrapping a gown around her, she slipped on her *Charley wote* (flip flops) and pulled back the sliding doors.

Out on the balcony the fresh morning breeze caressed her face. Leaning over the balustrade, she watched the ocean as it rolled gently to the shore. The smoky haze hanging over the hills had embraced the orange and red hues of the golden sun. The peacocks she'd received from Sheikh Idris of Arabia, for finding his fifth wife a palatial penthouse overlooking Lake Akosombo and its picturesque hills, strutted across the lawn, fanning their iridescent tails. She looked around the garden and smiled at the creeping bougainvillea, the roses, violets, tulips, lilies and sunflowers. Taking in a deep breath of fresh air, she observed the butterflies flying from flower to flower. The grasshoppers brought back memories of how she and Tamari would collect them in perforated jars and fed them with plants.

Zhara would have loved to spend the whole morning revelling in the splendour of nature, but there was work to be done, and a very busy day ahead.

Feeling invigorated, Zhara emerged from the bathroom with a towel around her waist. As she creamed her body, she scanned the wardrobe for something to wear. A dark brown pencil skirt caught her eye. That would look perfect with a green linen top, brown pumps and pearls, she thought.

After getting dressed, Zhara grabbed her brown shoulder bag, and was heading out when the phone rang.

"Hello?"

"Hi darling, how are you?"

The posh accent belonged to none other than Olympia, her cousin.

"Fine. And you?"

"I'm freezing, but I'll live. Since you hurriedly left England after the graduation I've been missing you like crazy! Anyway, just in case you've forgotten, my big three-O is looming. You are coming, aren't you?"

"Of course, I'll be there."

"The party is on Saturday 15th December. You know it won't be the same without you?"

"I do" said Zhara. "It will be nice to catch up with the boys. I can't wait to meet Auntie Samira, and your dad."

"I don't think Milo and Stavros can tear themselves away from their multi-million dollar empire. And Mum and Dad are on a cruise to the Caribbean, but I'll definitely see them when they return. Did I tell you what they are getting me for my birthday?"

"No, what is it?"

"A fully-furnished condo in the Hamptons. It's about half a mile from our house. We should go there together next year. I know you will love it…"

Zhara remembered the happy times she'd spent with Samira, Olympia's mother, and her father's only sister. Samira had told her that she and Kamil had been inseparable, until Georgiou eloped with her to New York. She had spoken with such sadness about the love affair that had nearly torn her family apart. The story had touched Zhara's heart.

It had all happened several years ago, while visiting their grandparents in Kano, Northern Nigeria. Samira, who was 18 at the time, had been on the way to the market with her 14-year-old brother, Kamil when a Land Rover pulled up beside them. The driver, a tanned good-looming man, asked Samira for directions. The teenagers had no idea that he was Georgiou Callimanopulos, the 35-year-old son of a Greek shipping magnate. After what seemed like a very long chat the car pulled away. According to

Kamil, his sister's behaviour began to change, and she would disappear for hours without telling him where she'd been. One evening the tanned handsome man showed up at his grandparent's house, bearing gifts. He'd come to ask for Samira's hand in marriage. He watched as the man was shown the door, and warned that if he ever went near Samira again he would be decapitated. The following morning Samira left for the market and never returned. Kamil prayed day and night for nothing bad to happen to his only sister. A few weeks after she disappeared Samira called her parents to inform them that she was in New York and planning to get married to Georgiou. Though her parents and grandparents could not hide their disappointment, they forgave her.

Kamil had been sad that he couldn't see more of his sister, but pleased that she was happy.

★ ★ ★

The sound of Olympia's voice brought Zhara back to the present.

Olympia could talk for England, and once she got started it was hard to get a word in edgewise. She kept on talking, unaware that Zhara's mind had been elsewhere.

"Really?" Zhara said, snapping quickly back into the present.

"Oh my my!" Olympia continued, "you have to see the guest list. The Ivy was my first choice but when I remembered how much fun we had at Claridges my mind was made up. And as you know, only the crème de la crème will be attending. Girl, ditch your glad rags and spend, spend, spend! Don't let me down; the party will be fab! Lawal sends his love. The poor guy is so miserable; please give him some love. Can't you be a little nice to him? It's time to give up the Virgin Mary and give the poor boy some! He adores you. Wait till I tell him you're coming. Amira and Pandora can't wait to see you either. Call me, and let me know when to pick you up from the airport. Darling, my mobile is ringing. It must be the judge I'm meeting this afternoon. I know what you're thinking, but sorry to disappoint. It's business, not pleasure, though I wish it weren't so. Must go honey! Give my love to uncle and auntie. Love you lots and lots and lots!"

The phone went dead.

Zhara replaced the handset, shut the door behind her, and made her way down the marble staircase.

A sweet smell of nutmeg and cinnamon floating through the air suggested that Kwansima was in the kitchen.

Kwansima had been working for the family for twenty years. She started as Zhara's nanny and retrained as chef and housekeeper. The petite lady in her late thirties had become indispensable and run the house like clockwork, overseeing the workers in the household. She particularly enjoyed baking bread in the early hours of the morning. It never failed to create a positive atmosphere.

Zhara waltzed into the kitchen. Smiling appreciatively she inhaled the freshly baked bread and fried omelettes.

"Good morning Kwansima."

Kwansima observed her keenly. "Good morning. You are looking exceptionally beautiful. Are you meeting someone special?"

"Not really. Just a few clients, and the architect working on the development at East Cantonment."

"What would you like for breakfast?"

Zhara mulled over whether to rush to work or stay for breakfast.

"Could I please have one, or maybe two bread rolls, and an omelette?"

"Certainly. Would you like it here or in the dining room?"

"Here, please. May I help?"

Kwansima turned the omelette. "No dear, I am nearly done."

Zhara took a seat and looked around the spotless kitchen with a gleaming work top."

"I've added baked beans" said Kwansima. She placed a plate of food on the dining table and poured Zhara a glass of freshly squeezed orange juice. "Would you like tea, coffee, Bournvita, milo, or Ovaltine?"

"Ovaltine, please." Zhara took a bite of warm sweetbread with melting butter. "Mmmmm ..." she hummed, "this is too good!" She could resist sweets, chocolate, alcohol and men, but when it came to freshly baked sweet bread and cakes, her willpower was abandoned.

Zhara was delighted when Araba and Kamil joined her

for breakfast. She told them about Olympia's birthday party and her intention to travel to London in a few weeks. She also intended to visit her grandmother, Maame Akua, in the village.

CHAPTER ELEVEN

December commenced with Harmattan. The dry dusty winds from the Sahara desert spread across the Gulf of Guinea and engulfed Mankessim, the bustling market town in the Central region of Ghana, in a cloud of dust, littering the streets and everything in its path.

Driving skilfully, Obetsebi manoeuvred around the potholes and maintained a safe distance between the overtakings, overloaded buses and lopsided trucks laden with people, goats, chickens and foodstuff. He'd been driving Zhara and her family for over ten years.

Zhara sat thoughtfully in the backseat. They had made good progress. After leaving Accra at 9 am, it had taken just over an hour to reach Winneba, and they hoped to arrive at Mankessim in about 30 minutes.

As they drove past fields of corn, sweet potato, plantain, cocoyam, banana, cassava and palm nut, Zhara was intrigued by the beauty and simplicity of village life. She watched women with babies on their back and a bucket balanced on their head making their way home from the streams, bare-chested children playing happily by the stream, young men grazing cattle and guinea fowls running around freely. As they neared the Mankessim roundabout, Zhara breathed a sigh of relief.

Flames burned from the depths of the coal-pot in Maame Akua's kitchen. The aroma of palm-nut soup with grilled grass-cutter, octopus, ewura-afua (salt fish), apofee (mollusc), snails, crab, goat meat and salted beef wafted through the large compound. The sound of pounding fufu echoed rhythmically with the talking drums which heralded the arrival of the paramount king. As crowds stood by to watch the royal procession, the sound of the drums unified their soul, gladdened their heart and moved them to dance.

Bentsiwa, Maame Akua's eldest daughter, raised the alarm when she saw the Land cruiser moving up the steep hill. Standing by the entrance of the thatched roof building with ten huts and a large central courtyard, she waited expectantly for her niece. Within seconds the courtyard was packed with excited relatives.

Maame Akua buried Zhara in her arms and held her for several minutes whilst the rest of the family; aunts, uncles, cousins, nieces, nephews and grandchildren waited anxiously to smother Zhara with hugs and kisses.

The younger children carried in the clothes, toys, sweets and provisions Obetsebi unloaded from the car whilst the older ones set the table.

Bentsiwa quickly checked the soup, then carried on turning the fufu (mixed cassava and plantain) around in the mortar with wet hands while her son, Ekow, pounded it with a pestle.

There was a buzz of excitement. The adults chatted merrily and the children ran around joyously.

With everyone quietly seated, Maame Akua gave thanks to the Almighty, vociferously:

Dear Lord, You said when two or more are gathered in Your name You will be present. Heavenly Father, we thank You for bringing Zhara safely home to us. May the light of Your truth bestow sight to the darkness of our sinful eyes. Enkindle in us the fire of Your love and let us share our faith and kindness with all mankind. Heavenly Father, we humbly ask for Your forgiveness. Please instill in each of us the gift of truth, humility and honesty and bless us and what we are about to eat. Shield us from sin, evil and temptation. Lord, we pray for the starving, the oppressed, the sick, the dying, the weary, those in great distress and those who cannot sleep. May Your holy name be praised, now and forever, Amen!

Later that night, radiated with the glory of The Lord, Maame Akua prayed with a rosary running through her fingers, for her entire family, her community, the nation and the whole world. She also prayed for those who never make it to church and those who were yet to know the Lord. Then she hugged every single person in her household, sang a couple of hymns and fell soundly asleep.

Zhara lay on her back, staring around the room where she had been born. Her eyes wandered from the four poster queen-sized bed to the mosquito net draped over it, before moving from the ceiling fan to the light blue walls. The black and white framed photo of her grandparents stared back at her from the wall. It was obvious from the way they were looking into each other's eyes that they'd been deeply in love. She snuggled into the white cotton sheets, wondering what it felt like to be in love.

CHAPTER TWELVE

Maame Akua woke up just after 4 am. After giving thanks to the Lord, she showered, put on her favourite black and white cloth, plaited her thick shoulder-length grey hair and wrapped a scarf around her head. She then opened her jewellery box and took out a gold necklace with a cross pendant. It had been a gift from her late husband, and was the only jewellery she wore, apart from her wedding ring.

She looked at the reflection in the mirror, as she wore the chain. Then she placed her hand on the cross and closed her eyes. Suddenly an image appeared in her mind's eye. It was her late husband, Thomas, smiling at her as he used to, with those funny eyes. Her heart quickened and blood thundered through her veins, just the way it had, over fifty years ago.

She had been the youngest of ten children, seven boys and three girls. Although she didn't see anything special about herself, many people took it upon themselves to tell her how smart, charming and beautiful she was. Some even referred to her as the prettiest girl in the village, which caused a great deal of embarrassment, especially when men from all corners of the land sought her hand in marriage. Maame Akua refused to marry the doctors, engineers, lawyers, politicians, wealthy aristocrats and high-ranking government officials, much to her father's annoyance. Then she met Thomas. She didn't think much of him either, initially, but Thomas was persistent. To him, she was the most beautiful girl on earth. Regardless of how many times Maame Akua told him to get lost, he carried on waiting by her compound after work, hoping she would one day stop and talk to him. Even catching malaria didn't stop him. When she heard he'd been admitted at the local hospital Maame Akua felt sorry for him. Then it transpired that he'd been bitten by a scorpion while laying in wait for her. She could not believe anyone could be that foolish. One day, while returning from the farm Maame Akua came face to face with the blue-eyed Scottish accountant. Against her better judgement she stopped and asked how he was. The more they chatted, the more she liked him. His jokes and the funny faces he pulled made her laugh so much that she didn't realise she was falling in love. In the weeks that followed they saw more of each other. Thomas went to see Maame Akua's father, to ask for her hand in marriage. He was devastated when he was turned down. Seeing how miserable his daughter had become, Maame Akua's father begrudgingly agreed that Thomas could marry his daughter. Though labelled by some as a 'sell-out', she had never set out to marry outside her race. Thomas just happened to be the only man she ever got to know and befriend. With his love she was able to withstand the hate. He had made her incredibly happy and given her three handsome caring sons and two beautiful kind-hearted daughters. She loved him with every pulse in her body and relished the 50 blissful years they had spent together.

"What God has joined together no man can put asunder", whispered Maame Akua. She opened her eyes and let go of the pendant. It was 5:15 am. Moving pensively, she opened the front door and took a cleansing breath of fresh air. The morning breeze was lovely and crisp. She walked leisurely towards the swing-chair in the centre of the compound and sat on it. From there she could see the whole village. She watched farmers hurrying to their farms, women loading foodstuffs on lorries bound for the market and young maidens sweeping their compound.

A hint of a smile appeared on her lips when the cock crowed. She admired creatures of habit, particularly those who begin work at sunrise, like fishermen, farmers, some wives and mothers, those who plough the fields, bakers and market sellers. Then at twilight, after the menfolk have wended their way home and settled down with a calabash of palm wine, the ladies prepare dinner, share the latest gossip and sing folksongs.

"Good Morning Nana" said Zhara as she neared the swing-chair. She looked lovely in a dark blue kimono embroidered with a fire-breathing dragon.

"Good morning, my angel" said Maame Akua with a heartwarming smile. "Come and sit with me." She patted the seat next to her.

Zahra embraced her grandmother. "Good morning,

Nana." She was about to sit down when a bundle of white fur jumped from the edge of the roof and curled itself around her ankles.

Zhara stroked Chido, the Persian cat she'd received from Kukuwa and left with her grandma when she started college.

Chido purred contentedly between Zhara's legs.

"Did you sleep well, my angel?"

"Yes, Nana [grandma]."

"I am glad, the tranquillity here is magical."

"I know, and that is why I love it here." Zhara linked arms with her grandmother. Placing her head on her shoulder, she snuggled closer and inhaled the fresh citrus smell. Sitting in silence, they listened to everything around them, even when it was nothing but silence.

"Nana?"

"Yes, my angel?"

"Can you tell me what happened when I was born?"

"Certainly, my dear." Maame Akua exhaled. "What prompted that thought, my angel?"

"Sleeping in the room where I was born, I think. Mum said she is alive today because of you, me and daddy. She told me what happened, from when she was due to have me until when she was discharged from hospital, but I would love to hear it from you."

"Your mum came to stay with me about a week before you were born. Your father was in Geneva at the time and she was missing him terribly. On the day before you were born, Araba woke up very early in the morning. By 7 am she'd swept the whole compound, cleaned, dusted, washed and ironed. I was astounded by how much energy she had on that beautiful Sunday morning. She was still hyper when we returned from church. When she suggested accompanying Bentsiwa to the farm, I was concerned, because of her condition. I tried to coax her to stay with me, but she wouldn't budge. You know how stubborn she can be, so I urged them to be careful. They returned after a couple of hours. While they were cooking, your father called. Araba nearly burst with excitement. I left for night service around 10pm. Your mum, aunt and uncles were playing a recording of Louis Armstrong's Satchmo Summer Fest..."

Obetsebi emerged from the guest hut at 6 o'clock. He had a chewing stick in his mouth and a towel over his shoulder.

"Good morning Nana. How are you?"

"I am fine, by God's grace."

Obetsebi regarded Maame Akua with respect. At nearly eighty she had her own teeth, a full head of hair, a keen intelligence and wisdom. She was the only person he knew who could tell from looking at the clouds if it was about to rain, read the change in seasons from the colour of leaves, and could suggest herbs and spices for all manner of ailments. He was wondering how she managed to remain as fit as an ox and attractive, even in her advanced years when she coughed.

"Can I get you a drink, Nana?" He asked, gawping at her flawless dark chocolate complexion.

"Now that you mention it, yes. Would you mind getting me a coconut from the tree? Those big ones up there ..." she pointed at them, "they look like they are ready for plucking."

"I'll g-g-g-get them immediately" he stammered.

He took a few quick strides to the shed, and emerged with a pole saw and a machete. Gliding to the tree, he inspected it thoroughly and yanked off two large coconuts. He picked one up, chopped away the thick outer husk, cut the top off skilfully and presented it to Maame Akua with a dazzling smile. He then picked the other coconut, repeated what he'd done with the first one and offered it to Zhara with a look of fulfilment.

Maame Akua took a few sips of the sweet refreshing drink. "Thank you. I really needed that." She took another sip. "Go on, pluck some for yourself and take some with you for your family."

"Thank you s-s-so much, Nana."

Feeling replenished, Maame Akua carried on with the story.

"The atmosphere at church that evening had been lively and exuberant. Reverend Eshun observed each of the regulars peppered throughout the congregation and shouted, 'Praise the Lord, halleluiah'. His eyes were wandering from the not-so-actives to the once-a-month drop-ins and the new arrivals, when brother Thompson banged out All Hail the Power of Jesus' Name. Consumed by the spirit of the Lord, the Reverend elucidated the importance of the reading. He had envisaged himself somewhere between heaven and earth, speaking forth the word of God to the masses, when I saw your uncle, Kofi, moving swiftly towards me. I could tell he'd been running. Gasping for breath, he whispered that your mum was having the baby. As we hurried home he said he met a woman at Dorothy's house when he went to fetch her.

"Who is Dorothy?"

"She was a midwife, one of the best. She delivered most of the babies in the village successfully. Anyway, the woman told Kofi that Dorothy was not back from work. When she learnt that your mum was having a baby she told Kofi that she was a senior midwife at Cape Coast hospital and would like to help. Araba was doubled over in pain when we got home. The contractions were quickening. I was rubbing your mum's back and urging her to continue taking deep breaths when a woman waddled through the door. As soon as I laid eyes on the woman, I had an instinctive feeling of doom. Something about the woman didn't sit well with my spirit. Putting my fate in the hands of The Lord, I said a silent prayer and hoped for the best. Your mum's water broke at about 1 am and you rushed into this world at 1:05 am on Monday 31st August weighing six pounds seven ounces. You were tiny, and you sure had some lungs on you. I took you from the midwife and cleaned you up. Waving a white handkerchief in the air, Bentsiwa danced jubilantly and shouted out 'it's a girl, it's a girl'. Your mum was delighted when I put you in her arms. You were so beautiful. We couldn't take our eyes off you."

Maame Akua wiped a tear from her eye. "Life is not measured by the number of breaths we take, but by the moments that take our breath away." She squeezed her arms around Zhara. "It was one of the best moments in my life." Maame Akua turned solemn. "The midwife had a distant look in her eyes when she took you from your mother's lap. When she said she'd waited for you all her life and would never let you go, I knew we had a battle on our hands. Trying not to cause panic, I persuaded her to let me have you, but she was proving difficult. Bentsiwa wasn't as tolerant. She yelled so much that the woman got scared. I quickly took you from her arms and she bolted out of the house. Your mother started to cry. Just then we realised the placenta had not come out."

"Really?" Zhara looked shocked.

"Yes. I encouraged your mother to push, but she was exhausted. We heard screeching tyres. Within seconds the whole compound was illuminated. Your father rushed in and decided you and your mum should be taken to hospital immediately. The thirty minute journey took about ten minutes but it seemed like eternity. Your mum was rushed into the operating theatre. An hour later the German doctor informed us that they had removed the placenta but she had lost a lot of blood and was in a coma."

Zahra looked distraught.

"The doctor assured us he would do everything possible to speed your mum's recovery so we prayed and hoped for the best. He also advised that it would be best if you were kept in the nursery for a few days."

"Did you leave me and mummy in the hospital?"

"We had to, but we returned as soon as we could. It was reassuring to see you in good hands. The nurses were exceptional. They took turns to feed you, bathe you and comb your full head of soft curls. Finally, after a week in the nursery, I was allowed to take you home. I carried you everywhere I went and wouldn't let you out of my sight. When people complained that you were getting too big for my ageing back, I would tell them to mind their own business. You were adorable. You loved motion, light, colour, music, pretty pictures and soft textures, but your greatest love was water. I often watched you blowing shiny bubbles of sound while lying in the bath with your tiny hands and feet dangling in the air. When you'd had enough I would pick you up, dry you up, run talcum powder all over your body, get you dressed, sing to you, and rock you to sleep."

Looking into her grandmother's eyes, Zhara asked softly "how long was Mum in the hospital?"

"About four weeks. Your father grew thinner and weaker as the days went by. He looked unkempt and would not touch his food. We were concerned about his physical, psychological and mental health, especially after he began to show signs of stress and anxiety. One day, he returned from the hospital around 2 pm, which was very unusual. I asked if all was well. He smiled, and then he said it was time to get you reacquainted with your mother. You see, you had not been with your mother since you were born, because of her condition. Your father was determined to change that. He insisted that you deserved to be with your mother, and it didn't matter whether she was conscious or not."

"Did you agree with him?"

"To be honest, dear, I didn't know what to think, but I trusted his judgement. So I wrapped you in a shawl, placed you in the crib and handed you to him. He took you to the hospital and sat beside your mother. He said at one point he looked at you, and there was something in your expression that was so like your mother that it made him feel as if a knife had been twisted in his gut. He began talking to you and your mother as if you were both coherent. He said that he'd been talking for about an hour when he felt an eerie silence in the room. For a moment he felt uplifted. He said the sinister atmosphere he'd become accustomed to was replaced by an inexplicable serenity and calmness. The sudden shift of energy gave way to a frosty breeze. Goosebumps appeared all over his arms as he drew you to him. That was when he noticed that your mother's feet were moving; the left foot, then the right. He called for help. After a long wait, it was confirmed that your mum had regained consciousness."

Zhara sat up. "Daddy must have been excited."

"That is an understatement! He was over the moon and beyond. He was tearing up with joy when I arrived. You were asleep. Your mum was fully conscious but very weak. It took her a while to walk and talk properly, but it all came back. My fun-loving, energetic and tenacious daughter became whole again."

Zhara held her chin thoughtfully. "Nana, I can't figure out what was wrong with the so-called midwife."

Maame Akua cleared her throat. "She was not right in the head. I saw at once, a series of confirming traits the instant she took you from your mother. According to Dorothy, the woman had been a senior midwife, but she lost her job after a series of gross irregularities at the hospital where she worked. Dorothy believed that the unstable behaviour began when she was kicked out by her husband for not being able to bear him children."

"Why did Dorothy not seek treatment for her friend, if she knew she was unstable?"

"You would assume as a medic, she would know better, but you see, it can be very difficult to convince people with mind disorders that they need help."

"Mum said Uncle Kofi, Uncle Kweku and Uncle Kwamena were incensed by what the midwife did."

"They were, but that is only natural, my boys have always been protective of their sisters. But the gospel according to Matthew teaches us to 'judge not so that ye be not judged'. What the midwife did was heart-wrenching, but it was not done with malice, she needed help."

Bentsiwa emerged from the kitchen. "Maame (mother) and Zhara, breakfast is ready."

"Thank you," replied Maame Akua "we are coming."

With their hands clasped together, Maame Akua and Zhara got off the swing chair and joined the rest of the family.

CHAPTER THIRTEEN

The household staff gathered around the car. They had come to see Zhara off. Trying to conceal his sadness, Awuni maintained a wide grin. What he admired most about Zhara, in the ten years he'd been working as houseboy, was her thoughtfulness. Unlike the children of previous employers who had been insolent, Zhara genuinely cared for the welfare of each member of the household and treated them with respect and kindness. Her gifts and tips maintained his status as champion of the house helps in the affluent suburb. It made the maids flock to him like a bee to a honey pot.

Obetsebi was excited that in just a fortnight, Zhara would return from London, bearing gifts for him, his wife and his children.

Kwakuvi, the gardener, appeared gratified. He'd been working for the family for just over two years and yet he'd already made enough money to build a small house for his mother in the village.

Kwansima emerged from the front door at 7pm, followed by Zhara and her parents.

Zhara said farewell to Awuni, Obetsebi, Kwakuvi and Kwansima. Then she got in the car and was driven away.

With mixed emotions the household staff waved to the car as they watched it roll down the driveway and disappear into the moonlight.

Kwansima was glad that Zhara was finally taking a well-deserved break, yet gloomy because she left a void whenever she went away.

The sound of Jonathan Butler's soothing jazz eased the lecture on the birds and the bees. It was a mantra Zhara had heard since puberty, so she concentrated on the music.

Looking distinguished in a deep purple dashiki, Kamil steered the car onto the main road. He seemed centred, Adam's apple moving each time he swallowed. Whereas most of his contemporaries were losing their hair, having a midlife crisis or growing pot bellies, the forty-six year old had been barely touched by age. His chiselled bone structure had been maintained and his muscles were perfectly toned. Even the strands of grey in his dark wavy hair added character to his handsome features.

There was no escape from the bumper-to-bumper traffic as he neared the Polo Club, about a mile away from the airport. A logjam of horns ululated painfully as taxi drivers swore, motorbikes sped past and street-sellers descended like flies on a road kill. Aided by streetlights the pedlars dived from one car to another parading fruit, pastries, toys, sweets, drinks and replica goods. Adding to the mayhem, young girls with trays of plastic-wrapped water on their head cried out 'iced waaaateeer!' as they sashayed along the pavements.

He was looking through the rear view mirror, when Kamil's eye fell on his daughter. Memories of her as a child and the terror in her eyes when she had nightmares made his heart jump. He was reminded of how helpless he had felt when he couldn't ease his little girl's panic and anxiety. Moving swiftly from the unpleasant thoughts he focused on the things she did that made him laugh. He remembered clearly the day he found her mimicking her mother. He'd laughed so much when he saw her tottering in her mother's high-heeled shoes, wearing oversized clothes and jewellery, make-up all over her face and a handbag almost as big as herself hanging over her shoulder. Just like her mother, she swung her hips like a pendulum, fingers pointed and dishing out orders to her imaginary workers. The image of the adorable little face warmed his heart, and a laugh slipped from his lips.

Araba noticed it and gazed expectantly at her husband. "Come on sweetheart. Let us in on the joke."

"I just remembered Zhara dressed up in your clothes. She was only five at the time."

Araba observed her husband with interest. She could tell he was missing Zhara already.

"She will be back in a few weeks." Arabra reminded him.

"I know that", Kamil replied "but the precious memories never go away." From the corner of his eye he watched Araba. She was wearing a silk kaftan and looked as beautiful and elegant as ever. His eyes wandered down to her jewel encrusted sandals. He touched her arm, and glowed at the feel of the velvety smooth olive skin. "Do you remember when she appeared on GBC TV?"

"Of course! How could I ever forget that? It was her acting debut and she was playing the innkeeper's wife in the Nativity?"

Kamil chuckled. "The part I enjoyed most was the bit at the end, when the cast returned to the stage and danced to Everybody Wants Kung Fu Fighting. The joy on their little faces, as they bumped each other on the hip..."

"I know" Araba said tenderly. Then she turned around so she was facing Zhara. "Do you know that before the show aired your father announced to the whole world that you were appearing on TV? And as if that wasn't enough, an hour before it started we were summoned to the living room and glued to the TV, just in case you came on early. When you eventually appeared on the screen, you looked adorable in a tradeswoman costume. Your father beamed like a satellite dish."

"You can talk" said Kamil. "You forget that you summoned your entire staff to watch the show, and your mother ensured that those without a TV set assembled in her compound to watch her granddaughter."

They were all laughing when they noticed the commotion. Two policewomen were escorting an elegantly dressed lady into a van. The woman, possibly in her forties, looked normal except for the loud conversation she appeared to be having with herself. She would laugh for a second and turn angry instantly.

Kamil turned to Araba. "Isn't she the American

diplomat who returned from a conference in the Middle East and found her husband in bed with the maid?"

Araba preened her neck for a closer look. "Oh my God! It is her. What could have happened? Oh dear!"

Zhara was reminded of her classmate, Kwame, whom she'd seen while driving to Tamali's house a few weeks back. She'd been extremely shocked when she saw the once handsome and extremely popular boy parading the streets of Kaneshie in his birthday suit and dirt-ridden locks of hair. Lost in a world of his own, he laughed loudly while catching invisible insects from the numerous carrier bags on his arm. Tamali had told Zhara that he joined a bad crowd at Medical school and got hooked on drugs, thus ruining a very promising future.

Thoughts of Kwame stayed with Zhara even as she checked in her bags. When her parents flung their arms around her tears rolled down involuntarily. She hugged her father tightly and buried her face in his chest. Then she crumbled into her mother's warm tender arms and inhaled the fragrant smell of gardenia.

Araba tucked a few strands of hair behind Zhara's ears. Ordinarily, this would have led to a sulk, but on this occasion Zahra smiled and hugged her mum even tighter, wishing she could remain in her loving arms forever.

CHAPTER FOURTEEN

The BA jumbo jet took to the skies a few minutes after 11 pm. The streets, houses, fields, hills and rivers below continued to diminish until they looked like creases in a palm.

High up in the clouds, surrounded by stars and the Milky Way, Zhara dimmed the lights and meditated. She was reflecting on her encounters with strangers around the world; the short and long conversations, friendly smiles, hostile stares, fleeting moments and varied emotions when the stewardess broke her reverie.

"Champagne ma'am?"

"No thanks."

"Perhaps a glass of water, or fruit juice?" The stewardess continued with an endearing smile.

"Apple juice please."

She left hastily and returned with the juice, nibbles and menu.

"Here you go, ma'am."

"Thank you." Zhara replied.

She took a sip and reclined into her seat. The enthusiasm with which the stewardess carried out her duty reminded her of what she loved most about the UK; it was

the home of most of her favourite writers and poets -
William Shakespeare, the Brontë sisters, Jane Austen,
Agatha Christie, Charles Dickens, Barbara Cartland, Lord
Byron, Robert Burns and Thomas Hardy; it had some of
the grandest palaces, monumental buildings, bridges,
parks and museums in the world; restaurants to suit every
palate and budget; famed stores - Harrods, Selfridges,
Harvey Nichols, Fenwicks, Liberty, John Lewis and
Fortnum & Mason; places of interest - Westminster,
Piccadilly Circus, Trafalgar Square, Madame Tussaud's,
the Coliseum; and theatres, jazz clubs, discotheques, pubs,
specialist shops, renowned shopping centres and street
markets. The three years she had spent in the UK had
been a master class in fashion, sexuality, race and religion.
Before then, she had only known of Islam and Christianity,
but by the end of her first year at university she'd been
enlightened about Judaism, Hinduism, Buddhism,
Sikhism, Jainism, Juche, Scientology, Kabbala and others
she couldn't even pronounce.

She recalled the day she went into the HMV music
store to purchase a CD. After trawling through the
alphabetically ordered artists in the jazz section for African
Woman by Hugh Masekela she gave up and asked one of
their many attendants. The uniformed lad with tattooed
arms led her to a till and tapped in the artist's name. "We
certainly do", he'd said with an irritatingly smug look on
his face. Then he told her she would have saved herself a
lot of time if she'd looked in the world music section.
Zhara was not sure if she'd stormed out because of what

he'd said or his attitude, but she did find Hugh Masekela's *African Woman*, much to her delight, clearly displayed in the jazz section at the Body Music store.

She took a few more sips of juice and wondered why some supermarkets in the UK put food items from Africa, Asia and the Caribbean in separate aisles and yet displayed fruits from these same continents; lychees, coconuts, bananas, mangoes, pineapple and watermelons side by side with European apples, pears, grapes and strawberries. She was thankful for the shops that stocked yam, plantain, okra, sweet potatoes, chillies and scotch bonnets, irrespective of where they were located.

As the chill began to set in, Zhara tugged a pillow under her head and covered herself with a blanket. She cast her mind back to an article she'd read a few years earlier about the results of a research on the behaviour of people living in hot climates v cold. It had stated that those who lived in tropical countries were drawn to spicy food and colourful attire whereas those in cold climates preferred mild-tasting dishes and neutral/dark attire. The article had also stated that the English language differed in accent and pronunciation, from one country to another. Bearing that in mind, she was astonished that some of her peers at university hadn't gathered that she was likely to speak, act and dress differently. She reflected on her first year in the UK, which had been incredibly exciting except for a few unpleasant incidents. She believed it was her prerogative, if she said t -MAY-toh instead of t -MAH-toh, shed-ule rather than sked-yul or shed-yule or geAr instead of geEr, so she did not take kindly to those who tried to correct her diction. But that was nothing, compared to some of the comments she had received; 'you really look colourful!', 'how nice and summery!', 'that looks rather bright', 'whoa, that is colourful'. Firstly, she may have appreciated some of the remarks, if they had been made during spring, autumn or winter, but it was blooming summer. Did they expect her to wear sack-clothes? Secondly, she would have understood if Olympia had not ensured that her entire wardrobe met with the fashion dictates of Paris, New York, London and Milan. Thus, armed with the approved shades for spring/summer (white, cream, orange, yellow, green, red, lilac) and autumn/winter (black, navy, grey, dark brown, dark green, deep red, dark purple) she could not help feeling deflated. So, to get her own back, she embellished her trendy wardrobe with some very colourful outfits she'd picked up from East Street market and threw caution to the wind. Coming from a culture where dark shades are worn by the bereaved, she found it interesting that people from other countries had no qualms about wearing dark shades. She came to realise that many people, especially woman chose to wear black, because it made them look slim.

An experience that had left a lasting impression on Zhara flashed through her mind. It meant little at the time but had since resonated with her.

She'd been waiting for a friend at a café when a young woman, possibly in her early twenties, walked in with a pretty girl trailing behind her. The girl had big blue eyes and long blond hair and was clutching a rag doll.

Zhara gathered from the woman's outbursts that the girl's father, repeatedly referred to as a no-good thieving scumbag, was serving time in prison.

As the girl, no more than five, and her mother waited by the counter she asked very politely if she could have a hot chocolate and a bun. The woman, glared at the child with glazed angry eyes, lit a cigarette with quivering hands and took a long puff. She turned and scowled at a respectable-looking Chinese couple and their two young children on a nearby table. The waitress was serving them a full English breakfast with all the trimmings; toast, scrambled eggs, mushrooms, tomatoes, hash browns, bacon, sausages, baked beans, coffee, tea, and orange juice.

The girl repeated her question, louder and more persistent this time, "Mum, can I have a hot chocolate and a bun?" Zhara wished she could throw her arms around the adorable little girl and buy her what she'd asked for, but she wasn't prepared for a confrontation.

The girl yelled at her mother, "Why can't we ever have proper food like them?" Her index finger was directed at the Chinese family.

The fury in her mother's bloodshot eyes was terrifying. She pulled at the cigarette with hollowed cheeks, extracted it as if it were a weapon, and let out a cloud of smoke. "Barbarians like them come over here and take everything we got," she yelled. They come with nothing, and before you know it they have good jobs, money in the bank, nice cars and big houses. Filthy little shops start opening all over our country and they take every fucking penny they can get from us." She glared at the little girl. "They are the reason we have no fucking home and can't afford to buy chocolate and a bun. The fat ugly pig behind the counter won't serve us because we have no money. He can look down his big fucking nose at us, but no matter how rich they get, we will remain superior to the fucking cunts! What the fuck are you looking at? She shouted at the man who owned the café. "If you fucking belonged here, you'd be white with blue or green eyes. Go back to your fucking country, the fucking lot of you!"

With that off her chest she took another puff of cigarette and stormed out of the café, dragging the little girl behind her. Sad, angry and shocked faces watched in silence. Some tutted and others shook their head with repulsion.

She sat up and looked around the cabin. The middle-aged man on her right had his head buried in the Financial Times. The young lady behind him was fast asleep. The reading on the map indicated that they were two hours away from London. She remembered one of her grandmother's proverbs, hurt people, hurt people.

Zhara said a prayer for all the starved, abused and homeless children around the world who'd never asked to be born, yet endure so much pain and suffering. She wondered why the needless suffering just carried on from year to year, why people who couldn't afford to feed themselves never stopped to think before bringing children into the world, why people hated each other just because of the colour of their skin. Baffled by man's inhumanity to mankind, she tried to figure out how the venomous evil that lies within each of us could be eliminated; that which makes us deny our own, that which makes us indifferent to the brutality of those who are not like us, that which makes us turn against each other in ghastly ways. She reflected on the horrific crimes of violence and mass murders deliberately planned and carried out around the world in the pursuit of gold, diamonds, cheap labour and oil; the horrors of the slave trade - killing and maiming millions of Africans; the theft of land and mineral resources with guns, bombs, teargas and cannons in the name of colonialism; the pain and anguish of the Holocaust; the genocides of Rwanda, Biafra, Ethiopia, Cambodia and Vietnam; the segregation and lynching of African Americans in the United States of America and the criminal and inhumane acts of apartheid that were allowed to carry on in South Africa.

Zhara wondered why the powerful rulers of the world looked on while the killing and brutality continued. Aristotle couldn't have been any clearer, she thought, when he said Man perfected by society is the best of all animals; he is the most terrible of all when he lives without law, and without justice.

She wished the barriers that divide us could be shattered, together with the evils of otherisation, racism, religious intolerance, and tribalism.

CHAPTER FIFTEEN

BA flight 567 touched down at 05:45 am. The atmosphere at Border Control could be cut with a knife, a sharp contrast from Kotoka Airport, which had bustled with smiling faces chattering in Ga, Fante, Twi, Ewe, Dagbani, Hausa and English.

As the demands and pleas penetrated the bitterly cold air Zhara felt sorry for the expectant mothers and those with infants who looked tired and dejected.

Olympia hadn't seen her cousin since she had hurriedly left the UK a year and a half ago. Thinking back, she felt sad that she hadn't been able to pull off the surprise party she had organised to mark her graduation.

She hurried to the arrivals hall and checked the screen. There were lots of people around, even though it was only 6:30 am.

Olympia's heart quickened when she saw Zhara approaching.

Waving vigorously, Zhara moved swiftly into her cousin's outstretched arms.

"I've missed you so much, you naughty girl," said Olympia.

"Me too" whispered Zhara. Wrapped up in Olympia's

arms, she felt the warmth and softness of the full-length mink coat. Casting an eye over the matching hat and gloves she wandered down to the six-inch knee-length Prada boots.

"You look as stylish as ever," she said affectionately.

"And you look like you could do with a hot meal and a nap."

They had reached the car when a thought crossed Olympia's mind. A wicked grin appeared on her impeccably made-up face as she thought, better late than never. Turning to Zhara she observed her with admiration.

"It is absolutely fabulous that you are partner and CEO, but darling, working twenty-four-seven without a holiday for eighteen months straight is downright crazy! I understand you love your job, but you know what they say about all work and no play. Trust me, you have a lot of playing to catch up on and this time, I won't be taking no for an answer!"

Zhara smiled. She realised Olympia hadn't changed at all.

Flakes of snow fell onto the autumn leaves. It looked so beautiful, like a picture postcard.

Olympia talked non-stop about her plans for the party, the latest trends in fashion and her many dates, from the moment she pulled out of the car park at Heathrow airport until they arrived in Vauxhall.

The tenth floor apartment was just as Zhara remembered it, with imposing views of the capital, rose-white walls, thick cream carpets, plush leather sofas and all the mod cons.

CHAPTER SIXTEEN

Zhara nodded off as soon as she fell into the queen-sized bed.

She woke up at noon, freshened up and was tucking into scrambled eggs on toast when it occurred to her that her phone had been switched off.

Olympia had left for work and it was exceptionally quiet. Snow was still falling outside.

Zhara retrieved the phone from her bag and switched it on. It beeped suddenly, making her jump. She had 12 missed calls; four from Lawal, three from Kukuwa, one from Lydia, one from Amira, one from her mother and two withheld.

She called her mother, then Lydia, her PA, before dialling Kukuwa's number.

"Hi stranger!"

"Oh my God! When did you arrive?" Kukuwa screamed with excitement.

"I arrived this morning."

"Your mum said you'd left when I called yesterday. I am just about to board a flight to London. I can't wait to see you."

"That is so sweet of you. I'd planned to spend a few

days with you in Switzerland, but this is a lovely surprise. I will prepare the guest room for you."

"That is really kind, but we've already booked the Savoy."

"We?"

"Yes, me and Fráncois, the guy I told you about. Remember?"

"I do remember, but you only met a few months ago, I didn't expect you to be living in sin already."

"We aren't, not technically anyway. I need to see you, there is so much to tell you, but not over the phone. Would you like to come here or should I come to you?"

"Um, can you come to me?"

"Of course. Where are you staying?"

"I'm at Olympia's place in Vauxhall. I'll text you the address. It must be costing a fortune at the Savoy, why don't you come and stay with us? I'm sure Olympia wouldn't mind."

"You know I would love to, if it was just me, but my fiancé..."

"Your what?"

"It all happened so quickly. Before I knew it, he was asking me to marry him, and I said yes."

"Congratulations darling, I am so pleased for you. At least now I can sleep better knowing you are sharing a room with someone who intends to marry you. Sorry, but I can't help being old-fashioned!"

"See you soon."

"Can't wait. Have a safe journey."

Zhara was unpacking her suitcase when the entry-phone started buzzing.

An image of Amira in a thick suede coat and hat, and Pandora in a soft brown fur coat appeared on the security camera.

As soon as Zhara unlocked the door, they screamed and threw their arms around her neck, leaving her breathless.

"Honey I've missed you so much" said Amira.

Pandora kissed Zhara's cheeks. "I can't believe you are here, I've really missed you."

"Me too" said Zhara.

She led them in and took their coats.

Amira looked stunning in a navy suit and baby pink shirt.

Pandora's tweed miniskirt, thigh high boots and plunge-neck sweater, made her look stylishly elegant and her long toned legs seemed even longer.

Amira gave Zhara a sweeping look.

"Still looking fabulous! I am loving the long kinky braids. I hope you brought me some of the sexy beads you used to wear on your waist."

"How can I forget?" she asked indignantly, "when you text me every month with your demands? And by the way, who told you I was here?"

Amira rolled her eyes. "Did you think you could come to this country without us knowing? From what I hear, you arrived very early this morning. It's now..." she glanced at her watch, "1:30 pm, when were you going to return my call?"

Zhara was lost for words.

Pandora, who had been rummaging through the high glossed kitchen cabinets, stuck her head in the fridge and cried out, "Cristal, Dom Perignon, Moët, caviar, oysters, smoked salmon, olives, truffles. Don't you have proper food?"

Amira and Zhara looked at each other and shook their head.

"I could make you scrambled egg on toast?" Zhara offered. "You know as well as I do that Olympia doesn't cook!"

Pandora scowled defiantly and threw back her long red mane. "You have to be kidding! Do you think I came all this way for toast? No honey," she rolled her eyes, "that will just not do. I want proper food, like what you used to make at uni - jolof rice, fried plantain and beans, yam and palava sauce, fufu and groundnut soup, kenkey [boiled maize meal] and fish..."

"Please give her a break," said Amira. "And stop throwing your toys out of the pram. Now you know why Zhara didn't inform us that she was coming to London."

"So, my dear friend," said Zhara "did you come here because you've missed me, like you say, or because you were hungry?"

Pandora feigned a look of sadness. "Of course I've missed you." She threw her long arms around Zhara. "But I have to admit, I've really, really, missed your cooking. Ever since you left, I've been craving for your mouth-watering dishes. I've even tried to cook some of the dishes from the recipes you gave me, but I won't lie, they didn't taste half as good as yours. As for Amira, she is bloody useless at cooking so I didn't bother asking her for help."

Amira chuckled. "Pandora, you have really got it bad. I thought you were joking when you said Zhara's delicious meals was like a drug, and you didn't realise how hooked you were on them until she left."

"Zhara," Amira pleaded, "Please make her something, anything, so she can shut up."

"OK then," Zhara pursed her lips, "Let me run to Brixton and get a few things. Please behave yourselves and don't go poking your noses into Olympia's closets."

"Would we ever do that?" Pandora muttered in a childlike voice.

"Yes you would, but you better not, because she will skin the pair of you alive. Denzel's Mississippi Masala is on the video recorder. I know that will keep you out of mischief. Help yourselves to drinks. There is popcorn in the top cabinet. I'll be back before you know it."

Zhara returned to her room and threw on a woollen skirt, boots, a jumper, gloves, scarf and a coat. She grabbed her bag and walked briskly to Vauxhall underground station.

It took her six minutes to get to the station. Brixton was two stops away on the Victoria line, so she reckoned she could be back in just over an hour if all went well.

The advantage of commuting in London was that it could be fast and convenient, especially outside the rush hour, 8 am to 9:30 am and 5 pm to 6:30 pm. As it happened, she was in luck, and even had a choice of seats and room to stretch her legs. A majority of the passengers were dressed for winter but some seemed to be unaffected by the freezing weather.

Engulfed by the hubbub of announcements and moving trains, Zhara remembered the worst journey she'd ever had on the underground. She'd taken the train on an exceptionally humid Saturday in July to meet Olympia for dinner at the Langham. She had arrived at Paddington Station just after 5 pm and taken the underground to Bond Street Station. The first two trains had been packed, so she had waited for the next. Though it had arrived within minutes it had been packed with only a little space left for standing. She had got on, and all seemed well. But one stop away from her destination hordes of people rushed onto the train, forcing Zhara into in a tight corner, one side of her face squashed up against the window and the other lodged beneath a sweaty pungent armpit. That had been the beginning of her worst commuting nightmare. She had held on tightly to the rail, barely able to breath because of the stuffiness. Then as if that was not bad enough, the train had jolted. Passengers had been thrown about in the carriage and fallen over each other. With mutters of apology and nervous smiles they had jolted from shoulder to shoulder, trying desperately to recover their equilibrium.

Then an ear-wrenching announcement: "Due to an incident on the train ahead of us, we will be remaining here until further notice. We apologise for the delay to your journey." Panic had set in, then anger and frustration. The fear of being stuck in a tunnel with no means of escape had shaken Zhara to the core. Crammed up like a sardine and assaulted by a vindaloo breath, the person standing beside her had broken wind, rather violently. Holding her breath, she had prayed for the train to move. Amidst the revoltingly smelly carriage a few drunken louts had caused a furore. Armed with cans of lager they had shouted obscenities. Though their anger had been aimed at London Transport for making them late for the football match at Wembley, they had scared the life out of some of the passengers. The fact that they had been drunk, tottering and still drinking had been very worrying. After a few minutes the train had set off, to everyone's relief, but Zhara's predicament had not yet ended. Her attempt to get off the train at Bond Street had been another battle. First she had had to fight her way through the carriage to get to the door, then, faced with a platform full of people, she had forced her way out of the train. One would have thought it logical for people on the platform to stand back and allow passengers off the train before getting on, but faced with despair, common sense had been thrown out the window. Like a herd of cattle they had forged ahead while alighting passengers had fought tooth and nail to get out. Feeling as if she'd wrestled a bull, Zhara had vowed never to travel on public transport during rush hour, and she had kept her promise.

Zhara hopped off the train at Brixton. She got on the escalators, run up the stairs, turned the corner and strode down Coldharbour Lane. The market was vibrant with activity and people of every hue. She bought fruit, vegetables, spices, fish, meat, buns and patties. Then she made her way to the stall which stocked all the ingredients for the food she planned to prepare.

"Would there be anything else?" The young man at the till asked, in a strong Ashanti accent.

"That would be all, thanks."

"It comes to £53.95, but let's call it 50 quid."

The come-again smile was rather toothy but reassuring.

Zhara smiled, said "Me da ase (thank you)," and paid the bill. Laden with bags, she flagged a black cab and jumped in.

CHAPTER SEVENTEEN

Amira and Pandora were eyeballing Denzel Washington's backside when Zhara popped into the living room.

"Oh you are here," said Pandora. "Can I help?"

Zhara shook her head. "I would not dream of taking you away from Denzel's toned rear, but thanks for asking."

She changed into a thick jumper and leggings and returned to the kitchen. She liked to listen to music while cooking so she turned on the radio. Michael Jackson was singing Liberian Girl, one of her top ten singles.

It was whilst she was stirring the groundnut paste that Zhara remembered the first time she'd offered to cook groundnut soup for Amira and Pandora. Unlike Amira, who had been keen to try the Ghanaian dish, Pandora recoiled, narrowed her eyes and twisted her face into a scornful mess, then she hissed "Groundnut what?" Zhara had been surprised when Pandora inched into the kitchen when the soup was ready. Aroused by the scrumptious aroma she asked if she could taste the soup. The fear in her eyes had not only been of the soup, but of the ladle and the saucepan too. Somehow she had allowed a tiny bit of the smooth brown liquid to fall on her tongue. She had tasted it gingerly, allowed it to linger in her mouth for a while, then asked if she could have another drop. Amira and Zhara were flabbergasted when Pandora licked her lips and asked for more.

The doorbell curtailed Zhara's thoughts. She wiped her hands quickly and rushed to the door. She was delighted to see Kukuwa.

"Does your mother know what you've done to your hair?"

Kukuwa gave her a bone-crushing hug.

"I've missed you so much!"

"Me too."

Zhara gaped at the huge ruby sparkling against her butterscotch hands.

"Ooh, it is so beautiful. I am so pleased for you. I hope you've found true love."

"Thank you darling. I really do. I've never felt this way about anyone."

Zhara shut the door behind them and took her coat.

Even in ripped jeans and a T-shirt, Kukuwa looked like she'd just stepped out of a vogue magazine. The short tapered dark hair with mahogany highlights did wonders to her face and cheekbones.

Zhara observed Kukuwa worriedly. "You haven't answered my question. Has your mother seen your hair?"

Kukuwa shrugged. "Not yet."

"She will not be pleased."

"I am past caring. Had it not been for her obsession with my hair, we would have attended the same secondary school."

"But look at you now, it may have been for the best."

"Perhaps, but it is my hair and I'll do as I please with it."

She could not agree more. Even with her hair shaved off Kukuwa would look drop-dead gorgeous.

Zhara introduced Kukuwa to Amira and Pandora.

They had moved on from Mississippi Masala to Chris Rock's Bigger & Blacker.

Zhara returned to the kitchen with Kukuwa. She stirred the soup, checked the jolof rice and put the kettle on.

"We met at the conference in September." Kukuwa began. "We had been dating for a few weeks when François dropped a bombshell. He wanted to introduce me to his family. He picked me up from work one Friday, and we flew on his private jet to the south of France. François proposed while we were there. Can you believe it?" She glowed every time she mentioned François's name.

"You'd been dating for how long?'

"About four weeks."

"Wow! That soon?"

"Qui! I was shocked, confused and delighted, but it was too soon, so I asked François to give me some time." A month ago he asked if I would accompany him on a short trip. I said yes..."

"Where did you go?"

"Mauritius. We were taking a stroll on the white sandy beach when he went down on his knee and asked if I would spend the rest of my life with him."

"And?"

"I could not deny how I felt about him. He is a lovely man, and he spoils me to bits but I needed more time, so I said maybe."

"What?"

"His birthday was two weeks away. I planned to say yes then, plus it would give me time to introduce him to my parents."

"How did he take it?"

"He was very disappointed, but he understood that it was a big decision and I needed to be utterly certain. Just as I'd expected, my parents took to him. So on his birthday, two weeks ago, I told him I would like to be his wife. It was well worth the wait. I'd never seen him so happy."

CHAPTER EIGHTEEN

Olympia was elated that the long drawn-out case had finally come to an end. It still hadn't quite sunk in that Baroness Obi had been acquitted of all charges. What she had done was wrong, and even though Olympia did not condone her client's actions, she understood why she had done it.

The Baroness had quit school at the age of nineteen so she could do three jobs and put her twenty-year-old boyfriend through college. They got married shortly after he was promoted to manager. Years later he was made partner. Money started rolling in. Power followed, and with it came a very lavish lifestyle and a title. As they approached retirement, the seemingly happy couple bought several acres of land in the countryside and built a mansion with an indoor swimming pool, tennis court and stables. So the sudden announcement, barely a month after moving into their idyllic countryside pad that he didn't want to be married any more, broke the poor woman's heart. Initially, she blamed herself, but when she discovered that her 60-year-old husband was trading her in for his 25-year-old secretary, she went nuts. The jury concluded that only temporary insanity would drive a respectable woman and dedicated wife to shoot her husband ten times with an AK47 and sever his manhood with a cutlass. The brutal killing and emasculation were not premeditated.

As she pulled into the underground car park Olympia felt a great sense of relief. She was with Ngozi, her closest friend and Chelsea, her executive assistant.

Ngozi looked bewildered when the door was thrown open.

"Are we at the right house?"

The aroma of spices floating through the air in Olympia's home was very strange, because she couldn't even boil an egg.

"Please tell me you've hired a chef. Please, please," she cried "not another beggar from your late night rendezvous!"

Olympia ignored her and carried on walking with her chest puffed out.

Shaking her head vigorously, the 30-year-old accountant braced herself. The thought of another gold-digger creeping in the state-of-the-art kitchen made her skin crawl.

Olympia had deliberately not mentioned to either of them that Zhara had arrived. She couldn't wait to surprise them.

"I know you won't believe me, but there hasn't been any action here for quite some time, not after the bitter pill I had to swallow from the last bastard."

Kicking off her Manolo Blahniks, Olympia followed the sound of laughter to the living room.

"Meet my dearest cousin, Zhara," she said triumphantly to Chelsea and Ngozi.

Ngozi breathed a sigh of relief. "Welcome darling, what a great pleasure!" she hugged Zhara, then turned to Olympia. "Were you aiming to give me a heart attack?"

Olympia gave her a cheeky smile. "I love surprises," she said and carried on with the introductions.

Whilst their friends were getting to know each other, Olympia followed Zhara to the kitchen.

"Darling, you've really outdone yourself. I can't believe you cooked all this, mmmhhhh..." She licked her lips "beef kebabs, stir fried vegetables with tiger prawns, jolof rice, fried plantain, groundnut soup, sticky toffee pudding ..."

"You should thank Pandora. Had it not been for her nagging I wouldn't have stepped out today."

"Thank you darling. I had planned to take you out for dinner, but this will do just fine."

The food was received with a chorus of 'mms' and 'aahs' and devoured. Appetites appeased, Pandora, Amira, Ngozi and Chelsea shuffled along the corridor, from the dining room to the living room.

It was approaching 8pm. Tiny flakes of snow continued to fall.

Kukuwa snuggled down on the sofa and admired the intimate views of London's many recognisable structures.

Zhara turned up the heat in the marble fireplace and sat beside Kukuwa.

Olympia stuffed bottles of Cristal in an ice bucket and topped the decanters with brandy, whisky and vodka. She intended to make it a night to remember. After laying out an array of drinks and nibbles, she set the scene with Marvin Gaye's Let's Get it On.

"I would like to propose a toast to my dearest cousin, Zhara." Olympia said, and raised her glass. "She only arrived this morning, but she has managed to turn this place into a home."

"To Zhara!" they cheered.

"I would also like to propose a toast to Kukuwa, who recently got engaged to François. Congratulations darling, we wish you only the best on your wonderful journey of love."

Olympia took a long sip of her drink. "I've known Kukuwa for over a decade, even before her exclusive finishing school education, and maturity into a stunning debutante fit for French aristocracy."

Kukuwa blushed.

"Last, but not least," Olympia continued, "I would like to say a big 'thank you' to each and every one of you for being here. It means so much to me."

Pandora couldn't take her eyes off Kukuwa. She moved with grace and elegance and was incredibly warm and polite.

"Which of the Swiss schools did you attend?" Affection gleamed in Pandora's large green eyes.

"Institut Villa Pierrefeu."

"What did you study there?" Amira asked, equally intrigued.

"French, business management, international etiquette, protocol and savoir-vivre."

"Wow!" said Chelsea. "That sounds impressive. Are you working in London?"

"No, I work at the United Nations in Geneva."

"Did you meet your fiancé in Geneva?"

"No." Kukuwa smiled. "Actually, we met at a conference in Paris."

"Was it love at first sight?"

"Not exactly, but he grew on me."

"So you'd been dating for some time?"

"About four months."

Chelsea's eyes bulged. "And you are engaged already?"

"How romantic!" said Amira.

Pandora swirled the drink in her glass, "I hope you are not up the duff?" Her eyes were squinted suspiciously.

"She said she hopes you are not pregnant." Olympia translated.

"Oh I see. No, no, no. We want to do things properly; get engaged, get married, and then babies."

Ngozi sighed with relief. "Thank heavens! Many couples rush into relationships before they've had time to get to know and love each other..."

"What has love got to do with it?" Olympia sniggered.

"Love, love, love ... It's all bullshit! One day they are all over you, and you begin to think the sun shines out of their backside, then before you know it they can't stand the sight of you." She guzzled the drink in her glass and uncorked another bottle of Cristal. "Crap, crap, double crap!" She topped the glasses, took a long sip and sunk into the cream leather sofa.

"As I was saying," Olympia continued. "All this love stuff is a waste of time. What matters is that they care enough about each other and intend to stay together. Kukuwa is a hot catch, by any standards. Just look at her! And François is an astute businessman. He would not have asked her to marry him if he wasn't convinced that she was the real deal. He is incredibly good-looking and the sole heir to the de'Conde family's multi-million pound corporation. I can't wait for the wedding!" She turned to Kukuwa. "Have you set a date yet, darling?"

Kukuwa crossed her legs at the ankles. She had swapped her champagne for a glass of Evian with a slice of lemon.

"Yes," she said softly. It is scheduled for the 17th of September, next year. I hope you can all come."

"I won't miss it for the world" said Olympia.

Chelsea made a note in her Filofax, "count me in!"

"Have you met his family?" asked Amira.

"Yes. His father is very nice..."

"And his mother?" Pandora knocked back her wine.

Kukuwa held his breath. "She tries to be nice, but she can't help being arrogant and condescending. The first time we met, she refused to shake my hand and wouldn't look me in the eye, but she is getting better."

Pandora poured a large shot of brandy, threw in a few ice cubes, shook the glass and gulped it. A sardonic smile appeared on her face.

"The fact that you love François doesn't mean you should put up with his mother's bigotry."

"But what can I do?" Kukuwa said sadly. "François believes she acts that way because she rarely associates with people of colour. But you know, her chauffeur and many of the servants in her chateau are coloured."

Olympia observed Kukuwa thoughtfully. "Darling, the woman certainly belongs to the old school but her actions towards you may simply be from ignorance, and fear of losing her son. Put yourself in the woman's shoes. Her son wants to marry a girl he has only known for a few months. She is probably disappointed that he has abandoned debutantes from French aristocratic families for an African girl. I think her hostility stems from doubts about her son's choice, and nothing else."

"I am not convinced" said Pandora. "Kukuwa, what is François doing about his mum's insolence?"

Kukuwa smiled. "François adores his mother, and he believes she will come around. He is adamant that what we share is unbreakable. I hope he is right."

"I am sure he is," said Zhara. "And I am glad his father is on your side."

Kukuwa nodded. "He is a charming man and very down-to-earth. He believes his wife will be fine, once she's had time to digest the fact that I am not after her son's wealth or the family's heirloom. He once referred to her behaviour as nothing more than the fear of the unknown."

"Don't let it get to you, honey" said Ngozi. "Mothers-in-law will always find a way to hold on to their precious sons. There have been many times when I could have strangled Tunde's mother for some of the things that come out of her mouth. The woman is vile, but reacting will lead to disagreements between me and Tunde, so no matter how much she provokes me, I remain kind and polite."

"Really?" Pandora looked startled.

"I love my baby" Ngozi gushed, "and I wish he wasn't such a mama's boy, but he is, so my only option is to grin and bear it. Luckily, she lives in Lagos so I only have to put up with her when she comes to visit or we go there. After ten years of marriage you'd think she couldn't get any worse, but the woman has a way of getting under my skin, even before she opens her mouth."

Zhara chuckled, "I think ignorance should be made a crime. Do you remember the boy from Texas?"

"Uh huh, your admirer!" Amira chortled.

"Yes, I remember." Pandora sneered. "He was such an idiot. The nerd offered to take Zhara to Las Vegas if she agreed to date him. As if that would tempt her!"

"But wait for this" said Amira excitedly. "When she turned him down, he had the audacity to suggest that she lived in a tree.

"Oh no no no!" Olympia cried out. "Please say he didn't. He did not go there!"

"Oh yes." Pandora shrieked. "He went there!"

"What did you say to that?" Olympia glared at Zhara with her teeth and fists clenched.

"I had to be sure I'd heard him correctly," she said calmly, "so I asked him to repeat what he said. Suddenly he started to stammer. I am so sorry, I didn't mean to offend you. I just assumed people in Africa lived in trees."

Chelsea laughed so much, she fell off her seat. "And you said?"

"I said yes, Africans live in trees. I even added that when the Queen of England visits Africa, she and her entourage dwell in trees in the jungle with pythons, cobras, lions, cheetahs, leopards, rhinos and baboons."

Pandora and Olympia roared with laughter.

Ngozi and Kukuwa were doubled over.

Chelsea stared in stunned disbelief. "I have often wondered how people who are perceived to be educated can be so bloody ignorant. Did he believe you?"

"I think he did, at first," said Zhara, "but when he saw Amira's face, the penny dropped. You've got to be kidding, he said, that can't be real, the Queen of England on a damn tree? I gave him something to chew on and hoped he got the message."

Olympia topped up the glasses. Bob Marley's Crazy Baldheads was playing softly in the background. She turned up the volume and sang to the music.

The girls joined in.

... I'n'I build a cabin; I'n'I plant the corn:

Didn't my people before me

Slave for this country?

Now you look me with that scorn,

Then you eat up all my corn.

We gonna chase those crazy - Chase them crazy -

Chase those crazy baldheads out of town!

Build your penitentiaries, we build your schools,
Brainwash education to make us the fools.
Hate is your reward for our love,
Telling us of your God above.

We gonna chase those crazy -
Chase those crazy bunkheads -
Chase those crazy baldheads out of the town!

It was a few minutes after 10 pm. The weather outside was below freezing. People hurried along the streets down below while the girls danced the night away.

The teetotallers, Zhara and Kukuwa, were steady on their feet but the seasoned drinkers, Pandora and Olympia were all over the place.

Olympia knocked back a few more glasses of Red Bull with vodka and slumped into the sofa. "You won't believe how many men Zhara has let slip through her fingers."

"Really?" Chelsea looked intrigued.

"Yes. It began with Greg, the tall handsome dark chocolate hunk. He was a few years older than Zhara, and from what I hear, fabulous under the sheets. Young girls and very mature women flocked to the club where he worked as a part-time DJ, hoping he would practice his bedroom skills on them. And he did, to pass the time, but he had his eyes on Zhara, and would serenade her with Feel so good, loving somebody when somebody loves you back by Teddy Pendergrass, whenever he saw her. She never gave him the 50:50 luv he desperately wished for."

"Whoaaa," Pandora played with her hair, "he sounds like chocolate heaven."

"He was, and had a body just like Adonis, but she couldn't be bothered. A few weeks later Abedi came on the scene. She had just turned seventeen. The moment I saw him, I knew there was no hope. The guy had a cute smile, but he was a bit on the short side, and his Gerry-curl was longer than my hair."

"That is just too much hair for a man" said Amira.

Pandora cringed. ""Uh-uh, and a whole lot of grease."

"When she told me Larry was hounding her, I just had to laugh." Olympia continued. "I dated his twin brother for a while, you see, so I was quite fond of the guy, but he was a decade older than Zhara, bald, married and had a mistress or two in every area code in Accra."

"He sounds like a dog!" said Ngozi.

"He was, and proud of it. And he could bag any girl he wanted with his fleet of luxury cars, but not Zhara."

Amira took a long sip of her drink and looked at Zhara with a grin on her face. "Did you ever have lunch with Raja?" She asked Zhara.

"Who is Raja?" She stared vacantly.

"The guy who owned the antique shop in the arcade. Surely you must remember!" Amira huffed. "He said you reminded him of the Taj Mahal, and he narrated the story behind the beautiful castle to us. Each time he asked you out to lunch you would say you were busy so he developed a nasty habit of turning up unannounced at campus bearing gifts. He thought it would induce you to go out with him."

"Oh, him."

"Yes, him." Amira sighed with relief. How could you forget him. He vowed to build you a castle, if you returned his affection. He was soooo in love with you."

"You're a hard nut to crack." Chelsea commented.

Zhara jauntily tossed back her hair. "Not really. I didn't fancy him, so why would I want to have lunch with him?"

"It wouldn't have done you any harm to have lunch with the poor guy."

"Poor guy?" Zhara was losing her patience. "That is how it starts. First they give you something then they want something back. There is no such thing as a free lunch, and I don't intend to waste my time with any Tom, Dick or Harry. I have had it up to here with all of them" she said angrily, "handsome, ugly, old, young, fat, thin, tall, short, perverts, stalkers, rapists, murderer, castle builders..."

"OK dear," Olympia said soothingly "we get the message, but you can't discard all men while you wait for Mr Right. Wouldn't it be fun to have one or two hunks as your friends with benefits? That way, you could get to understand men better and get a taste of what's on offer, with no strings attached."

"I don't think so" she replied. "I know all I need to know about men."

Olympia prepared herself for the dangerous ground she was about to tread. "I don't doubt that, but darling," she said affectionately, "there is a difference between knowing about men and knowing them. Do you get my drift?"

Though she appeared calm, Olympia could tell from Zhara's eyes that she was fuming.

"Please tell me" said Zhara, "what happens after I have known one, two, three, four or even ten men, and I am still not happy with what they have to offer? Do I stop or carry on until I reach fifty, eighty or perhaps a hundred?"

"I sincerely hope not!" Olympia replied. "But you need to give them a chance. Even those that we think we know very well can develop multiple personalities and bad habits so there are no guarantees, but you can't let that stop you. Life is a gamble, some you win, and some you lose. It is all part of the learning curve."

Zhara took a deep breath. "I know you mean well, and I love you for it, but I will not waste my time with anyone I don't intend to marry. My body is a temple and will remain so until I marry the man I intend to spend the rest of my life with, for better or worse."

"What if he wants sex before he commits? Pandora asked.

"Then we are not meant to be. Anyway, if he really loves me, then he will understand. Of course, if he chooses not to wait until we are married then he doesn't deserve me."

"You rule!" Ngozi shouted. "I am impressed. It would be an ideal world if we could all live by those standards, but temptation and peer pressure gets in the way."

"I agree," said Kukuwa. Many girls succumb to the desires of their boyfriends because they are scared of losing them, but the boys leave them anyway, after they've had what they want."

"Have you heard from Lawal?" Olympia asked Zhara.

"Yes, he called while I was sleeping."

"Have you returned his call?"

"Not yet."

"I must say" said Olympia, "out of all your admirers, he is my favourite."

"Me too!" said Pandora. "Prince Lawal is handsome, gentle and caring, and ever so cute."

"Is he a real Prince?" Chelsea asked excitedly.

"Yes, as real as can be, and fucking loaded," said Amira.

"Wasn't he the guy who sent you a huge bouquet of roses and a giant-sized teddy bear when you caught flu about two years ago?" Ngozi asked Zhara.

"Yes he is," Olympia replied. "I didn't think you would remember."

"He sounds divine," said Chelsea. "How did she meet him?"

"They met at college. He was a year ahead of her. Though they've remained friends, I know he secretly pines for her and would love to take things a step further, if she'll let him."

"What is it with you and men anyway?" asked Pandora. "Don't you love him at all, not even a tiny itsy bitsy weeny bit?"

"Lawal is a great guy," said Zhara. "I like him a lot, but I don't love him."

Olympia threw her hands up in the air. "I give up!" She turned and looked steadily at Zhara. "How would you know about love when you refuse to be loved? Lawal is handsome, intelligent, charming and very thoughtful. Moreover, he comes from one of the most highly respected royal families. What more do you want?"

Amira held her chin thoughtfully. "There must be something else. She has turned down every single guy who has asked her out. Come to think of it, she has never had a boyfriend, and she sure isn't getting any younger."

"Has it occurred to you that she may have experienced some sort of abuse?" Chelsea said, looking askance at Zhara. "Mental, physical or sexual abuse either witnessed or experienced can put people off men."

"Absolutely not," Amira cried out.

"I wonder if it has anything to do with the stalkers." Olympia commented thoughtfully.

"What stalkers?" Pandora demanded and hastily turned towards Zhara.

"The first incident occurred when she was eleven." Olympia explained. "An elderly man, a chief, had been stalking her for days. Apparently none of his seven wives could bear him a son and he'd been told by a fetish priest to look for a virgin bride. Why he picked Zhara is still a mystery. Anyway, he showed up at her home with one of his many wives to ask for her hand in marriage."

"Hell no!" Amira yelled. "The cheek of it!"

"Needless to say" Olympia continued, "they were shown the door."

"Some men can be such ignorant pigs," said Chelsea. "Bloody pervert!"

"That sort of thing happens quite a lot in some parts of the world." Ngozi remarked. "I think anyone who harbours sexual desires for a child should be castrated."

"I concur!" Kukuwa said vehemently.

The next incident happened in London." Olympia continued.

"Another one? Really?" Kukuwa sighed deeply. She had a sneaky feeling that something awful may have happened to her friend. "Will you tell us what happened, Zhara?" She said with a sad smile.

"I was on my way to a friend's birthday party in Anerley, South London. While waiting for the No. 3 bus at Brixton, a black Mercedes pulled up beside me. The driver, a middle-aged white man, stuck his head out of the window and asked if I wanted a lift. I looked away. He shouted, 'hello gorgeous, I could take you anywhere you want.' I moved away and stood behind a group of girls waiting for a bus.'"

Amira leaned forward, eyes wide and alight, "And?"

"I assumed he had left and put him out of my mind. I got on the bus and was thinking about the party when a young man approached me. He'd got on the bus at Herne Hill Station. He said while he was waiting for the bus the man in the car behind us had asked him to tell me he would be waiting at the next stop for me. I turned and looked behind. Right there, behind the bus was the black Mercedes. I asked him how he knew it was me and not any other person on the bus. I nearly died when he pointed out that I was the only young lady on the bus and the description he gave of me was very accurate."

"What did you do?" asked Chelsea.

"I knew instantly that I had a stalker on my hands and he wasn't kidding so I moved swiftly to the front of the bus and waited anxiously for the conductor to finish her rather intimate discussion with the much younger bus driver. 'What you want!" She yelled at me. I am sure she thought I had nothing better to do than to listen in on their conservation. I told the forty-something uniformed woman with a mouth full of gold teeth that I had every reason to believe that I was being followed by the man in the car behind us."

"And?" Amira asked with her mouth wide open.

"She laughed her face off. 'Chil, 'e don' mean no harm, 'e soon gone' she said.' Throwing back her dreadlocks, she walked leisurely to the back of the bus and squinted at the car behind us. Then with one hand buried in her hip pocket, she bit through a Kitkat and rolled it around in mouth. About a mile away from Crystal Palace, she began to panic. By then the only people left on the bus were the conductor, the driver and me! The conductor had been gaping at the Mercedes for some time. Suddenly, she let out a loud piercing cry and lunged to the front of the bus screaming 'Blood clout! Bambaclout!' As we turned the corner into Crystal Palace Bus Station she yelled 'Call the Police, Babylon! Looord!' She was hyperventilating when we reached the final stop. The police arrived in less than a minute. I was very impressed."

"That was because the police station is just round the corner. I know the place well," said Ngozi. "Where was the fucking bastard?"

"Parked behind the bus and waiting." said Zhara, "and he made no attempt to move, not until the policemen, all four of them, finished talking to us and moved towards his car. Just as they neared him, he reversed and sped away."

"Oh honey," said Kukuwa, "did you make it to the party?"

"I did, but by then I was in no mood for partying. The police kindly gave me a lift to my friend's house on William Booth Road."

Pandora poured a long shot of brandy and rested her feet on the rosewood table. "He sounds like those predatory stalkers who haunt their victims, rape them, kill them and dispose of their bodies. I still can't believe he actually followed you all the way from Brixton. That should tell you how determined the nutter really was. I'm so glad you got out of that one unscathed."

"And to think he actually asked someone to pass on a message" said Kukuwa, looking nonplussed, "that he would be waiting for you at the next stop, that is seriously disturbing."

Zhara moved to the fireplace and warmed her hands.

Kukuwa joined her. "You poor thing! Why didn't you mention any of this to me?"

Zhara remained silent.

As they stared into the flames, Kukuwa put her arms around her and held her close, wondering what else she'd kept to herself.

Chelsea took a long shot of brandy and topped it with ice

cubes. Easing into the sofa she shook the glass gently and took a sip of the drink.

"Sometimes, it is best to be free of love," she said dolefully, "and thus free of fear, hurt, pain, complexity, doubt, weakness, longing, jealousy and sadness. For love can be the essence of all these feelings. It is only without love that we can truly have hope."

"But that can't be true," said Pandora. "How can anyone have hope without love?"

"It's a long story." Chelsea said, forcing back the tears.

Amira rubbed her arm. "You don't have to do this, if you don't want to."

"But I love long stories" said Pandora. She filled a plate with tortilla, guacamole, crab and lobster stuffed mushrooms and olives, and stuffed her face.

Olympia poured a long shot of Rémy Martin and took a handful of Brazil and cashew nuts while humming to Jocelyn Brown's Somebody Else's Guy.

Pandora tutted disapprovingly. "Please, Chelsea" she pleaded.

It was approaching midnight.

Holding her chin in quiet deliberation, Chelsea poured a very long shot of brandy and threw most of it down her throat. It sent a rush of colour to her cheeks.

"On the surface he seemed like the perfect gentleman," Chelsea said, looking dejected. "Just thinking about him would send my pulses racing, and when he smiled, oh my, I floated up above the skies to the heavens. At first I wondered what the 26-year-old entrepreneur saw in me, a plain-looking 17-year-old from the wrong side of town. When I heard wealthy sugar mummies all over the world were throwing themselves at him, I was flattered. I know how dumb that sounds, but I was young and naive. Some of my friends told me they'd seen him in a compromising position with women old enough to be his grandmother, but I wasn't deterred. I was furious when they suggested that he might be a gigolo? I guess it was easier to think they were green-eyed monsters. And why not?" she laughed, "he was drop-dead gorgeous. His shirts matched his Italian leather shoes and designer belts and his eau de cologne lingered hours after he'd left the scene. It never crossed my mind that the house he lived in, the shop he claimed to own and all the cars he drove may not be his. The rolled up notes and white lines on his dressing table were really none of my business, and the joints he smoked made him sweet and mellow. He didn't have to explain to me that the stream of ladies and gents who flooded his shop were business associates, but I was glad he did. And as for his frequent disappearance for months on end without a word of warning, that was fine, he didn't have to justify himself to me. A few years down the line I grew wiser and even swore to leave him. He'd been gone for over six months and hadn't bothered to call. But the minute he returned, his sweet smile and warm embrace obliterated the niggling doubts and all my intentions were thrown out of the window.

"So, my dear friends, nothing prepared me for the brutal truth until I heard he'd been arrested for battering the woman he had shared a home with for six years. She also happened to be the mother of their four-year-old daughter and the owner of the house he said was his. Can you believe that he made me believe his daughter was his niece and her mother was his brother's wife?"

"When was that?" asked Amira.

"Very early in the relationship. We had been dating for about a year and I was as dumb as they come. He picked me up from college, and was driving me home. They were in another car and waved at him when we stopped at the traffic lights. Of course, I bought his lies but only God knows what he told them about me. I can't believe how foolish I was. The blinkers peeled off when I realised I'd wasted six years of my life with the lying scumbag.

"As if that wasn't humiliating enough, he wanted me to forgive him and take him back."

"Did you?" Kukuwa asked.

"I probably would, if I had not found out that his mother was his pimp. She started working in Amsterdam's red light district when he was only a child. After several years in the business she became very popular and owned one of the biggest brothels in Europe, but out of all her prostitutes, strippers, dancers, escorts, money launderers and drug pushers, her son was her top earner. I cried my eyes out when I found out the truth about him. I immediately booked an appointment for a full health assessment. I had to be sure he hadn't given me any diseases. Waiting for the results was like waiting for a life sentence. Thankfully, all the tests came out negative."

"Has he been in touch since you broke up?" asked Pandora.

"He calls persistently, but he doesn't stand a chance in hell. I am content with my single status."

"Surely you can't remain single forever?" said Pandora.

"She can if she wants to" Olympia retorted. "You should count your blessings that Balotelli worships the ground you walk on."

"Is that her boyfriend?" asked Kukuwa.

"Yes honey." Said Olympia. "She is dating a forty-two-year-old property tycoon, but you'd never guess he is twice her age, with his fit body and perfect tan. He wants to make a decent woman of her, but she won't let him. I've tried to convince her that as a wife, she gets a share of his wealth and properties, should anything go wrong, but she won't budge.

"But it shouldn't just be about money," Kukuwa stated emphatically.

"I know that," said Olympia "but bearing in mind the number of stick-thin bimbos waggling their oversized boobs in his face, I wouldn't keep him waiting, if I was her. The temptation out there is overwhelming."

"I've said I'll marry him when I graduate from medical school." Pandora said indignantly. "I won't change my mind, so stop fretting."

"What will you do if he decides not to wait for you?" asked Olympia.

"My medical career means a lot to me, so if he can't hold off until I complete med school then we don't have a future."

"You certainly haven't thought this through," Olympia

said bluntly. "Do you think you will have a future if he decides not to pay your fees? And what will you do if he kicks your ass out of the luxury flat?

"Let me be worry about!" Pandora snapped.

"Would anyone like a strawberry tart?" Zhara asked, hoping to diffuse the strained atmosphere.

"Yes please," said Chelsea.

Zhara passed the mini fresh fruit tartlets around and smiled at Pandora.

"Don't be grumpy. Olympia says it as it is, but she means well. I think you are right though. You must finish your studies before taking the plunge."

"Why don't you get engaged," Ngozi suggested to Pandora. "That will assure him of your love, buy you time, and hopefully keep the bimbos away."

"Why would anyone want a bimbo when they can have a stunningly beautiful medical student?" Kukuwa asked, smiling fondly at Pandora.

"Has Jamal been in touch with you?" Ngozi asked Olympia. "I hear he is in London.

Olympia shook her head.

"Who is Jamal?" Amira asked, excitedly.

Ngozi looked at her watch. "It's almost 2am," she gasped.

"So?" Amira said. "I haven't had this much fun in a long time and I am not done yet."

"I've enjoyed myself too," said Ngozi "but unlike you, I have a husband and children to go home to."

Olympia winked at Ngozi. "Please put the bitch out of her misery."

Ngozi rolled her eyes. "He was infatuated with Olympia, from the moment he laid eyes on her. After a short but very intense affair, he left for a business meeting in Dubai. She was devastated. That was when the moaning began."

Amira looked confused. "What was the moaning about? It sounds to me like they had a good time!"

"Olympia was in so much pain, she walked funny for days."

"What was wrong with her?" asked Amira. "Why she walking funny?"

"I don't think she was making it up, but why she never complained about the size of his manhood when she was practically living in his hotel suite baffles me. It was as if they couldn't have enough of each other."

"Maybe it was a delayed reaction." Pandora said zestfully. "Like when you work out strenuously and seem to be enjoying it at the time but find it difficult to move the next day because all your joints hurt."

"Wow, that sounds like a twelve inch work-out!" Amira sneered. "I can feel her pain."

Ngozi giggled. "I never heard her complaining when she was working her tongue down his throat."

"Ha ha ha", Chelsea laughed. "Sounds like she finally met her match."

"You bitches really need a life" said Olympia. "Amira darling, I hear Conrad went back to school?"

"Yes, he's at St Andrews. He lost his job when the slump hit the FTSE. Rather than look for another job, he decided to study for his PhD."

"Are you sure he spends every night by himself?" Olympia asked with a sneer. "All the way out there? My guess is that he has one or two Scottish beauties on the side."

"I trust Conrad," said Amira. "He never cheated on me when he worked as a top city trader and lived life to the full. Why would he cheat now? Not all men are dogs!"

"Meaaoow," Pandora purred mockingly at the standoff.

Olympia took a swig of whiskey, screwed up her face and took another. Wiping her mouth with the back of her hand, she stood up, staggered to the edge of the room and looked longingly at a huge portrait of her father on the wall.

"All men are dogs!" she slurred. "I fell for the biggest motherfucker! After doing everything I could to make the bastard happy, what did I get in return?" she asked disparagingly. "Disgrace and humiliation! I should have kicked the moron out when he squirmed his way into my bed. I gave that fucking tramp a home and replaced his rags with designer clothes, but that wasn't enough. Sometimes I wonder why I felt the need to make him better than he was, why I paid for his tuition, opened a bank account for the beggar and set him up in business." She staggered back to her seat and fell in it.

Zhara moved closer to Olympia. It was the first time she'd heard her talk openly about her failed marriage, and even though it hurt to see her tearing up, she was glad that she was letting out the pain.

"I should have known he was up to no good when he

offered me coke. He told me it would make me feel good, and I believed him. When I was high, there was nothing I wouldn't do for him, and he knew that. I taught him how to wine and dine his clients in Michelin star restaurants and he taught me how to roll joints. With my head in the clouds and my heart in the palm of his hands, he squeezed the life out of me. I should have sent him back to the gutter where he crawled out of. Dad was right when he said he should have drowned on the fucking boat that brought him to England!"

Zhara rubbed Olympia's arm. "Don't let him get to you," she said, "that was a long time ago. Let bygones be bygones and let's dwell on the future."

"Bastard!" Ngozi spat. "He knew he couldn't fool me with his shifty eyes and fake American accent, so he tried to keep us apart. I tried to warn you but you wouldn't listen. He turned you into a mumu (idiot). I still think he put some juju (charm) on you. I wish I'd shaken my beads and turned it back on him," she said snapping her fingers.

Olympia sighed. "My parents must have sensed he was a fake. They looked so miserable when we announced our engagement. Their only wish was that I brought home a decent hardworking man from a respectable family who loved me and was determined to make me happy but I couldn't even grant them that. Bonded by a mutual hatred, our mothers moved tooth and nail to split us up, but couldn't. His mother had expected a glamorous three-day wedding, with all expenses paid for. After all, they had boasted to all their friends and family that their son was marrying a multimillionaire's daughter, who would become their cash cow." She filled her glass with Evian water and drank it.

"My parents braced themselves for the wedding." she continued. "It was at Skibo Castle, a fabulous location, even for the cynics. Dilip grinned nervously throughout the ceremony. He even got the shits when Superintendent Parker arrived. He thought he was an immigration officer." Olympia laughed. "I was given away begrudgingly. Even though my father felt dejected and my mother's spirit was squashed, I had no reason to doubt that my marriage would succeed. If only I'd known about what went on at the stag-do, the whole damn charade could have been brought to a halt. I wish I'd listened to my parents."

"What happened at the stag-do?" Kukuwa looked askance at Zhara.

Olympia took a deep breath. "The signs were there right from the start, but I was too damn stupid to do anything about it. I suspected Dilip was cheating on me, with men and women, a few weeks before the wedding. There were many rumours about his participation in sex orgies, but he vehemently denied it, and I believed him."

"Men and women?" Kukuwa looked bemused.

"I have nothing against how people choose to live their lives. I am no saint either, but from the day we made our vows, I expected us to remain in a monogamous relationship and be faithful to each other. So to hear that he'd been carrying on with men after our wedding was like putting the last nail in the coffin."

"Who told you that he was carrying on with men?" Pandora asked.

"His ex-friend, Steve. But I'd hired a detective by then, just to confirm my suspicion."

"How did Steve know?" Amira enquired.

"He walked in on Dilip and his best man. They were butt naked and romping in the hotel room like dogs on heat."

"When did he tell you this?" asked Amira.

"About six months after the wedding. We met in Mayfair and I asked him why he didn't come to the wedding. It just set him off, and he told me everything. I closed our joint account, changed the locks to my apartment and filed for an annulment."

"How long had you been married?" Amira asked.

"Weren't you paying attention?" Pandora snapped, "she said six months."

"But that is awful." Amira said sadly. "He sounds like an asshole."

"He was an asshole!" Ngozi quipped.

Olympia sniffed. "I had come to learn that no matter how much you comfort a snake, in the end, it will surely bite. I was up to my eyes with his habitual lies, late-night business meetings and weekends away with his 'mates'. I also noticed that he was spending my money like it was going out of fashion."

There was a sudden chill in the room. All was quiet except for Rod Stewart's husky voice singing 'The first cut is the deepest'.

It started with a sob and quickly erupted into a gigantic wail. Olympia was inconsolable.

"Let it all out!" Ngozi shouted. "You are better off without the gold-digging rat anyway. Look at you now, the youngest senior partner in your firm. You certainly wouldn't have got your head screwed on if he was around feeding you coke and all his bullshit! We are so proud of you, darling, and so are your parents.

"I dread to think what would have happened to you, if you hadn't left him." Zhara said consolingly, "what happened was dreadful, but our bad experiences can only shake us up and make us tougher, stronger and wiser."

After long hugs and kisses, Zhara and Olympia's friends departed at a quarter past four.

Zhara lay in bed that morning, thousands of miles away from home. She was glad she'd taken a break from her hectic schedule of site visits, meetings with clients, real estate agents, bankers, investors, accountants, architects and engineers. She'd almost forgotten how refreshing it was to be young and carefree.

CHAPTER NINETEEN

The streets in the West End of the City looked colourful with festive lights and Christmas decorations. Attractive shop windows and discounted sale prices enticed shoppers from every corner of the globe, and like a melting pot of varying shades they filled the shops, streets and markets.

Olympia was glad to find a parking spot next to Pâtisserie Valérie. She and Zhara popped in for breakfast. Though she loved shopping for clothes, her busy schedule made it impossible for her to do so as often as she wanted, and hiring a personal shopper took the fun out of strolling through the shops.

They began their shopping spree after breakfast. Starting from Harrods, they moved on to Harvey Nichols and trawled through New Bond Street to Old Bond Street, Selfridges, John Lewis, Fenwicks, Liberty, Carnaby Street and Piccadilly Circus. Olympia's six-inch Prada boots looked great, but her feet ached badly. Zhara had opted for low-heeled comfy Clark boots, and it certainly served her well.

Armed with enough clothes, shoes, handbags and accessories for the year ahead, they flagged a black cab to take them where the car had been parked.

Olympia swore when she saw the parking ticket tucked underneath the Range Rover's wiper. Fighting the urge to show the traffic warden her middle finger, she took a deep breath, exhaled and channelled positive thoughts.

Their next stop was Bliss, Olympia's favourite spa, for a much needed pampering session - facial, deep tissue massage, manicure and pedicure.

Hugh Masekela's Grazing in the Grass lifted Zhara's spirit as she watched Olympia manoeuvring the car over uneven surfaces, potholes and ramps.

Road closures, road works and speeding buses took the fun out of driving and overzealous traffic wardens hovering like flies in the inner city areas made a bad situation worse.

The sound of revving engines alerted Olympia to check her rear view mirror. The car behind her was literally up her rear and picking up pace. The temptation to slam her brakes was overpowering, but she resisted it, and carried on driving. The revving stopped for a few minutes and started again but this time with a clicker and flashing headlights. The car behind had inched over the yellow line and was aiming to get past her. Olympia tapped her brakes like a Morse code; just enough to make him nervous. He was adept at being a menace. Olympia slammed on the brakes at the double yellow line, putting the bumper rider back in his lane. With no other option than to leap over her car, he managed to stay put.

As she approached the traffic light on the A302, Olympia heard raised voices. A fight was just about to break out.

The red-faced skinhead, possibly in his thirties, stuck his head out of a battered Ford Mondeo and bellowed, "Oi tosser! Go on, sling your hook, you fucking wanker!"

A tall skinny lad, possibly in his late teens, turned down the music in the white Audi TT convertible and yelled, "You talking to me? You fucking cunt!"

"Don't you fucking get me started!" The skinhead roared.

"Well I just fucking did. What are you going to do about it?"

"Bollocks!" the skinhead screamed. Suddenly he was out of the car and heading for his opponent, pulling up his trousers to cover the builder's bottom.

The young lad jumped out of his car and rushed towards the skinhead.

Zhara quickly dialled 999.

The skinhead threw a heavy punch.

The lad ducked.

A crowd gathered, but no one tried to break them up.

Olympia wasn't sure whether to intervene or wait for the police.

With jeans so low that most of his Armani briefs were showing, the lad jumped on the older man and finished him off with a succession of blows. The skinhead was left in the middle of the busy street, barely conscious.

Adjusting his oversized jeans, the young man glanced at his wrist, to ensure the Jacob & Co watch was still in place. He then swaggered to the sparkling new Audi, slid into the driver's seat, turned up the volume and sped off.

There was still no sign of the police.

Luckily the older man stirred, got up slowly and hobbled to his car.

With the show over, those caught in traffic and the others who had stopped to watch walked on by.

CHAPTER TWENTY

Months before the fashion show, Agyeman had envisaged exactly how he wanted his new collection to look. He translated his ideas into a storyboard, added a few sketches, sifted through various pieces of material and came up with a design that pulled on the heartstrings of couture. Each of his pieces had colours, textures, cuts and styles that exploded with modern design and innovation.

Buyers for major departmental stores, fashion editors, fashion moguls, celebrities and paparazzi arrived at Milano Malpensa Airport for the fashion extravaganza. Among them were designers from top fashion houses and a young up and coming Ghanaian designer, Agyeman Johnson, whose bespoke collection had recently won him the African Fashion Designer of the Year' award.

As his models hit the catwalk, Agyeman held his breath and hoped for the best. He had not expected the crowd to go berserk with excitement. Astounded by how well his collection had been received he breathed a sigh of relief and braced himself for what lay ahead.

His first signing was with a buyer for a large chain of boutiques in London and New York. They agreed to meet in London to finalise the deal. There was a lot of interest from American celebrities, Arab businessmen and African movie stars.

Delighted with his success at the show Agyeman prepared himself for a stopover in London.

The Alitalia flight from Milan touched down at Gatwick Airport just after 4:30 pm. It was a bitterly cold winter. Flurries of snow and icy winds blew in from the east, reducing the temperature to minus ten degrees.

Agyeman felt the chill when he emerged from the terminal. Looking like an Eskimo in a thick coat, tweed cap, woollen scarf and leather gloves, he flagged down a taxi and gave the driver the name and address of the hotel he was heading to. Even though he wasn't keen on the bitterly cold weather, he was enchanted by the blue skies, falling autumn leaves and white blanket of snow.

"Isn't it beautiful?" he said enthusiastically to the taxi driver. "Nothing beats the serenity of Mother Nature."

The driver, a fifty-something year old Zimbabwean, had many things on his mind but the beauty of nature wasn't one of them. He talked at length about living in London, which he'd done for over twenty years, and why he had to drive a taxi even though he had a master's degree in Economics.

Something about the elderly man reminded Agyeman about his father. Casting his mind back to his childhood he wondered how his life would have panned out if his father were still alive.

The last few moments with his father flashed before his eyes. He remembered his last words, 'Son, my life is nearly over, but yours has just begun. I am sorry I can't be with you to see you grow into a man, but I will always be with you, anyway I can. Please forgive me for what I'm about to tell you. I want you to know that I did what I thought was right at the time, what I believed was best for you, my dear son. Dora has loved you like any mother would love her child, but she is not your real mother, not biologically anyway ...'

He had been shocked, angry and terrified at the same time. There were many questions he had wanted to ask, but he held his father's hand and let him speak.

"... your mother, the woman who gave birth to you, is Princess Yaa Asantewa. She is the Ashanti King's youngest sister. We met at the palace when I was Minister for the Ashanti region. Her elder sister, Princess Pokuwa was married to the Ambassador. She introduced me to your mother. We started off as friends but it soon turned into a very loving relationship. But I couldn't leave Dora, so I decided to end the affair. Your mother was pregnant with you by then. I came to see you when you were born and I begged her to let me have you. She wouldn't let me at first, but she finally agreed, when I came to see you on your second birthday. Giving you away was the biggest and most painful sacrifice she had to make, but she did it because she loved you. She knew how much I adored you, and she realised that it was important for us to maintain that bond. So, if you must blame anyone for what we did back then, it must be me. We planned to tell you everything on your sixteenth birthday, but as you can see, death has no regard for plans or promises when it rears its ugly head. I have loved you from the day I held you in my arms and I will continue to love you, even after my last breath, never forget that!" Agyeman's father had started to cough. Moments later the doctor pronounced him dead.

Agyeman's whole world came crushing down on him. His father, who had been his rock, was no more. To add insult to injury, he had no idea who his real mother was. The fifteen year old had felt as if his heart had been ripped out of his body. Time, place, reality and imagination were all muddled up as he went through the motions of getting acquainted with his birth mother and the Ashanti royal family. Although present at his father's wake, funeral and burial, it had all seemed unreal, as if he was watching a movie. Lost and alone amidst the clatter, well-meaning smiles, hugs and condolences, he bottled up all the pain inside him and nothing could shift it.

Dora and Agyeman's mother, Princess Yaa Asantewa, tried everything they could to console Agyeman, but nothing could shift his anguish. Playing with his cherished rabbits gave him some solace but he continued to remain torn and secluded.

By his nineteenth birthday the smart, charming, witty and artistic sportsman had dropped out of school and was drinking, smoking, and partying like it was going out of fashion. He kept a string of girls, none of whom lasted more than a few days. He had no time for love, and felt nothing for any of them. They were just for sex, a momentary thrill and something to do to pass the time.

He returned home late one night, high as a kite. The dark brown tender eyes were red and fearsome. Plagued by sorrow and bitterness, his heart had also turned into a stone with no room for love or affection. He collapsed onto his bed and was lost to the world. When he came to, it was noon. The sun was peeping through the curtains blindingly. He remembers sitting up, rubbing his eyes, then he noticed a photograph he'd taken with his father. He was five years old and presenting a bunch of flowers to Queen Victoria. His father appeared to be bursting with love as he smiled at him. The medals and gold figurines he'd received for winning the inter-college table tennis championships, coming third in the national swimming competition and scoring the most goals in the junior football tournament were arranged side by side with the photograph. He remembered how elated his father had been when he received each of the medals. Overcome by a sudden wave of emotion he'd cried out, and sobbed bitterly. He'd felt better after that. It was as if he'd released all the anguish he'd been holding back since his father's death and finally surfaced from the darkness. Instead of going out that day, he cleaned his room, helped around the house, fed his rabbits and played with his dogs. He also decided to return to school. Though well behind his peers academically, he still excelled in sports.

His talent for fashion and design emerged during his apprenticeship with a bespoke tailor in Kumasi. His skill and dedication opened many doors and he was able to set up his own fashion house when he turned 25. His deepest regret was that his father had not been able to share his success.

The taxi pulled up at Leigham Court Hotel just after 6 pm. Agyeman took out his bags, thanked the driver and added a huge tip to the fare. Strolling confidently into the hotel he had an instinctive feeling that his father would have been proud of him.

CHAPTER TWENTY ONE

Agyeman woke up with a huge smile on ninth December. Everything was going according to plan. He had finalised the deal on his collection, ordered all the fabric, threads and other items required for the next season's collection and had even had time for a little retail therapy. He still had a week and a bit before returning to Accra, and he planned to make the most of it.

He got up, made a few phone calls, spent a couple of hours in the gym, showered, got dressed and popped into the restaurant for a late breakfast.

Agyeman left the hotel at noon and took a quick stroll to his cousin's salon just off Streatham High Street. He'd arranged to meet one of his friend's there.

The receptionist was having an animated conversation on the phone when he arrived. She had been rather liberal with her make-up; thick layer of foundation, pink cheeks, purple eye shadow and bright red lipstick.

As his eyes glazed over the gold-tipped purple talons Agyeman could not help but wonder why the receptionist had gone to such lengths with her appearance, when she could have looked younger and prettier with just a hint of make-up or none at all.

With receiver to ear like a large sausage and a chandelier in each earlobe the receptionist caressed the butterfly tattoo on her neck. It was obvious she was having a private conversation on the job, but she made no attempt to cut it short, even with customers waiting.

"Jay and I go way back, he is one of my crew dem. Wha? ... I can't believe that guy just dissed her like that. You get me though! Init? ... If any of my baby father tried that with me... He keeps flexin' though... and the bling bling... init though? And she is well... Joan, I need to go." She said hastily. "It's getting really busy here and Rottweiler's spy just walked past me. I'll catch you later!"

She put the phone down, blew up the gum in her mouth and popped it. Then she pulled up her trousers, adjusted her top so her boobs would stop creeping out, and forced a smile.

"How may I help you, sir?" she asked, fluttering the louvre blade lashes.

"I'm here to see Serwa."

"Do you have an appointment?" she asked, pulling up the tight fitting top that barely covered her midriff.

"I don't." He replied. "But she will be pleased to see me."

Agyeman was tempted to advise her that if she went up a size or two, her clothes would look more flattering on her, and she would feel more at ease, but he decided to bite his tongue.

"May I take you name?"

"It's Agyeman." He said politely.

"Please take a seat over there." She said, pointing to a little area near the staircase.

Agyeman was watching a music video of Prince's When Doves Cry when he felt a draught directly above his shoulder. He tilted his head to the side. It was the receptionist.

"Can I get you a drink?" she asked seductively.

"No thanks." He said, hoping she would stop invading his personal space.

She moved closer. "Are you sure you don't want a drink?"

"I am quite certain!" He said, eyes focused on the screen. He could feel her breath on his cheek.

It looked for a moment as if she was transfixed but the sound of clicking footsteps got her moving hastily to the front desk.

A tall lady pushing fifty came rushing down the stairs in an immaculate cream suit.

"Nana [Prince] Agyeman! What a lovely surprise!" She fell into his arms.

"Good to see you, Serwa." He said affectionately. "It's been a long time. About two years, if my memory serves me right."

"Yes, two long years," she smiled sweetly, "but you are here now, and I want to know everything about what you've been up to. I heard your show in Milan was fantastic. Well done!"

"It was awesome, much better than I anticipated." He

picked up a huge bag beside him. "Here, I got you a little something."

She rummaged through the bag, eyes sparkling like a child with a new toy.

"Wow!' She shrieked. "Thank you so much! I can't believe you got me all the new season must-haves. Please promise you'll spend a few days with me. I want to spoil you so much; you won't want to rush back to Accra. Can you wait for a little while or would you like to come back in a couple of hours? I would love to take you out to dinner."

"Actually, I've asked Tony to meet me here. We are heading to North London to meet up with some friends. Can we make it tomorrow?"

"Of course!" she said sadly, tugging at the silk scarf around her neck, "but first..."

The receptionist was hovering anxiously in the background.

"Shaniqua, anything the matter?" Serwa asked sharply.

"Your one o'clock is here. She is a bit early. Can I ask one of the stylists to attend to her?"

"No, I need to see to Olympia myself. Take her upstairs and offer her a drink. I'll be up shortly."

Serwa turned to Agyeman, clutching the bag possessively, "Honey, could you please give me a few minutes?"

"Take your time," he replied. "Tony should be here soon, anyway."

"Promise you won't disappear when he arrives." She said sternly.

Agyeman laughed. "I won't leave without telling you. I promise."

She blew him a big kiss and hurried up the stairs.

CHAPTER TWENTY TWO

Tony found a parking spot opposite the salon. After inserting a few coins in the meter he crossed the road and walked briskly to the salon.

He spotted Agyeman as soon as he entered the salon. Ignoring the eagle-eyed receptionist he moved swiftly towards him and tapped his shoulder.

Agyeman shot up cheerfully, locked hands with Tony and hugged his shoulder.

"Charley! (mate). How be? (how are you?)" Tony said zestfully. "It's so good to see you. He took a long look at Agyeman, skimming over the paisley cravat, Black Armani shirt, Hermes belt, Indigo Versace jeans, the gold Daytona Rolex set with sapphires and Church's shoes. "You are looking well my friend!" he said, patting him on the back.

"Thank you. Things have finally started to take off. Charley! You don't look so bad yourself. How is life in London?"

"It's not easy, but what can we do?" he said miserably. "You work hard to make a living but before the money comes the taxman takes one-third and most of what is left goes towards the mortgage, insurance, gas, electricity, water and my high maintenance wife. It's a rat race, man."

Agyeman laughed heartily. "And how is your beautiful wife? I must see her before I leave."

"Still as demanding as ever." he said grumpily. "Count yourself lucky that you are still single. Women!" he sighed deeply. "If I'd known she would turn into a nag, I would never have put a ring on her finger. Honestly, sometimes I feel like packing it all in and coming back home, without her."

They were deep in conversation, reminiscing about the past, when Shaniqua drew near. "Is there anything I can do for you, gents?" she asked, blinking obligingly.

"Could I have a cup of tea?" Tony asked, rubbing his hands together.

"How do you like it?" She smiled mischievously.

"Strong, I mean black with one sugar."

"Just the way I like it! She tittered.

"What about you, luv?"

Agyeman was taken aback by the casual use of 'luv', by Shaniqua, whom he guessed could be eighteen or nineteen but certainly no more than twenty.

"Nothing for me." he said, and carried on with the conversation.

Shaniqua returned a few minutes later with a cup of tea. As she handed it to Tony she deliberately brushed her arm against his.

Tony moved his arm hastily. The drink spilled onto the tiled floor.

"Oopsie daisy," Shaniqua cried. She set the drink on the table dashed to a room at the far end of the salon and returned with a mop. Bending over slightly, she mopped the floor. The top half of her bottom was hanging out, and so was her red lace thong. She inched closer to Agyeman, mop in hand, eyes buried in his crotch. Licking her lips, she whispered, "I could give you a wash and trim, with a massage thrown in for good measure." She leaned forward. "It will be the best head massage you'll ever have in your entire life. It will rock your world, and keep you coming."

Agyeman shifted uncomfortably. He'd had more girls than hot dinners, but this one was getting way out of hand. There was a time when he would have given her what she was asking for, and some, until she begged for mercy, but that was back then, he thought, and he intended to keep it that way.

"The girl has a crush on you." Tony whispered to Agyeman without taking his eyes off Shaniqua's backside. "It's as serious as a heart-attack!"

She turned abruptly. "Whatchoo looking at? Pervert!" She said, much louder than Tony would have liked. With a venomous stare she pulled up her jeans, adjusted her boob-tube and kissed her teeth. Then, flicking her hair over her shoulder, she flounced past Agyeman.

All eyes were on Tony. Feeling flushed he buried his face in a newspaper.

"What is going on between you two?" asked Agyeman.

"Nothing, except that the HO thinks she can hustle a hustler."

"I know, but you moved your arm too quickly, you must have hurt her feelings. You know what they say about a woman scorned. She gave me attitude when I arrived and switched to flirting. I wouldn't touch her with a bargepole but while we are here, just try to be cordial."

Tony threw down the newspaper and run his fingers through his dark wavy hair. He looked around frantically. "Charley, we need to make a move." He looked desolate. "I can't stand people staring at me."

"Don't get paranoid. No one is staring at you. Just remember, she is young and misguided, everyone can see that."

Several thoughts flashed through Tony's mind, all unpleasant. "Young and misguided?" He sneered. "She was all over you, begging to be straddled. All I did was look at what she was exposing to the whole bloody salon. The bloody cheek! You'd think she would want to hide the muffin top, not adorn it with a belly-ring."

Agyeman held his chin. "Is that what you were looking at?" he said derisively.

"Yeah!" Tony replied, "pardon me for looking at the fat wobbly ass with tattoos all over it."

"Are you being mean because she caught you leering at her backside? Or is it because she called you a pervert?"

"I am not being mean!" He snapped. "Firstly she shouldn't be putting it out there if she can't handle people looking. Secondly, she is not much to write about. That tiny head on a spherical body doesn't do it for me. Thirdly, she shouldn't be hustling older men at her age. Finally, how on earth does she wash herself with those talons? I accept that a little make-up goes a long way but layers of paint in rainbow-colours? And as for her fake lashes, they could seriously take her eye out, not to mention the fake nylon hair down to her ankles. That is taking falsehood to a whole new dimension!" he said with derision. "If you ask me, she would be better served in a bordello. You need to tell your cousin that!"

"OK." Said Agyeman, I get the message. Let me find Serwa and tell her we are leaving."

He stood up. Took a few strides toward the staircase and stopped in his tracks. He could not take his eye off the lady with smooth chocolate legs, left over right, under the saffron-tinted dryer. Even though her face was partially covered by an Estates Gazette, he had a gut feeling that he was fated to be with her.

Oblivious of the gawping eyes zooming in on her, Zhara carried on flipping through the magazine.

Tony noticed Agyeman hadn't made it past the staircase and decided to find out what was keeping him.

"Please stick your tongue back in your mouth," he said vehemently. "Don't you know it's rude to stare? Anyway, what are you gaping at?"

"Isn't she beautiful?" Agyeman said, without taking his eye off her.

Tony shook his head. "I can't believe it. What is it with you and skirts?"

"You should be asking yourself that question." Agyeman retorted. "I am young, free and single and can do what I please with the fairer sex; you on the other hand cannot, because you are married."

"Yes, you may say that, but I was only looking and by the look on your face, you don't intend to just look."

"She is not just any skirt. This one is special. Trust me, I can tell."

"OK Casanova. If you mean the lady under the dryer, yes, she is definitely a babe. But there is a slight problem," he said mockingly. Without seeing her backside, how can you tell if she meets your criteria?"

"What criteria?"

"You know!" Tony slapped him on the back. "38-26-48," he illustrated with his hands. "The hour-glass figure" he continued, "big boobs, tiny waist, large hips."

"You know me too well," Agyeman chuckled "but I have the inkling that she will pass the figure test. And even if she doesn't, I can look past that."

"But I thought we were leaving."

"We were, precisely!"

"It is sad what a natural beauty with innocent Bambi eyes can do to a grown man." said Tony, "I guess the boys will just have to wait, now that you've found someone to keep your bed warm in this terribly cold winter. You sure are whipped! The receptionist didn't stand a chance, did she? She was miles out of your comfort zone. But this one, I think she will fit perfectly, just like a glove, but please make it quick, some of us have homes to go to."

"Please take your mind out of the gutter and come with me."

With a self-satisfied grin Agyeman led the way.

They found Serwa on the top floor working her magic

on one of her customers. Not wanting to interrupt her, Agyeman leaned against a pillar and waited, hands buried deep in his pockets. He was not aware that he was tapping his leg repeatedly.

Serwa noticed the men. Ordinarily she would have carried on but she decided to let her senior stylist take over. She knew Agyeman well enough to know that he only tapped his leg when he had something on his mind. It was a habit she hoped he'd quit.

"Nana, I hope you are not leaving already," she said with an arm around his broad shoulders. "Tony, its, good to see you, it's been a long time. I hope you are well?"

"I am fine. I see you haven't changed a bit! You are looking as gorgeous as ever!"

"I am?" She said, revelling in flattery. "Thank you. I hope you are not taking Nana away just yet."

"We were intending to leave, but he may have other plans!"

"Plans? Am I included?" she looked askance at Agyeman.

"You are, in a way," he said hesitantly. "You see, there is a lady here that I need to meet. She is downstairs. Would you mind coming with me?" he asked with a bashful smile.

Serwa blinked rapidly, and followed them. She did not take kindly to being interrupted, especially for a girl, but she could hardly say no to her dearest cousin. If only they were not related, she thought.

When they reached the bottom of the stairs Agyeman directed his gaze at the lady he'd taken a shine to and smiled sheepishly.

"Who is she?" he whispered in Serwa's ear.

"I am not sure." Serwa said wistfully. "Leave it with me, I will do some digging. Are you looking for someone to warm your bed tonight?"

"No, this one is something else. I don't just want to sleep with her, I would like to get to know her."

"Whew," she said, "that's a first!"

"I need to spend some time with her. Please, anything you can do to hook us up will be greatly appreciated."

She rubbed Agyeman's shoulder affectionately. "There is nothing I wouldn't do for my favourite cousin, you must know that." she said with conviction. "Boys, make yourselves at home and do let me know if anyone bothers either of you."

"What makes you think we are being bothered?" Tony asked.

Serwa tapped the side of her nose. She is a tart, I know, but please bear with me. With that she winked at Agyeman and hurried up the stairs.

It is a well-known fact that hairdressers are the biggest gossips ever. With their customers' heads in their hands an intimacy is created. It allows the customers to let go of their guard and this tends to break down some of the barriers. Usually, whatever the customer reveals is treated anonymously, and being very good listeners, and talkers, only saying what the customer wants to hear they are able to coax out lots of information from their customers. With this in mind, Serwa went to work on Olympia, making all the right noises. She was certainly skilled at her craft and knew how to make her customers feel special.

"Wow, you look fabulous," she said to Olympia. "and I am not just talking about your hair. Could it be a new diet or a new hunk?"

"Definitely not a diet and I wish it was the other."

"Look at the length of your hair. Didn't I trim it two weeks ago? Please tell me you are not on horse tranquillisers, else I may need to start taking some! The brown sugar and white lollies aren't doing it for me anymore."

They laughed hysterically.

Positioned firmly behind Olympia, Serwa pumped the chair up vigorously until it was at a level she could work with.

"Joan," she yelled at her senior stylist, "bring Olympia her usual; an extra hot cappuccino, with lots of chocolate. And remember to add some biscotti."

Serwa knew how to flatter and pamper her customers and they loved her for that.

"I know Ike has worked a treat on your hair." she continued. "Bless his cotton socks! But can I try something new today? And as for the big three-O, I have something that will have all eyes on you, like they should."

"OK." Olympia smiled with gratitude.

"Trust me. I have the perfect coiffure for the belle of the ball."

Looking over her shoulder she snapped her fingers.

"Tina, pass me my bag of tricks. George, be quick with the highlights. The towels need to go in the wash, and don't forget to take some refreshments to my cousin and his friend. And please send Portia to reception. Shaniqua can do the sweeping and tidying up." She sighed deeply. "That girl is stressing me out. After promising to turn a new leaf she comes in dressed like a hooker and leaves nothing to the imagination. If not for her children, I would have kicked her ass out of my salon months ago.

"Children?" Olympia huffed, "but she is barely out of nappies."

"I know dear. Who would believe that with all my talk about education, enlightenment and contraception, the nineteen-year-old is stupid enough to have three kids under the age of three with three different fathers, just so she can get a council flat, dole money and child benefit. What happened to standards, morals and just saying no? I have given her my very last warning, if she doesn't get her act together and keep her hands off my male customers, I will have no option but to let her go. I run a classy salon here, not a bloody brothel!"

Seconds later she gave Olympia one of her sweetest smiles and whispered furtively. "My I ask who the drop-dead-gorgeous lady is? I mean the one you came with."

"Oh, it's Zhara, my cousin. Sorry, I should have introduced her to you."

"No worries, we can do that later. So what does Zhara do? Is she...?"

Olympia did not disappoint. By the time her hair was done Serwa had all the information she needed.

As soon as she'd finished with Olympia she made her

way downstairs to meet the lady who she was certain would be the next notch on her cousin's bedpost.

"Good job, Divine." Olympia said to the junior stylist. "Let me take over here. You can see to Mrs Smith."

Positioning herself behind Zhara, Serwa gave her a megawatt smile.

"Hello Dear, I hope Divine has been taking good care of you."

"Yes, she has."

"Good." She put a comb through her hair. "Wow, I love your dimples!"

Thanks."

"You must be Olympia's cousin?"

Zhara smiled. "Yes, that's me."

"I'm Serwa, and you are?"

"Zhara." she replied, observing the tall masculine lady with interest.

"I'm not sure if you have a style in mind but I have the perfect style for that cute face of yours and it will highlight your cheekbones. Not that you need it, mind, they are perfect but I want you to walk out of here looking better than any supermodel."

"OK, thanks." Zhara said quietly.

"Laweh, pass me the straightener! Do get a move on" she yelled, "my two o'clock will be here soon, and this could take a while."

Serwa observed Zhara keenly from the mirror.

"Long thick lustrous curls, I would kill for hair like

that." She said, flipping her perfectly layered bob. "So, honey, where are you from?"

"Ghana."

"I guessed, but you don't look like a full Ghanaian."

"Oh, I see. My mother is half Ghanaian, half Scottish and my father is half Ghanaian, quarter Nigerian and quarter Arabian."

"Interesting." Said Serwa. "So what does that make you?"

"Predominantly Ghanaian with a bit of Scottish, Nigerian and Arabian thrown in."

"I like that!" Serwa said, looking bemused. "But it explains a lot about your unique features. Your parents must be really proud of you. I can't believe that you are running a successful property development company in Accra."

"I don't run it alone, it's my mother's company and I just happen to be one of the partners. The company was doing great before I joined."

"You're too modest. To be honest," Serwa continued, "not many people are fortunate enough to have a job immediately after graduation. You must have been born with a silver spoon in your mouth."

Zhara wasn't sure if she should answer back or not, so she didn't.

Serwa pressed on. "Do you have a special person in your life?"

"Yes, many - my parents, my grandmother..."

Serwa shook her head. "You are funny, but I am not

talking about your family, what I mean is someone special, like a boyfriend..."

"I have friends who are boys" Zhara said with a hint of sarcasm, "but I am not dating anyone, if that's what you mean."

"How come? I would expect them to be all over you. Some of us struggle to get the attention of common cleaners, but you..."

"I've been busy," Zhara interrupted, "with other things, and haven't really had time for dating."

Serwa grinned broadly. "In that case, I have the perfect man for you. And I promise, you will not be disappointed."

"The last thing I need right now is a man," she said politely, "but thanks anyway.

Serwa was stunned. She had assumed that Zhara would be pleased that she was hooking her up with a man. How could anyone in their right mind turn down her cousin, she fumed. It seemed to have skipped her mind that Zhara didn't have a clue as to who the perfect man she'd referred to was.

Embittered by the knock back Serwa decided to change tactics. Any affection she might have had for Zhara had completely evaporated by then. Damn bitch, she thought, how dare. She concluded, in that instant that Agyeman would be better off without Zhara, and devised a plan that would ensure their paths would never cross.

"I don't know if you have noticed," she said, forcing a smile, "but that man standing by the pillar hasn't taken his eye off you since I started styling your hair."

"Not really." Zhara said, without bothering to look up. She could tell from the sour look on Serwa's face that she was upset.

Serwa carried on talking. "You don't need the likes of him. If I were you, I would run a mile if he so much as smiled at me. He is as bad as they come. The minute he has his wicked way with you, you are history, like all the ones before you. I hope you don't get lured into his trap. They all fall hook, line and sinker and he doesn't discriminate; ghetto, trashy, elegant, sophisticated, rich, poor, young, old, ugly..."

The more she talked, the more Zhara understood why the girls at the salon referred to her as a Rottweiler.

In an effort to find out who Serwa had been talking about, Zhara glanced in the direction of the pillar. Two men were chatting. One of them was looking intently at her. He was tall, dark and very handsome. She locked eyes with him. He continued chatting but his eyes were fixed on her. He smiled. She returned his smile. She felt funny all over. His lips curled into a smile and the tip of his tongue emerged from the beautifully sculptured full espresso lips. It prompted feelings she'd never felt before. A sudden rush of heat pulsated rapidly through her veins.

"Sometimes I wonder why they bother..."

Oh no! She thought, Serwa had been talking all along, what if she'd asked her something and she hadn't heard, that would be so rude. Zhara looked at the man she was being warned to stay away from and returned her gaze to Serwa. Something was up, she thought. It just didn't make sense. She felt a churning in her stomach. Somehow her instincts were telling her to keep an open mind. The stirrings within her gave way to emotions she'd read about in romantic novels. No one had ever had that effect on her. She took a deep calming breath and let it out slowly.

CHAPTER TWENTY THREE

Agyeman did not know what to believe. He had shared heartwarming smiles with Zhara and thought he felt the chemistry between them, and yet Serwa was adamant she didn't want anything to do with him. Though it sounded far-searched he knew she would not lie to him. Serwa had also told him Zhara was stuck-up, rude and dull, and she couldn't rub more than two words together, which he thought was rather spiteful. From the way she spoke fondly of Olympia and described her as intelligent, charming and perfect for him, he wouldn't put it past her to be bad-mouthing Zhara so she could pair him up with Olympia. Even though he valued her opinion and Olympia wasn't bad to look at, he intended to follow his heart, and only Zhara fitted the bill. He had no desire whatsoever of dating a cougar.

Agyeman decided to settle Zhara and Olympia's bill. He was sure it would give him a little time with Zhara and he could find out for himself if what he felt was just a figment of his imagination.

Serwa bounded towards Olympia and Zhara. "Please put your money away. It's already taken care of, darling."

"You can't be serious?" Olympia gave her a quizzical look.

"I am, let me explain." She pulled her to the side. "My cousin, his royal highness Nana Agyeman, happens to be in town. He popped in to see me. Anyway, when he saw you, he mentioned how fabulous you look. And you know me, I got carried away and let slip that you were celebrating your 21st birthday yet again, and it will be the grandest party in town. Being the generous soul that he is, he decided to give you a little birthday treat. You must meet him."

"That is really thoughtful of him. Of course! It would be a pleasure."

"Do come with me," she said, leading the way.

Olympia took Zhara's hand and followed her.

"Nana Agyeman, Tony, I'd like you to meet Olympia, a very good friend of mine, who also happens to be among my favourite customers. This is Zhara, her cousin."

Agyeman shook Olympia's hand. He lingered when he got to Zhara. She looked even better up close.

Zhara tried to avoid his eyes. She had a lot on her mind. After what Serwa had said about him she was shocked to hear he was her cousin. Her feelings hadn't changed though, and being near him made it worse.

"Thank you so much," said Olympia. "I am overwhelmed by your kindness." She gawped at Agyeman's massive manly hands, wondering how they would feel on her body. Then she moved down to his polished leather shoes; size 12 or 13, she guessed, and swallowed, convinced he was undoubtedly a real man in every sense. "Nana Agyeman," she said lasciviously, "since you've given me a present for my birthday, perhaps you would let me make you the guest of honour at my birthday party."

"Ehmm, when is it?" he hesitated.

"Next Saturday. I would be delighted if you could attend, and you may bring a friend."

"I would be delighted to attend," he said enthusiastically, "but on one condition."

"And what would that be?" Olympia asked.

"That you and Zhara join us for a quick drink."

"Done deal!" Olympia said cheerfully. She was feeling peckish and could do with a drink or two. She was beginning to enjoy herself. It had been a while since anyone had bought her a drink, not that she couldn't afford it mind, but it was nice to be asked every now and again. And as for getting her hairdressing bill paid, that was a first.

Olympia checked out the younger men as they said goodbye to Serwa. She liked, liked, liked! Agyeman was six foot two, dark chocolate, had a natural flair and looked eminent. The deliciously tempting lips, broad shoulders and rippling muscles had her captivated. Tony was about six foot and several shades lighter. The danger in his dark grey eyes was unnerving. Olympia was partial to a bit of rough and he looked like he was up for the challenge in his faded denim, black leather jacket and Doc Martens. Like a kid in a candy store, she was spoilt for choice.

"I know a place not far from here." Agyeman said to Olympia and Zhara, perhaps you would like to come with us?"

"Oh, OK." Olympia nearly jumped out of her skin.

"We will follow you, please lead the way."

"My car is outside. Would you like to join us?" Tony asked Zhara, hoping she would say yes, and give Agyeman a head start.

"No thanks." Zhara replied. "We will follow your car."

The boys crossed the road and got into a Porsche Cayenne SUV.

Zhara and Olympia got into their car. It was parked a short distance away. Just as they came up towards the boys Tony indicated and drove ahead of them. He veered off the main road into Leigham Court Road, drove for about a mile and arrived at a Victorian mansion with a quintessentially English charm.

Agyeman and his guests were welcomed by the butler and led to a cosy room with a lit fire, dimmed lights, overstuffed couches and soft velvet cushions. The smell of jasmine and sandalwood lingered in the air as the butler took their coats and a waiter arrived to take their orders.

"Hmmm, this is lovely" said Olympia as she eased into the couch. "Could I have a Cosmopolitan?"

"And you madam?" the waiter asked with a pleasant smile.

"Lemonade, please."

"With a touch of Cinzano!" Olympia added.

"I don't think so" said Zhara.

"Please honey," Olympia coaxed, "a little drop of alcohol won't do any harm."

"OK," she relented.

"And a few cans of Tennent's super strong lager." said

Tony.

Agyeman sat next to Zhara. After the chef had taken their order he inched closer to her.

"Hi Zhara!" His voice was deep and sexy.

"Hi Nana Agyeman." she said softly. She liked the way he pronounced her name.

"Your have a very beautiful name, just like you. Do you know what it means?"

"Thank you. Yes, I do, it means flower of the world."

"I should have known," he said affectionately, "it is a very special name."

"Do you know the meaning of your name?"

"Yes." he said. "It means courageous warrior."

"That sounds pretty special too. A warrior prince."

Smiling, he cast an eye over her crimson cashmere jumper.

"That colour looks great on you, it compliments your skin tone."

"Thanks" she murmured.

He smiled. The sensuality in her curves and the way she carried herself blew his mind, and definitely met all his criteria.

"Do you live in London?" Serwa had given him chapter and verse but he didn't want her to know that.

"No, I'm only here for a short visit. I live in Accra." She noticed his pearly white teeth.

"Isn't that a coincidence?" he said, observing the smooth flawless face, eyes that touched his soul, the long thick natural lashes, dimpled cheeks and full luscious lips.

The waiter interrupted his train of thought.

"Your drink, sir."

"Thank you." He said politely and took a sip.

Serwa had given Olympia the impression that Agyeman was keen on her, so she was rather cheesed off that he hadn't sat by her. Engaged in a heated debate with Tony about the virtues of men, she was thrilled when the waiter served her drink. It wasn't that she did not fancy Tony, he was a fine young man, but Agyeman ticked all her boxes. He has a certain je ne sais quoi that charmed the pants off her. Much to her chagrin, she had noticed that Agyeman only had eyes for Zhara, and judging by the ridiculous grin plastered on his face, she knew she stood no chance, not that she would ever want to come between him and Zhara. It didn't stop her from wondering why someone with his reputation would lust after a naïve, inexperienced lady when he could have had her, a seasoned sex kitten who could match him in every position. His loss, she thought. After the third Cosmopolitan she couldn't care less about Agyeman or the fact that Tony was married.

"The moment I saw you," Agyeman said, gazing into Zhara's eyes, "I knew I couldn't let you walk out of my life."

The dark heated eyes sent a quiver down her spine.

"I would really love to see you again," he continued. "Can I pick you up tomorrow?"

Avoiding his eyes, she focused on the neatly trimmed

moustache.

"I'm busy tomorrow."

"What about the day after tomorrow?"

"I can't. I am meeting up with friends" she lied.

He looked disappointed. "Can I call you?"

"Of course." She scribbled her number on a piece of paper and handed it to him.

"Here" he said, giving her his business card. "You can all me any time, night or day. I'll be waiting."

They were discussing the effects of extra-marital affairs, something Agyeman and Olympia were very passionate about, when the chef arrived with a platter of sizzling dishes.

"Now that's what I call a spread!" Tony said, with a big smile on his face. "I am starving!"

"Me too," said Olympia. "It looks and smells delicious."

They ate ravenously and continued drinking and chatting until Zhara nudged Olympia that it was time to go home.

"But it is only just after 10 pm on a Saturday. Can't we stay a little longer?"

"I am tired. Can we go, please?"

"OK, OK," she said, looking peeved and very drunk. Can I finish my drink!"

Shortly after 11 pm Zhara thanked Agyeman for a lovely evening and drove home with Olympia.

CHAPTER TWENTY FOUR

After seeing Tony off Agyeman returned to his suite. Zhara had been gone for over an hour and yet he couldn't stop thinking about her. That was when it dawned on him that what he felt for her was not just sexual, but a deep emotional longing. It was the first time he'd felt a bond with anyone since his father's death. The desire to hear her soft sweet voice was overwhelming. Unable to resist it anymore he picked up the phone and dialled her number.

She answered on the second ring.

"Hello?"

"Hi, it's me. Just checking you got home safely."

"Hello Nana Agyeman, thanks for taking the time to check up on us." Her heart started pounding. Flashes of their last few minutes together came to her; she could still smell his alluring aftershave and the feel of his lips on her cheek had got her reeling. Could it be a passing infatuation, she thought, or the real thing?

"It is always a pleasure to hear your voice, but please drop the Nana."

"Why is that? Don't you like being called a Prince?"

"The truth is, I don't, but I wouldn't want my mother to hear that. She would practically skin me alive. Zhara," he paused for a moment. I really enjoyed your company last night. I would love to see you again. Can we meet

159

again, soon?"

"I don't think so. Are you coming to Olympia's party?"

"My plan was to spend a few days in London but..."

"Are you saying you accepted the invitation even though you knew you couldn't make it?"

"Yes, I did, but things are different now?"

"Really? How?"

"Because you stole my heart and I want to spend more time with you."

Zhara could feel her heart pulsating.

"What are you doing now?"

"Getting ready for bed."

"Can I come and join you?"

"No thanks," she giggled.

"What is funny about that? Would you like to come and tuck me in? Seriously, I could send a car to pick you up. I'm in room 102. Don't get me wrong, I don't just want to sleep with you, I really really like you."

She felt the sincerity in his voice. "I really like you too, but not enough to share your bed. To be honest, I don't think I am the type of girl you are looking for."

"Why do you say that? Of course you are. You are what I've been looking for all my life!"

"I can only agree to a friendship at this stage, nothing more."

Agyeman realised Zhara was going to be a hard nut to crack, much harder than he'd anticipated. The only girl friends he had were those he hadn't slept with yet and she was certainly way out of their league. "OK." he said, "I can deal with that." He didn't like it but he would rather have her any way he could, than not have her at all. "When can I see you?" he pressed on.

"At Olympia's party." She yawned.

"What about tomorrow?"

"I'll be busy."

"And Monday?"

"I have a lot on this week."

"That's a shame. I would have loved to see you before I left for Accra."

"But I thought you said you had changed your mind."

"Yes, I did. But that was because I thought you wanted to see me. If you don't want to see me then there is no point hanging around."

"So you lied to Olympia?"

"Perhaps, but I would have said anything for a chance to spend time with you."

"So stay then, and I promise to see you on Saturday?"

"OK I will, but you better not disappoint me."

"Olympia will be delighted you changed your plans so you could attend her party. Thank you."

"I am staying because of you, not Olympia or her party."

"I am touched," she teased.

"You will be, when I get my hands on you."

"Good night."

"Good night."

Zhara could not wipe the smile off her face. She barely knew the man and yet he'd found a way to consume her mind, her thoughts, her body and her soul. Though she didn't want to admit it, not even to herself, what she felt for him had 'love' stamped all over it.

CHAPTER TWENTY FIVE

The Christmas-themed birthday party was in full swing when Agyeman arrived. He was accompanied by one of his closest friends, Captain Akatapori. They were guided to the ballroom, a grand room embellished in rich reds and golds, and candelabras swagged with velvet in trailing ivy. The sound of smooth jazz, the fresh smell of pine and uniformed waiters proffering trays of champagne, caviar and a menu of cocktails created a buzz of excitement.

Agyeman was searching the crowd of suits and ball-gowns for Zhara when he heard a familiar voice.

"Hello you! I'm so glad you made it." Olympia looked stunning in a white topless fitted gown with Swarovski crystals. Her hair was pinned up elegantly and diamonds sparkled in her ears, around her neck and on her wrists.

"Happy birthday!" said Agyeman as he hugged and kissed her! You look amazing."

"You look fabulous," she said, eyeing his tuxedo. And who do we have here?" She asked leering at his friend.

"Please meet Captain Akatapori."

Olympia extended a hand to the dashing man with a deep scar across the left side of his face. He took it and raised it to his lips. She blushed, all over.

"Is there an airport close by, or was it just my heart taking off?"

Olympia was intrigued by the deep rich accent with hints of Bolgatanga and the American Deep South.

"Are you a comedian?" she chuckled.

Akatapori smiled. "Not really, but I would love to become one, just to see you smile."

"You are just too much!" she laughed. He was growing on her, rapidly. The tall muscular physique was sheer temptation and even though the scar sent a shiver right through her, she couldn't wait to find out how he got it.

"Can I take a picture of you so I can show Santa what I want for Christmas?" he asked with a straight face.

"Sure. With a body like that you may have anything you want honey! Are you a sportsman?" Olympia licked her lips seductively.

Akatapori smiled. "Not any more, but we dabbled in sports in our youth. Agyeman was the real sportsman, at one point he couldn't decide whether to play professional football, table tennis or concentrate on swimming for his country."

"Wow, that must have been tough" said Olympia.

"It was, but that was years ago." said Agyeman. "Akatapori was the budding football star until his parents decided he needed a proper career and sent him to the flying academy."

"Are you saying he is a pilot?" Olympia loved men in uniform. Her ultimate fantasy was to be made love to in a cockpit.

"Yes he is, and single."

Olympia's heart bounced off her ribcage. It was as if all her birthdays had come at once.

Agyeman could feel the growing passion between Olympia and Akatapori. He'd brought him along so he could pair him off with Olympia and it seemed to be working. His job was done, he thought; it was time to find Zhara.

"Is Zhara here?" he asked Olympia.

"Yes, she is around somewhere. Let me find her for you."

"Don't worry. I'll go and look for her."

Agyeman was offered another glass of champagne as he strode through the crowd. He was leaning up against the piano when he saw Zhara coming towards him. She looked delectable in a luxurious red chiffon gown.

"Hi gorgeous." He kissed her on each cheek. "I am delighted to see you again."

"Hi. I'm glad you made it," she said bashfully. She felt a shiver run through her body. He was like an aphrodisiac, paralysing and unnerving her with his dark piercing eyes. She couldn't trust herself around him.

He smiled licentiously and was about to say something, when they were distracted by a petite blonde. She moved rapidly towards them, in a figure-hugging sequinned gown. One arm was clutching the hem of her dress and the other was waving frantically at Agyeman. Tottering in ten inch sequined stilettos, her steps quickened as she neared them, hips swaying vigorously from side to side. The 48KKK boobs and pink blown up lips reached Agyeman before she did.

"Hi luv," she sniffed, "sorry to budge in like this, but I had to come over and find out for myself. Were you one of the designers at the Milan fashion show?"

"Umm, yes." Agyeman said dryly.

"Oh my god!" she squealed. "I knew it! I just knew it was you!" She turned and waved at an elderly man in a grand boubou. He was a few feet away and looked flushed. "I told you he was at the show in Milan." She extended her hand to Agyeman, blue-green eyes twinkling with awe.

"My name is Lola, and this is Chief Olusegun Obasanjo." She winked at the Chief. "I really loved your show and your collection is to die for. Anyway, if you ever need a model, please don't hesitate to give me a call." She dug out a card from her sequinned purse and handed it to him.

"Do you have an agent?"

"I did, until a week ago when the creep started to get on my tits, so I told him to sod off. Anyway, don't forget to give me a tinkle. I will be waiting."

Zhara was wondering what Lola could be doing with a man old enough to be her grandfather, when Olympia threw her arms around the Chief.

"I am so glad you could make it. Where is Victoria?"

The Chief pursed his lips and shrugged. "I tried to persuade her to give up the bible," he said in a strong Ibo accent, "just for one night, but she refused. So when she left for all-night vigil I called my ever-ready Lola." He looked affectionately at Lola and took her arm possessively. "Sweetie-pie, meet my Greek-African goddess. She knows how to keeps me out of trouble. Beneath the beautiful face is a barrister's brain that surpasses all her peers."

Lola looked impressed. "Hiya. You must be really clever."

"Don't take it literally" said Olympia, "he likes to make me sound more important than I really am. But enough of Chief, tell me about yourself."

Lola grabbed another glass of champagne. "I left school at 16 to become a model. After four years of having doors slammed in my face I had my first big break last year, but only after the boob job, nose job, tummy tuck, lipo, botox, lip enhancement and work on my teeth."

"But surely you didn't have to put yourself through all that to become a model?"

"I wasn't ugly, but I had to, and it wasn't cheap either. As luck would have it, all my dreams started to come true, from the moment I bumped into Chief. He was dead against it at first, but he realised it was the only thing that would make me happy, so he paid for the lot." With eyes filled with love and appreciation she kissed Chief passionately on the lips and left him breathless.

"So how did you two meet?" Olympia asked.

"Olympia, you are too inquisitive," the Chief said, "but since you want to know, I will tell you myself.

He took a long sip of orange juice. "I went to Selfridges for a few things, but my biggest mistake was taking Victoria with me. We'd been there for over three hours and she still hadn't finished shopping. I lost my patience and went outside to get some fresh air. All of a sudden this skinny pretty little white thing bumped into me and fell flat on her face. She said sorry but I was more concerned about her. Next thing she was crying like a child. It made me feel bad, like I'd done something to her."

"Honey!" Lola said gleefully, "You could never make me cry." She turned to Olympia. "He's the sweetest, kindest man I've ever known. Honestly, he would give me the world if I asked for it. The reason I was crying was because I'd just been turned down by yet another modelling agency, for being too fat, even though I was a size ten and I felt like throwing myself over a bridge. You came to my rescue when I was lost and alone and had no-one. And you were so kind, even though you didn't know me. That was what made me cry. Until I met you, my whole life was full of upsets, heartbreaks and disappointment. There was no room for anything else."

"You make it sound like your parents didn't love or care about you" said Olympia.

Lola laughed hysterically. "Parents? Love? Care? Those are just words to me, not reality. First of all, I had no father, just a mother who couldn't recall which of her many men had produced the sperm that conceived me. After years of sexual abuse from her many boyfriends I left the council flat in Penge, the only home I'd ever known, and dossed on my best friend's couch in Peckham. I've never returned to the stinking pisshole and don't ever intend to."

"Don't you miss your mother?"

"Not really. When I told her what her boyfriends were doing to me she did nothing about it. All she cared about was getting pissed out of her brains. She preferred them to me anyway, so why should I care about her? Chief was the best thing that could have happened to me. Now I have a flat in Chelsea, a new wardrobe every season, a BMW and money in my account, thanks to him."

Chief drew Lola closer to him. "My little chicken, you need to come with me to Abuja so I can spoil you more. You'll have your own mansion, servants, cars, a yacht and a private jet."

Lola couldn't wait to go to Africa with Chief, just for a short visit. She adored him for his kindness and thoughtfulness, but there was no way she would leave her modelling career and become his sixth wife. She grabbed a glass of champagne from a passing waiter and downed it, then another. After about six glasses of champagne, a selection of cocktails and a few shots of tequila she was ready to party.

Chief stayed clear of the vol au vent and caviar blinis but didn't hold back on the lobster with hot pepper sauce. "This is too good!" he said as he neared Agyeman. "Young man, I hear you did very well at the fashion show and your clothes were of exceptional quality. How can I get my hands on an exclusive selection of your suits? I want a few suits like the one you're wearing; it makes you stand out from the crowd. I will also need a few classic shirts, short sleeved ones with a mandarin collar, suitable for Africa, and some long-sleeved ones for when I'm in Europe."

"That shouldn't be a problem." Agyeman said with a broad smile.

"Excellent! Here is my address. Shall we say tomorrow at eleven o'clock?"

"Fantastic!"

Delighted at the prospect of bagging another client, Agyeman clinked glasses with Chief, wondering where Zhara had got to.

Akatapori was heading back to the ballroom when he saw Zhara. He remembered seeing her with Agyeman and figured she must be the girl he'd been raving about.

"Hi, I don't think we've met." He extended his arm and smiled broadly. "My name is Akatapori."

Zhara shook his hand. "I'm Zhara."

"I know," He smiled warmly. "Agyeman has told me a lot about you."

Zhara looked puzzled. "Really?"

"Yes. I believe you've captured his heart."

"That's news to me. What else has he been saying?"

Akatapori raised his bushy eyebrows. "Hmm, that I couldn't make you laugh. Could you do me a favour?"

"It depends..." she said warily.

He reached behind her dress and pretended to read what was written on the tag. "Yes, just what I thought!" he tried not to laugh. "Made in heaven."

She laughed.

"I knew I could make you laugh!" He said, looking thrilled with himself. "OK, now that I've proved Agyeman wrong, can I let you into a little secret."

"Of course!" She said, wondering what it could be.

"OK, I think you should know this," he whispered. "Agyeman is madly in love with you and it scares the hell out of him because he's never felt like that before. Please try not to break his heart."

"I see you two have met." Agyeman said, interrupting the tête a tête.

"Your friend is funny" said Zhara.

"I know. He should have been a comedian."

"Enough about me, where did you find such a precious jewel?"

"Here in London, just like I said. And where have you been? I've been searching all over for you."

"Around" Akatapori said with a cheeky smile. "I'll fill you in later."

"Later? I want to know now."

Zhara left the boys to banter. She was looking for Olympia when she felt a tap on her shoulder. It was Kukuwa. They hugged each other.

Kukuwa looked exquisite in a green chiffon gown. Her long, graceful neck and ear lobes sparkled with rubies. A tanned, dashing man stood beside her, in a luxurious dark grey suit with a red cravat and piercing blue eyes.

"François, meet Zhara, my best friend," said Kukuwa.

Blue eyes widened, giving way to a broad smile. "I am delighted to finally meet you. I've heard so much about you." A few strands of golden hair shifted around his shoulders. He took Zhara's hand and raised it to his lips. "You are more beautiful than I imagined."

"Thank you" Zhara said demurely. She had expected a French accent and was pleasantly surprised by the pronounced English drawl.

The MC's voice travelled across the ballroom. "Ladies and gentlemen, please take your seats, dinner is served."

Ngozi bounded towards Olympia, clutching the hem of her purple gown. Her place at Olympia's table had been given to another guest, and she wasn't pleased.

"I've just found out that I am not on your table."

"Sorry hun, I should have told you. There was a last minute change. I hope you don't mind?"

"Of course not, but you should have told me. So who is it?" she enquired.

"Captain Akatapori." Olympia's face lit up.

"I should have guessed it would be a man," she said crossly.

"You have to meet him." Olympia said jubilantly and walked away.

Kukuwa placed the tablecloth carefully on her lap. She'd noticed the change in Zhara's demeanour when she was with Agyeman and was glad they had been seated together. They had a lot of catching up to do.

"Lawal is glaring at you and the Ashanti Prince hasn't taken his eyes off you since he sat down" she whispered. "I must say, he looks trés cool and from what you've told me, I am convinced that you are in love." She smiled joyfully. "Does he know how you feel about him?"

"Not yet, and I intend to keep it that way."

"Honey, he needs to know how you feel. It is obvious that he fancies you, and you look good together. He's perfect for you."

"Perfect? How?"

"Well, he is mature, tall, very handsome, polite and incredibly stylish. OK, he may have been a player, but if he is willing to change then I think you should give him a chance. Damn, I bet he knows things Lawal hasn't even heard about. Don't get me wrong, Lawal is a nice guy but beyond the wealth and education he's just an empty shell. I don't think he knows the needs and desires of a woman, not like Agyeman does."

Zhara caught Agyeman eye. He winked at her. Trying to keep her emotions in check she concentrated on the lobster in ginger sauce and ate it with relish.

"Did you notice the way Agyeman's friend was ogling you?"

"I didn't, François did. He threatened to chop off his balls if he came near me."

"What planet is François on? Have you seen Akatapori's humungous biceps? That alone will crush François to pieces. All he needs to do is trust you to be faithful. Didn't he know what he was getting himself into when he proposed to a drop-dead-gorgeous lady? I hope his mother is behaving herself, else I'll be forced to tell her some home truths."

"François is very possessive, and it drives me mad. His mother seems to be turning a new leaf, but very slowly." Kukuwa picked at her food. "I have never doubted that there is nothing but friendship between you and Lawal. What I don't understand is why you insist on being friends with Agyeman when you are clearly in love with him."

Zhara took a sip of water. "Sometimes I think you know me better than I know myself. The truth is, much as I like Lawal, we just don't click. Our fathers are connected by religion, politics and heritage, but beyond that, there is nothing. When I'm with Agyeman I feel passion, emotion and intense sexual chemistry, but he has a reputation and I don't want to be anyone's plaything. I need to be sure that he means it when he says he wants to be with me and only me. He's my ideal man, but I want to love and be loved for better or worse. I can't settle for anything less. I will only commit to true love, with all the bells and whistles."

"Oh Zhara, I am so pleased for you!" said Kukuwa. "I think you've definitely found Mr Right. If he has any sense he will be true to you. He seems sincere though, so I'm sure it will work out. You must follow your heart sweetie, don't fight it." She took a forkful of food and ate it slowly. "Anyway," she said thoughtfully, "what is it with you and princes? First, the Crown Prince Lawal, and now His Royal Highness Nana Agyeman, are you a prince magnet?"

CHAPTER TWENTY SIX

Olympia picked up a handmade tartan cracker and pulled it with Akatapori. A shoehorn, a crown and a joke dropped on the white linen tablecloth.

Akatapori picked up the shoehorn and handed it to Olympia with a slight bow, "Your highness, you will need this for your killer heels."

Everyone at the table laughed.

Kukuwa and François pulled the next cracker. It contained playing cards, a crown and a joke.

All eyes were on Agyeman and Zhara as they pulled the next cracker. It contained a crown, a joke and a ring.

"It's a sign!" Olympia said exultantly.

"Can I be best man at the wedding?" Akatapori asked with a wicked grin.

"You are destined to be together." Kukuwa whispered with elation.

Agyeman picked up the ring and placed it on Zhara's index finger. His eyes were full of passion as he gazed into her large indigo-rimmed eyes.

Zhara felt her muscles clench.

The MC's voice attracted everyone's attention. He invited Olympia to open the dance floor.

She jumped up from her seat, took Akatapori's arm and led him to the floor. As they danced to R Kellie's Bump and Grind they were joined by many of the guests. There was no letting up when the MC played Keni Burke's Hang Tight. Everyone got up to dance. The atmosphere was electrifying.

Taking Ngozi's hand Olympia twirled around the break-dancers, hip-hoppers, toe-tappers and finger-snappers.

Agyeman loved music, but was not keen on dancing. Perched by the wall, he felt a pang of jealously as many men asked Zhara if they could dance with her. He noticed that one of the men wouldn't leave her alone, and it made his blood boil. He was pleased when Akatapori took her hand and led her away from the man. He watched them dance. Zhara was definitely the queen of the dance floor. She moved gracefully to the beat and spun around like a carousel, lighting up the room with her infectious smile.

Ngozi pulled Olympia to the side. She appeared not to have got over the business with the table plan. "Honey, you know I care about you, but please don't treat me like an idiot. You've only just met this loser and yet you treat him better than me. Why can't you control yourself when it comes to men? If you're not careful he will trample all over you, just like the others."

"A loser? Please. If you must know, he is a very accomplished pilot. You don't have to badmouth him because of what I did, the whole table business was my idea, he had nothing to do with it." She took a deep breath. "You are right, we've only just met, but he is a decent man. Believe me, he is not like any of the men I've been with."

"So what exactly were you doing with him in the suite?"

"I hate to break it to you, darling, but if you must know, he took me through the mountains, up the clouds and beyond the Milky Way. I saw the stars twinkling like I'd never done before and in the little time we had, he unearthed places I didn't even know existed. Trust me, this one is a keeper. I will do everything it takes to make him mine."

Ngozi could not believe her ears. "You are despicable!" she hissed. "Here?"

"Yes darling and it was the best birthday present ever! Millie Jackson hit the nail on the head. What she said in her song, the Ugly Man, it is sooooo true. You must try it."

"I swear you need help." Ngozi scowled. "And there is no way in hell I will be trying it. Just in case you've forgotten, I'm a married woman. And for your information, even if I weren't married, I would never go where you've been. I pray that what he feels for you is love, not just the usual 'wang bang thank you mum'."

"I hope so too, but don't be a hater. Let's go find my boo (lover)."

Olympia swung her hips towards Akatapori and beckoned Agyeman to join them.

Grudgingly, Agyeman moved to the dance floor. Zhara's warm and inviting smile egged him on. He took her hand and pulled her to him. Marvin Gaye's Sexual Healing blared through the speakers. Zhara tried to pull away. He wouldn't let her go. He wrapped his arms around her tiny waist and inhaled her enticing smell, wondering if she knew the effect she had on him.

The feel of Agyeman's masculine arms around her body sent shudders through her. She buried her head in his chest and tried to remain calm. He smelt so good she could stay there forever. As they danced, she felt the sparks. She drew a deep shuddering breath.

"Are you cold?" he whispered, drawing her closer to him. He could feel her soft breath and her warm supple body.

"I'm fine," she whispered.

"Zhara, I know you want us to be just friends but I can't help the way I feel about you. You know that, don't you?"

"Mhmm," she mumbled.

"And the ring in the Christmas cracker," he continued, "that was not a mere coincidence. I believe it is our destiny."

"Really?"

"Yes, and in time you will believe me. It breaks my heart that I will be leaving tomorrow. Please promise you will keep in touch."

"Tomorrow?"

"Don't say that. It will only worsen my agony, knowing I won't be seeing you for a while, but I will be in touch. I don't just want to be your friend, I want to love you, I need to share my life with you; I want you more than you will ever know."

"OK, I will keep in touch."

"When do you intend to return to Accra?"

"In a week or so."

"Promise you will come and see me."

"You don't ask for much, do you?" she giggled.

"Zhara, I think you want me as much as I want you, even if you don't want to admit it but if I am wrong please tell me and I will leave you alone. But if I am right, let's not play a cat and mouse game. Please let me love you like you deserve to be loved, don't fight it. Do you promise to come and see me when you return to Accra?"

She sighed deeply. "OK, I promise".

"Cross your heart?"

She giggled. "Yep."

Just as she raised her head he lowered his. Their lips brushed against each other. They looked into each other's eyes and the world stood still.

CHAPTER TWENTY SEVEN

Zhara was keen to head back to Accra. She yearned to wake up to the sound of the crowing cockerel, watch the sun rise over the Atlantic Ocean and listen to the sound of crickets at night. She loved bright hot sunshine, every single day of the year.

With her motherland in mind, she packed her suitcase with boundless joy, checking and rechecking her long list of items; Swiss voile, embroidered lace, organza, brocades, Holland wax prints, silk head ties, sandals, shoes, handbags, perfume, lingerie, French Polynesian black pearls, cream baroque pearls, classic white freshwater pearls. "OK," she muttered to herself, "that covers Mum, Grandma, Aunty Bentsiwa and Kwansima." Returning to the list, she ticked off the Santos Cartier watch, cotton and linen shirts, cufflinks, black, brown, white and grey socks, aftershave, white cotton pants and singlets. "That's Dad sorted," she said joyfully. The rest – clothes, toys, gifts, books, gadgets, sweets and two boxes of gourmet cat dinners were for the people who worked with and for her, her cat, her nieces and nephews and children in the village orphanage.

After saying goodbye to Olympia and Akatapori, Zhara got

in the taxi. She was glad Agyeman had brought Akatapori to Olympia's party. They were dating and seemed perfect for each other. He was down to earth, hilarious and made Olympia very happy. And considering what she'd been through, she deserved a good man.

The taxi arrived at Heathrow Airport just after 12:30 pm. Zhara's luggage was piled on two trolleys. She rolled the trolleys towards the departure lounge and cringed when she reached the check-in desk. Her oversized handbag was within an inch of bursting. Avoiding eye contact with the uniformed attendant, she handed him her ticket and tried not to think about the excess luggage charge.

"Ma'am. Did you pack your entire luggage yourself? He asked, desperately seeking her eyes.

"Yep!"

"Has anyone tampered with your bags or asked you to pack something for them?"

She was tempted to say 'Yes. My cat, friends, aunt, uncles, nieces, nephews, distant relations and people I haven't even met yet,' but she settled for a polite "No", and was surprised that he didn't ask if she had a fridge in her handbag.

Observing her severely, he weighed the luggage.

"Ma'am, do you realise you've exceeded the required weight for your luggage?"

She knew that, but decided to remain silent.

"Your excess luggage charge comes to…" He looked at her, then back at the screen, as if considering how much to charge her. From Zhara's calculations it was about one hundred and fifty pounds but she decided to let him say it.

He looked up again. She averted her eyes, determined not to make eye contact.

He hesitated. "Would you perhaps be interested in an upgrade?"

She smiled and made eye contact, briefly.

"In that case I'll move you to seat 1A in the first class cabin."

"And the excess charge?" She stammered.

His smile got wider. "Let's pretend we never had that conversation."

"Thank you."

After a few clicks he gave her an award-winning smile and a boarding pass. "Have a pleasant flight!"

Zhara moved quickly past the families laden with trolleys. She even managed to overtake the unnaturally fast-moving businessmen and the stewards who moved in a smooth continuous motion, as if their mechanisms were jammed on the wrong setting. With 40 minutes to spare she whisked through customs to the duty-free shops.

Stretched out with a glass of lemonade high up in the sky she tried to read a book, but couldn't. She could think of nothing else but him; his voice, his smell, his touch, his smile. Memories of their dance and the brush of their lips played on her mind. She loved him with every pulse in her body, but she had to be sure it wasn't infatuation, so she decided to avoid contact, only until she was sure of her feelings.

The plane touched down just after 8:30 pm on 22nd December. Passengers on the aircraft clapped and cheered, which seemed unusual for those who were travelling to Ghana for the first time.

Zhara stepped out of the aircraft and walked down the metal staircase. The air embraced her, filling her lungs with warmth. She looked up at the black velvet sky covered with twinkling stars and was delighted to hear the crickets welcoming her back to the motherland.

CHAPTER TWENTY EIGHT

It was the middle of January. Agyeman had called Zhara many times but was yet to hear from her. As he paced the room, doubts started to creep into his mind. Had he meant anything to her, he wondered. It was nearly three in the morning and yet he could not sleep. He tried to put her out of his mind, but he wasn't having much luck there either. The sleepless nights had started to take a toll on his work and his health.

He fell into the king-sized and stared blankly at the walls. The pain in his head was becoming unbearable and his eyes stung. He cried out and buried his head in the pillow.

The sound of the doorbell made him jump. He ignored it. Seconds later it rang again. He cursed out loud, jumped up, stomped to the window and pulled back the curtain. The gate was firmly locked and there was no sign of life within his house or the surrounding area. The bell went again. He grabbed a dressing gown and pulled it on, unlocked the glass doors and proceeded angrily towards the balcony. The bulky frame of Al Hassan, the night watchman with his enormous neck, giant-sized shoulders and thick biceps in a white jellaba and cab caught his eye.

"Al Hassan," he called out, "did you press the bell?"

"Yesah!" Al Hassan shouted. He moved towards the front lawn so he could get a better view of Agyeman. Removing his cap, he scratched his head and bowed.

"Sah, I see say you no de sleep, only waka waka teeeee for three days now. Ibi when I hear say you de shout wey only you dey for house that I de start to worry." He sighed deeply. "Wooyooi Allah! That be the time wey I dey press bell make I check sey na everything be well well for you." He shook his head vigorously. "Wollahi, Allah!"

A smile appeared on Agyeman's lips as he observed the middle-aged ex-army officer who it appeared had been keeping an eagle eye on his nocturnal activities instead of just guarding the house as he had been paid to do. Even though he had a ferocious glare, which scared the hell out of most people, he also had a heart of gold.

"Al Hassan" Agyeman shouted. "Thank you for your concern. As you can see, I am fine. I can't sleep because I have a lot on my mind. There is nothing to worry about."

The worried look on Al Hassan's face was replaced by a broad toothy smile. "Thank you sir. Allah bless you well well!"

Agyeman shut the door behind him and headed for the bathroom. His head was pounding and his body felt like it was burning, even though the air conditioner was on the coldest setting. Agyeman nearly fell over with shock when he saw himself in the mirror. He did not recognise the gaunt, dishevelled man staring back at him. It gave him a reality check. I need to sort myself out and get a life, he muttered to himself. He made a mental note to erase

Zhara from his life, eat properly, stop being a recluse, sleep more and stop having audible conversations with himself.

Shrugging off the bathrobe he stood under the shower and let the water run down on him.

He headed down to the kitchen and took some aspirin to numb the pain. The house was silent except for the humming noise from the fridge freezer. Ignoring the chilled Star beer, he opted for a bottle of water. He warmed the soup the chef made the previous day and ate it with a bread roll.

He was halfway up the stairs when he remembered he'd left his phone in the workroom. Turning back around he took a few strides and opened the door to the workroom. The uniforms he'd sketched for the airline were exactly where he'd left them a couple of days ago. The suits he'd been designing for the groom and his mates were nowhere near completion and the wedding was only a month away. The phone was blinking away on the desk. He pushed the loudspeaker and listened to the messages, all fourteen of them. The aspirin kicked in after about an hour and he was beginning to feel himself again so he decided to work on the sketches.

By 7 am he was completely shattered. He grabbed the phone, dragged himself to the bedroom and collapsed on the bed.

Agyeman thought he was dreaming when he heard the phone ringing. Turning over he grabbed it. "Hello?"

"I hope you're not sleeping at this time of the day."

"Hi," he said groggily.

"What happened? You didn't show up at the jazz club on Friday night or the party yesterday. I dread to think what you could be doing in bed at two o'clock on a Sunday afternoon when there is a football match on. Whoever you've got in bed with you must be good. You sound like you are completely wiped out."

Agyeman rolled onto his side. "Sam, I left work early on Friday and have been home since, and alone."

"Are you kidding me? You? Alone? Pull the other one!"

"You know what, you are right, he said grumpily "I am exhausted so if you don't mind I would like to catch up on my sleep. I will call you when I wake up."

"Are you OK?" Sam said fretfully.

He could sense that something wasn't quite right. Agyeman never flew off the handle without good reason, and he was clearly ticked off. But at what, he wondered? There had been talk that success might have gone to his head, but he knew Agyeman too well to believe any of that rubbish. He had noticed subtle changes after Agyeman returned from Europe but he put it down to fatigue. Even though the guy enjoyed his work, it never stopped him from hanging out with his friends. He figured there was a reason for the reclusion.

"Not really, maybe it's malaria. I don't feel too good."

"You're not the sickly type. What is really wrong?"

Agyeman had known Sam for over 20 years and when he was on to something he was like a dog with a bone. He tried to put him off. "You've disturbed my sleep, called me a liar and won't get off my phone. Must you always be a nag?"

"Not always," Sam replied, "only when I suspect you are holding something back. And you shouldn't. You are like a brother to me and I want to be there for you. I hope you can trust me with whatever is eating you up and keeping you out of circulation. A problem shared is..."

"OK, OK, I hear you." Agyeman sat up. "I met a girl in London...."

"Yes, so what? You meet them all the time. Nothing new there."

"Listen!" he huffed, "this is different, I mean she is different. She lives here in Accra. I like her very much. I thought she liked me too, but now I know she doesn't. The problem is that I can't stop thinking about her. The one time I'm prepared to give my heart to a woman she doesn't want to know. It's driving my insane!"

Sam could not get it. "What exactly is the problem? Why doesn't she want to be with you? Is she married?"

"No, she is single."

"But that doesn't make sense. Doesn't she know who you are? How can she turn down His Royal Highness, our Prince, the renowned successful fashion designer? Does she realise that you're the original ladies' man?"

Agyeman shook his head. "I knew you wouldn't understand. All that nonsense doesn't mean anything to her. She is different."

"Did you hit it?"

"Don't be silly, she is not that type of girl."

"You haven't even shagged her and she's already dumped you? Fuck her! There are plenty more fish in the sea."

"I wish it was that easy."

"I thought it was your dick that made contact with the chicks and nothing else. It sounds as if your heart got there first with this one. She must be special."

"Something about her just blows me away. The way she moves, the way she talks, the way she smiles. For once, sex didn't even matter. I just wanted her to be by my side. It meant more than sex or anything else. I was sure she wanted to be in my life but now..."

"Damn," said Sam, "you better stop there before I start tearing up. This is some serious shit!"

"I know. I so wanted her to be a part of my life. I want to love and cherish her. The thought of never seeing her again scares the hell out of me."

"Holy crap! You have certainly found your match, someone who makes you want her but doesn't need you. I like her already. And you say you haven't slept with her? She must be classy, unlike those who just can't wait to jump into bed with you. You can't let her go. No, no, no, man! Maybe she has heard about your antics and doesn't want to get hurt. You must find her and tell her how you feel."

"I don't know. I told her everything in London. She even promised to come and see me when she got back to Accra but she hasn't. I can't go in search of her when she won't return my calls. I will get over her, somehow, I know it."

"I hope you do. If she doesn't give a hoot's ass about you, then fuck her. On the other hand, if she does care about you, like you do about her, then you'll find each other. Maybe she's playing hard-to-get. Some of these classy chicks they love that game. If so, she'll come to you, when she's ready. Let's meet for lunch tomorrow. I'll pass by your office."

Agyeman felt relieved. "Thank you for shouting at me. I feel better already. See you tomorrow."

CHAPTER TWENTY NINE

Zhara left home around 10 am to meet a client at one of her properties. As she passed the University of Legon she remembered Agyeman had said he lived close by. The thought of him stirred feelings she'd been trying very hard to fight, without much luck. Though she'd tried many times to return his calls she hadn't been able to go through with it. Each time she picked up the phone Serwa's words would ring in her ear and she would be besieged with an irrational fear.

She arrived earlier than planned and was inspecting the property when she felt an overwhelming urge to call Agyeman. Ignoring the warning voices in her head, she reached into her bag and took out his number. With trembling fingers, she tapped the number into her phone and waited. One, two, three rings. A click, a breath, a woman's cheerful voice...

"Hello?"

Zhara clicked off. The depth of feeling she had for him was disturbing, and she knew that, but jealousy? That was totally expected. Taking a deep, calming breath she tried to control her emotions and concentrated on the job at hand.

Pleased with the outcome of the meeting Zhara returned to her car. Instead of starting the engine she dialled Agyeman's number and braced herself. This time she was determined to see it through, no matter who answered the phone.

"Hello?"

She hesitated. It was him, she thought. "Hello. Can I please speak to Agyeman?" The sound coming out of her mouth sounded nothing like her. She wondered what had happened to her voice.

"Hello, it is Agyeman. May I ask who I am speaking to?"

His tone was very formal and distant, she thought.

"It is Zhara, remember me?" She hesitated for a moment, "we met in London."

"Oh yes." He said indifferently. "How are you?"

She'd expected some enthusiasm, not this. Damn, she thought, why did she call him? He had clearly forgotten all about her. Where was all the love and passion he'd talked about? She decided that calling him was a big mistake.

"Fine. I promised to call, remember?" She said coldly.

"Yes, you did. You also promised to come and see me. Do you intend on keeping that promise?"

There was a note of sarcasm in his voice, but he was definitely getting warmer.

"Iii do," she stammered, and bit her lip. "Actually, that's why I called. I just finished a meeting with a client in the Legon area. I could pass by if you are not busy, but if you are not to worry, we can meet at another time."

"I am not busy," he said very warmly. "I would really love to see you. Do you want me to pick you up?"

That was more like the Agyeman she knew, she thought. She was delighted that she called.

"That's OK, I am driving."

He gave her directions. "Zhara, if you haven't eaten I could rustle something up, and I promise not to bite."

"I didn't know you could cook".

"There's a lot you don't know about me. I can compete with the best chefs in the world, if I need to. See you soon."

Zhara powdered her nose and applied a thin layer of metallic bronze lipstick. She straightened her black pencil skirt, adjusted her short-sleeved lemon shirt and stepped on the engine. The chic and professional image was exactly what she wanted to portray.

As she approached the black wrought-iron gate, Zhara's stomach lurched. The man guarding the gate grinned broadly and let her in.

The house was much bigger than she'd expected for a bachelor. A beautiful selection of tropical flowers added colour and warmth to the manicured garden.

Agyeman watched Zhara park the S-class Mercedes. A ray of sunlight fell on her hair a she stepped out of the car. His heart skipped a beat. She looked even sexier in the sunlight.

He threw his arms around her and kissed her dimpled cheeks. "You look stunning."

"Thank you" she said demurely. "It's good to see you too."

Her heart flipped when she saw the long, toned legs in shorts. They were perfectly moulded, and the best legs she'd ever seen on a man. A refreshing sight, she thought, unlike the cassava sticks she often saw paraded around in shorts.

"This way" he said, leading her through the house and into a large, airy sitting room. She leered at the rippling biceps in the sleeveless T-shirt.

"Please take a seat." His voice was warm and husky.

She sank gracefully into the sofa.

Cocking his head to the side he regarded her intently. "What can I offer you?"

"Water, please."

"Sure. What would you like with your meal? Champagne, wine, beer?"

"Muscatella, if you have it."

"I don't, but I know a man who does."

She stared shamelessly at his backside with the image of Adonis in mind and looked around the room. The soft mint walls, white corniced ceiling and crystal chandeliers blended nicely with the black decor.

"Your house is beautiful. Did you decorate it yourself?"

"Yes" he said with a wry smile.

Gregory Isaac was belting out Night Nurse from the state-of-the-art music system. Sunlight poured through the glass doors and windows creating an ambiance of calm and serenity.

Agyeman left the room for a few minutes and returned with a glass of chilled water. It was while he was opening a concealed cabinet containing an impressive collection of LPs and CDs that her eyes fell on the photographs. One was a signed portrait of Bob Marley. It read:

Until the philosophy which holds one race
superior and another inferior
Is finally and permanently discredited and
abandoned
Until there is no longer
First class and second class citizens of any nation.
Until the colour of a man's skin
Is of no more significance than the colour of his eyes
Everywhere is war.

The other photo was of a very young boy in a suit presenting a bunch of flowers to Queen Elizabeth of England. An older man stood beside the boy. He was very handsome and impeccably dressed in a dark suit with a cravat and a handkerchief in his breast pocket. His hair was short and wavy with a side parting. He was looking at the boy with immense pride. The resemblance between the boy and the man was uncanny.

"Is that you and your father, with the Queen?" She asked Agyeman.

"Yes, that is my dad." He said proudly.

"You look just like him."

"I know." He cocked his head to the side. "He was a

very special man."

"Was?" Zhara stared with bulging eyes.

"I am afraid so, he passed away many years ago."

"I am so sorry." Their eyes locked. She looked away. "The house is massive. You must have a big family?"

"I do, but I consider myself an only child and I live here alone. Is that what you wanted to know?"

Damn, she thought, must he read her mind? "Um, I was just wondering if the woman who answered your phone lived with you."

"Did someone answer my phone?" He raised a bushy eyebrow.

"Yes. I called this morning, about an hour before we spoke."

"You must have spoken to my aunt. She arrived from Kumasi this morning. She's gone shopping with the driver, but she should be back soon."

Zhara was not entirely convinced, but she chose not to dwell on it.

Zhara was impressed when Agyeman served a mouth-watering spread of sliced kenkey, fried snappers and shrimps, blended onion, scotch bonnets and tomatoes, sardines and shito (hot chilli oil).

"This is delicious," said Zhara appreciatively.

"I'm glad you like, but I must confess, I did not cook any of it."

"I know." She laughed, maybe next time, but I appreciate your honesty. "Where did you buy the shito? It is among the best I've ever tasted."

"I have a weekly order of kenkey (boiled maize dish), fish and shito from a lady at the Kenkey supermarket at Osu. She is the best in the business."

"Really?"

"Uh huh!" He took a long sip of chilled Star beer. "It is my favourite meal. I can eat it every day. I will get you a few bottles."

"Thank you." She said gratefully.

They were stretched out on the sofa, he sipping beer, she sipping muscatella when he pulled her into his arms.

She didn't protest. Her pulses started racing.

Gregory Isaac's Tempted to Touch moved them into musical bliss.

"Zhara," Agyeman whispered, holding her tenderly. "You know how I feel about you. Is there any hope for us?"

"Yes." Her voice was barely audible. Her heart was pounding.

"Waiting to hear from you..." he paused. "It has been torture. I don't think I can go through that again. I need to know that you feel the same about me. I think I love you."

"I care about you too," she said. "Why do you think I came to see you today? I don't make a habit of visiting men in their homes and allowing them to put their arms around me. It took a lot of courage to get me here. When you answered the phone, I was so pleased, but you sounded distant. I began to doubt if you really cared about me."

"I do, you must know that. I love you so much it hurts. How could you be in Accra all this time and not return my call? I thought you didn't want to know me."

"I've never felt this way about anyone. I needed time to process my feelings. I needed time to think. I had to be sure that the feelings I have for you are real."

"And?"

She held her breath. "I know it now. It is real. I can't fight it any more. It must be love, because I can't seem to stop thinking about you. You are constantly on my mind."

"I've missed you too, too much."

His mouth crushed over hers. She pulled back and was saved by the doorbell.

Agyeman was fuming as he went to answer the door but the frown melted away when he saw his mother's sister.

"Hi Auntie!" He hugged the elegantly dressed elderly lady and led her to the living room. She was wearing a richly woven Kente cloth and thick gold bracelets.

"Auntie, meet Zhara, the lady I hope to marry, if she'll have me. I believe you two may have spoken. She called this morning."

"Hello dear, I'm Nana Konadu." She proffered a hand.

Zhara shook it. "I am really sorry, I didn't mean to hang up on you. I thought I'd dialled the wrong number."

Nana Konadu chuckled. "Don't worry dear, it is a natural reaction. When a woman calls her man, the last thing she wants to hear is another woman's voice. I understand. It shows you care about our Prince. You two look like you are made for each other. His mother must hear this. I must warn you though," she said "she is very protective of her son and headstrong. Sometimes I wish she could be more easy going and liberal minded."

Turning to Agyeman she whispered in his ear. "She is pretty and very polished; please make her our princess. Those child-bearing hips can bear us many beautiful babies."

CHAPTER THIRTY

They had been dating for a month, yet it felt as if they'd known each other for ages. Zhara had introduced Agyeman to her mother and he'd introduced her to his stepmother and flown her to Kumasi to meet his mother. They knew each other's friends and seemed very much in love. Like the ideal couple, they shared similar interests and an inexplicable familiarity. There was something about his demeanour that resembled characteristics of her father, and it drew her to him.

He loved that she was smart and fun to be with and couldn't resist her soft voice, her dimples, especially when she smiled and her thoughtfulness and generosity to the less fortunate.

She had noticed his complexities, the dark side to his seemingly pleasant nature and the mood swings, which swayed from exhilaration to subdued and withdrawn, but she hoped to ease his plight with love and affection. She had also become aware that beneath the charm and confidence was a vulnerability that resonated with her. There was so much she wanted to tell him, but she decided it was too soon.

Zhara arrived home just after 7 pm. In order to meet her client's deadline she had skipped lunch and was feeling very hungry. A delicious aroma was wafting out of the kitchen. She opened the door and was pleasantly surprised.

"Mum, it's you! What have you done with Kwansima?"

"I gave her the afternoon off." Araba wiped her hands with the apron. "Don't look so surprised, come in and give me a hug."

"How was your day?"

"Wonderful!" she said.

The kitchen was a mess. Pots, pans, crockery and half the contents of the larder was scattered on the granite worktop.

Araba pushed a stray lock of hair behind Zhara's ear. "I may be a hard-nosed businesswoman, but nothing gives me more pleasure than cooking for my family."

"I know Mum," she said cheerfully "Daddy will be delighted!"

Zhara placed her briefcase on a chair and began tidying up. The aroma of the sizzling lobsters was irresistible.

Araba liked to put her heart and soul into everything she did, so even though she rarely cooked, when she did, it was nothing short of Michelin Star quality.

She had noticed the glow in her daughter's eyes and her instincts told her it was love.

"Sit down dear," she said. "How are things with you and Agyeman?"

The sound of his name made Zhara's heart sing.

"Fantastic! I really like him, mum. He is kind, thoughtful and just perfect!"

"Do you love him?"

"I think so. When I'm with him I have a funny feeling..." She lit up. "A really good feeling."

Araba took her daughter's hand. "Finding someone who makes you this happy means a lot to me. After you introduced him to meet me at the office, I did some digging."

"Mum! You didn't!" She flushed.

"Uh-huh!" she said, with an endearing smile. "Sweetheart, you deserve the best of everything. Did you know that his father passed away when he was very young?"

"Yes," Zhara nodded sadly. "He mentioned that his father passed away many years ago."

"Well," Araba continued. "Apparently he went a bit crazy after that, but he has straightened up and is doing very well. He comes from a good, respectable home and his mother is the Ashanti King's younger sister. Everything I've heard so far is positive, apart from the womanising. But I hear he hasn't been seen with anyone since he returned from London. You will need to tread carefully though, his heart may be in the right place but I'm not sure if his head is yet. Take your time and get to know him very well before you commit to anything."

Zhara threw her arms around Araba. "Thank you mum, I think I know what you mean. He is the only man I've felt this way about."

"Then you need to follow your heart. He adores you and I think he is worthy of your love."

"I love you, mum. What would I do without you?"

Araba pushed back the tears. Knowing she could talk to her about almost anything gave her great pleasure. Zhara was the best gift she could ever have wished for.

"I think you better get changed," she muttered, "dinner will be ready soon."

CHAPTER THIRTY ONE

For the third day running he'd woken up with a smile on his face. Pulling back the curtains, he sensed another beautiful day ahead. The sun came shining in and filled him with joy. He thought about her before he fell asleep and woke up with her on his mind. She was hard work, much harder than he'd anticipated. He had never worked so hard for any girl, but she was worth it, he thought. The short time they'd spent together had been more fulfilling than all his affairs put together. She brightened his life like the rays of the sunshine and the many colours in the rainbow and turned him on with her sweet smile. Smiling to himself he glided into the bathroom and burst into song:

"She is my last stop, my beautiful, smart and incredibly sexy flower of the world. She will remain my last stop if it kills me... I need no other girl: good, bad, pretty, sexy, no no no, self-indulgent, bitchy, bimbos, asinine gold-diggers, hell no!"

He emerged from the bathroom feeling refreshed. The singing continued, but this time it was R Kelly's Forever, not one of his made up songs.

"... say marry me, (Marry me) marry me (cause I love

you baby Marry me), marry me (there's no ...marry me, marry me, marry me, marry me ..."

CHAPTER THIRTY TWO

The DHL courier arrived just before noon. Liora, Agyeman's assistant, had been expecting it all morning. In the three years she'd been working for Agyeman she had never seen him date anyone for longer than a week, and she was glad that he had turned over a new leaf.

Straightening her dress, she took a quick glance in the mirror and hurried to his office. She hesitated for a moment and tapped on the door.

"Come in."

She opened the door and smiled. "The package you were expecting has arrived". She handed it to him.

"Thank you, Liora." She turned and shut the door behind her.

He took the package and unwrapped it carefully. Then he opened the box. It was exactly what he wanted. He picked up the phone and dialled Rolihlahla number.

Before they had met at the Johannesburg fashion show, Agyeman had no idea what it was like to be a black South African in the apartheid regime. He heard how young and old men conscripted to work in the mineral mines travelled from the hinterlands of Southern and Central Africa to work day and night in the most pitiful conditions, labouring in the belly of the earth, digging and drilling for the shiny mighty evasive stone, so they could send money home to feed their families. It had made him wonder how they coped with the anguish of not knowing if they would ever see their loved ones again whilst they slaved for a meagre salary from the greedy pigs who gained enormous wealth from the diamonds. Rolihlahla was one of those men, until he found a way to partake in the fortunes of his country. After setting up his mining company he had employed as many of his former colleagues as he could afford and gave them a decent wage, better working conditions and accommodation where their families could come and visit. It was Rolihlahla's philanthropy that sealed their friendship. They had remained good friends ever since.

After a long chat Agyeman thanked Rolihlahla for the ring and carried on working.

Later that evening he called Zhara.

"Hi sweetie," he said with the biggest smile.

"Hi."

"I need to see you. Can we meet after work tomorrow?"

"Sure, what time?"

"I could pick you up from work at 6:30."

"That sounds good, see you then."

At exactly 6:30 pm the next day Lydia received a call from the receptionist.

"Hi Lydia, we have a gentleman here to see Zhara."

The 35-year-old PA knew Zhara's schedule like clockwork. She was a graduate from the University of Legon and spoke fluent Fante, Twi, Ga, Hausa, Ewe, Dagbani, French and German.

Moving swiftly to Zhara's office, Lydia peeped through the door, smiling radiantly. "Your carriage awaits."

"Thank you so much. I'll be down in a few minutes."

Zhara wondered how she could ever cope without Lydia around. She was loyal, efficient, dedicated, conscientiousness and such a lovely person. She switched off her computer, powdered her nose and said goodbye to Lydia. On her way down the stairs she checked her reflection in the mirror and smiled contentedly.

Agyeman's driver was waiting by the black Bentley. He acknowledged Zhara with a dazzling smile and quickly opened the door for her. As she slid into the backseat Agyeman put his arm around her and kissed her.

"You look sensational" he whispered, eyes alight with passion, taking in every inch of her hourglass figure.

"Thank you" she said. She was wearing a figure hugging lime green Chanel dress, which she had matched with black Louboutins and a Chanel purse.

A strange emotion connected somewhere deep inside her as she glanced at Agyeman. He looked strikingly handsome in a dark blue tailored suit.

"Where are you taking me?" she asked.

"Chicken George. It's a Jazz Club. Have you been there before?"

"Not really."

"Have you been to any clubs?"

"Nope!"

"So how come you dance so well?"

"I practise a lot. I dance when I am bored, when I am happy and when I am cooking. I dance to anything really, but I do not do much partying, clubbing or discoing."

The club was packed when they arrived. The atmosphere was buzzing and everyone seemed to know Agyeman.

Taking her hand possessively he led her to a private section of the club where a table had been reserved for him.

A waiter scurried over to them. "Nana, will you be having your usual?"

"Yes, a bottle of Pouilly Fumé and grilled guinea fowl."

"Certainly!" He scurried away.

With hands entwined, Agyeman and Zhara bopped to be-bop, hard bop, jazz-blues and soul-jazz.

They left the jazz club at 9:30 pm and drove to the Mandarin restaurant at Osu where they were guided to a beautifully laid out table with a red rose in a vase and candles.

Agyeman passed the menu to Zhara and ordered a bottle of their finest champagne.

The waiter uncorked a bottle of Dom Pérignon and filled their glasses. Moments later he returned with the first course.

Zhara noticed that Agyeman was a bit tense and wondered what was on his mind. The Bee Gees were playing one of her favourite songs, Love You Inside And

Out. She finished eating the oyster tempura and was laughing at something he said when the waiter brought in the main course.

Agyeman stroked his chin thoughtfully. Suddenly he was by her side, down on one knee, holding her captive with his eyes. He pulled out a red box from his breast pocket.

"You once told me you wouldn't go out with anyone you didn't intend spending your life with." His gaze was so intense, she felt as if he was looking into her soul. "We've been going out for a while now, and I want to spend the rest of my life with you. I think you are the missing piece in the jigsaw of my life and I can't bear to spend another day without you. I would like it very much if you could be mine, forever. Zhara, will you take this ring..." he clicked open the box "and make my life complete?"

Zhara had figured he was up to something, but it never crossed her mind that he was planning to propose to her. She gasped at the beauty and size of the ring, and was shocked and excited at the same time. Words eluded her. The whole evening had been very special. And to top it all, the ring was her birthstone, a peridot encrusted in yellow diamonds. She could feel her heart beating like the kete drums. As she starred at the vivid green gemstone sparkling in the candle light she remembered that they were both Virgos; they shared the same birthstone and zodiac sign. She also remembered the ring in the Christmas cracker and even though it sounded like a lot of mumbo-jumbo at the time, she was beginning to think that it was too much of a coincidence. Maybe fate really had brought them together, she mused.

He looked pleadingly into her eyes, like a lost child. "I am deeply in love with you. Please say you will be my wife. There is no one else I would like to spend my life with but you. Please say yes."

"How can I say anything else?" she said softly. "Yes. I will marry you."

He took her hand and slid the ring on her index finger. Then he licked his lips, stood up and pulled her into his arms. As he kissed her passionately, he felt a million braids brushing like waves against his cheek.

"I would love to wake up beside you every day for the rest of my life." He whispered in her ear.

"I wouldn't mind waking up beside you either." She said breathlessly.

Agyeman raised his glass. "Let's make a toast to us." He took his glass to her lips and she took her glass of champagne to his lips. They looked into each other's eyes as they sipped.

Zhara placed her glass on the table. "There is more to me than meets the eye," she said with a distant look in her eye.

"I know that!" he laughed. "Why do you think I am so crazy about you?"

"I don't think you do," she said softly. "It's not what you think. I have a lot of baggage and a not-so-pleasant past."

"Please tell me about it, I want to know everything there is to know about you." The sincerity in his voice moved her. She felt she could trust him implicitly. "I will, but not here."

"OK, I understand." He pulled her close and kissed her sweet-scented braids. "I guess we need to make a move."

She nodded. "And thank you for a very lovely evening."

"But we are not done yet," he said. I was planning to take you to Funky Town, it's a discothèque, I want to see you dance."

"Can we do that another day?" she said with an endearing smile.

"As you wish, my love."

Taking Zhara's arm, he escorted her out of the restaurant and into the car park.

Agyeman unlocked the car and opened the door for Zhara.

"What happened to the driver?" Zhara asked, as he started the engine.

"He's gone home."

"Oh?"

"He lives just around the corner so I asked him to go home. Even though he has been driving me since morning, he was still reluctant to leave, but I had to insist. His family needs him more than I do. I believe the best way to have good people around you is to be kind to them and treat them with respect."

Zhara couldn't have agreed more. As they drove past a hair salon on the high street she remembered the conversation she had had with Serwa.

"I need to clear the air about something," she said, turning towards him. It had been playing on her mind for some time.

He threw her a quick glance.

"Did you do anything to offend your cousin, Serwa?"

"Not that I know of. Why do you ask?" He kept his eye on the road.

"Because what she said about you was not very nice especially as it was the first time she had seen me."

"What did she say?"

"She said quite a lot about your affairs. I got the distinct impression that she was trying very hard to put me off you."

"Are you sure?"

"I am very sure. In fact, if she hadn't gone on and on about you, I probably wouldn't have noticed you."

"But that can't be right," he said, looking concerned. Why would she talk about my affairs when she knew I was keen to meet you? She was supposed to hook us up."

"Well, something must have gone wrong, because she warned me to run a mile if you so much as smiled at me. She said you were as bad as they come and that as soon as you got your wicked way with me, I would be history."

"I don't doubt you," he said trying to remain calm, "it's just that I can't figure out why she would say that to you. Why would she try to put you off me? She seemed eager enough to get us acquainted when I asked her for assistance, and she would have told me to back off, if she had any objections. She's certainly not backward in coming forward!" He ran his fingers through his hair.

"She was no shrinking violet!" Zhara chuckled. "Do you know she asked if I was dating? When I said I wasn't, she said she had the perfect man for me. I had only met the woman, how could she have known who my perfect man was? Anyway, I made it quite clear that I wasn't interested. I think I must have hurt her feelings because things sort of went downhill after that. It was obvious from her demeanour that she was livid. When she asked if I'd noticed the man staring at me, I said I hadn't without bothering to look up. But as she carried on talking I got curious and looked up. That was when I saw you..." she smiled tenderly at him."

"I am glad you did!"

"Me too" she continued, "isn't it ironic? Her attempts to keep us apart is what brought us together."

"I am glad it backfired," he said cheerfully. "To be honest, I don't give a damn about her intentions, what matters is that you are here with me, and I don't intend to let you out of my sight."

They were a short distance away from Zhara's house. Instead of taking the turn to her road, he drove into a quiet lane and switched off the engine. It was a few minutes past midnight.

"Have you forgotten where my house is?" she asked.

"No, but I am just not ready to let you go yet," he said with a wicked grin.

"But it is late," she said looking at him suspiciously.

"When are you expecting your parents back from Mauritius?"

"Tomorrow evening. Why?"

"Would you like to come home with me?"

"Please don't do this to me," she said softly. "I have told you, no sex until we are married!"

"I know, but you will be all alone in your bed and me all alone in mine. Why can't we keep each other company? I promise, there will be no sex."

"I like being alone in my own bed."

He knew she meant every word and didn't intend to push his luck. "In that case, do you mind if we talk for a little while?"

"It is very late," she said, glancing at her watch, "but I guess we could talk for a while."

He put his arm around her. "I have to be honest with you," he began, "because you will hear about my affairs and I can't deny that I have had my fair share. The truth is, before I met you, I never thought I would fall in love with anyone and I never dreamt of giving myself wholeheartedly to anyone. The first time I looked into your eyes, I felt something; it was the most intense feeling I have ever felt for anyone. I knew then that anything I did before I met you wasn't worth my while." He looked into her eyes. "Darling, you mean everything to me; your warmth, your sincerity, your kindness, your dogged determination; they are just a few of the unique qualities I have grown to love about you. I want you to know that what I feel for you is very special, you are the irreplaceable love of my life, and I mean that from the bottom of my heart. I admit that whatever Serwa may have said, or anything else you may have heard about my casual affairs is true, but that was before I met you. I have no desire to ever cheat on you. I hope you believe me."

"I believe you," she said calmly. "I wouldn't be here if I didn't, and I certainly wouldn't have agreed to marry you if I had the slightest doubt."

"I am pleased to hear that," he said, stroking her face tenderly. "I will never let you down." He traced the contours of her lips with his hands. "What you mentioned at the restaurant, about your baggage, would you like to share it with me?"

She looked around, and tried to suppress the overwhelming feeling of panic that gripped her whenever she cast her mind back to the awful incidents. "There have been many scary, strange and inexplicable occurrences, from as early as I can remember. I've managed to get to grips with most of them and hope you will too, but if not, you have the opportunity to back out of this relationship before things get complicated."

He squeezed her tightly. "Nothing will ever change how I feel about you."

Feeling secure in his arms, Zhara told him everything - the nightmares, ghostly encounters, her struggles with paedophiles and even the witchcraft incident. By the time she was through, her emotions had got the better of her.

Wiping away her tears Agyeman buried her face in

kisses. "Honey, don't cry," he whispered. "You've been through so much, and yet it hasn't stopped you from achieving your dreams. How you remain content and unruffled is beyond me. Right now I feel like strangling those men, especially the fat ugly perverted swine..."

"You don't know what you're letting yourself in for!" Zhara sniffed.

"I do, but together we can handle anything that life throws at us."

She breathed a sigh of relief. "Well, if you're sure..."

"I am!" he said positively. She kissed his forehead.

"Now that you've agreed to marry me, I think it's time I asked your parents for your hand in marriage."

Zhara cheered up. "I will arrange for you to meet them when they return from their trip. I know mum will be delighted, but you may have to work your charm on daddy."

"Don't worry," he said, "I will make him like me, no matter what it takes."

"I hope so," she giggled, you do know that even though we are technically engaged, he has the final say."

"I do, and I know he will say yes. I can feel it in my bones!"

"I am sure he will like you."

He took her hand. "I would love to meet the man who has the key to my happiness."

She held his gaze. "I am sure he would love to meet you too. Thank you for a wonderful evening. The restaurant was an excellent choice. It has been my favourite since childhood."

"Really?" he said, pulling her to him, "and you've kept that to yourself, all this while?" He kissed her gently at first, then passionately, shattering her pulses.

CHAPTER THIRTY THREE

Agyeman's heart began to pound as he approached the affluent suburb with lush green lawns and manicured hedges. It was four o'clock on a beautiful sunny day, the tenth day of March. The skies were the bluest he'd ever seen. He took his time, observing the chirping birds as they flew past. The eagle-eyed security guard recognised him from the previous night, and let him through the gates.

The sweeping driveway led to the elegant mansion with massive glass and iron doors. There was utter silence, except for the ocean waves and the musical splatter of the neon-lit fountain in the rose garden.

Having rehearsed the momentous words over and over again, Agyeman hoped everything would go according to plan. Earlier that morning he had remembered one of his father's sayings, eloquent words are not appropriate on a fool's lips. Bearing that in mind, he'd come prepared; clean shaven, neatly trimmed hair, white cotton shirt tucked into dark trousers hanging perfectly over well-polished shoes, belt, cuff-links and a dash of his favourite cologne.

Raising the brass door-knocker, Agyeman let it drop gently.

The door was opened instantly.

"Good evening Your Highness," said Kwansima, with a welcoming smile. "They are expecting you."

Agyeman returned the smile and followed the immaculately dressed petite lady into the house. He guessed she was pushing forty even though she looked a decade younger.

She led him through an entrance hall with high ceilings and an imposing crystal chandelier to a pearl-laminated family room.

Kwansima offered him a seat, asked what he would like to drink and slipped quietly out of the room.

Agyeman looked around the large family room with a gorgeous mix of sophisticated details including ebony-shaded lamps, antique mirrors, paintings, carvings, a massive book collection and uninterrupted views of the Atlantic Ocean.

He was admiring a dark-wood carving of a large bossomed woman with a baby on her back when Zhara bounded into the room. She looked effortlessly chic in a strapless silk baby-doll top with white denim shorts. Her long legs reminded him of a gazelle.

"Hello!" she beamed, "how are you feeling?"

"I am good," he said coolly and gave her a peck on the cheek.

"Don't worry. You will be fine," she said, "daddy's bark is much worse than his bite."

"You look ravishing," he said, ogling the smooth chocolate flesh around her shoulders.

"Thank you," she said demurely.

He gave her a wink, trying his utmost to squash the lustful thoughts running through his head.

Kamil strode into the room in a white tunic. Araba followed, looking elegant in a mint summer dress.

"Welcome to our home." Kamil said warmly.

Agyeman rose to his feet. "It's a pleasure to meet you, sir." He'd seen Kamil on TV but he looked much better in the flesh; younger, slimmer and much better looking.

"The pleasure is ours, said Araba with a delightful smile. How are you?"

"I am very well, thank you."

Kwansima emerged with a tray of tall glasses containing pomegranate juice, guava juice, mango juice and chilled sparkling water. She seemed to know what each of them wanted, so they sat in respectful silence until she left the room.

"Zhara said you wanted to see us." Kamil said, looking relaxed.

"I do," Agyeman said, sitting up and clasping his hands in front of him. He'd made a conscious effort not to tap his leg. "Ever since I met Zhara in London, I have found it impossible to be without her. I came to see you because I would really like to take the next step..." he paused, "and I hope you will permit me to make her my wife."

Zhara gave him a reassuring smile.

Kamil cleared his throat. After taking a sip of

pomegranate juice, he smiled thoughtfully. "There have been many suitors, some of whom she doesn't even know about, but I have always known that when the time was right, she would make the right decision. She is a very principled lady, and knows what she wants, so if she agreed for you to see me, then she must feel the same way about you..." He glanced at Zhara and turned to Araba with a knowing smile. "judging by the radiant smile on her face, I think she is ready to settle down. By the way," he continued, "she showed us the ring. It is beautiful. I am sure it must have cost a fortune."

"I would have come to see you first, but I had to be sure she would accept me."

Kamil's lips curled into a wry smile. "I understand. She is not one to be taken for granted." He crossed his legs leisurely. "Tell me about yourself."

"I was born in Kumasi, but I have lived in Accra most of my life. My father was the late Dr Francis Johnson and my mother is Nana Yaa Asantewa. After leaving school I did an apprenticeship in fashion design and set up my fashion house a few years ago."

Kamil listened carefully. He liked Agyeman's youthful charm and the fact that he appeared to be intelligent, hardworking, responsible and very humble.

"I knew your father well." Kamil said sympathetically. "We met initially when he was the Northern Regional Commissioner, and again at a function when he was made Ambassador to Canada. He was a fine man, a great man indeed, and highly intelligent." He cocked his head to the side. "How is your stepmother, Dora, these days? Is she still baking her mouth-watering cakes?"

"She is fine, and her cakes are arguably the best in Accra."

Kamil had a distant look on his face, as though he was reminiscing about the past. "Dora is one elegant lady," he said wistfully, "a typical polished Fante woman, very much like my Araba here." He smiled fondly at his wife. "I hear you took Zhara to meet Dora and your mother, Princess Yaa Asantewa."

Agyeman nodded.

"She turned quite a few heads back then, you know. Is she still a hot-head?"

"I'm afraid so" Agyeman said quietly.

Kamil's remembered that a number of statesmen and dignitaries had their eye on the princesses but he'd never anticipated that Dr Johnson would have an affair with the princess.

"I think your talent for fashion stems from your father," said Kamil. "Did you know he only wore bespoke suits from London's Savile Row?"

Agyeman nodded. "Yes, my mother mentioned it."

"It is what earned him the nickname 'Foreign'. He had excellent taste in clothes and the ladies loved him because he was what they call a perfect gentleman; opening doors for them, taking off his hat, and putting them first. I was much younger then but I learnt a lot from him."

Kamil had never been able to figure out was why the princess gave her son to Dr Johnson to raise him or how he managed to escape the wrath of the Royal Family. How ironic, he thought, that Dr Johnson's lovechild would be seeking his daughter's hand in marriage. Placing his elbows on the chair he smiled kindly at Agyeman and lit a cigar.

Araba sensed it was time to leave the men alone.

Zhara quickly followed her mother.

"Are you in love with Zhara?" Kamil asked, staring blankly at the grand master piano in the far corner of the room.

"Yes, I believe so, deeply," said Agyeman.

"As you probably know, love can be an addiction, just like smoking. I know it's bad for my health but can't kick the habit so I restrict myself to one a week. My wife thinks I smoke when I'm stressed, and she may be right, but it helps me unwind."

Puffing on the thick cigar, he continued. "There are two types of love. The first type begins with great enthusiasm and passion but slowly wears away; one day you wake up and it's all gone, completely drained. The second type of love is hard to notice at first, but like an oyster making a pearl it grows slowly, adding a little bit to itself day by day; gradually, grain by grain, a jewel appears from the sand, a beautiful pearl."

He placed the cigar in the ashtray. "We have been though some really tough times, and at the time, I wondered if my wife would stay with me, but the thought never crossed her mind because of her deep and profound love for me. To her, for better or worse meant just that, there was no way out. There have been occasions when everything had to be measured, my time, her health, money, friends, family and even what we ate and drank. Every single thing seemed to have a limit, except our love and dedication to each other. It filled our hearts abundantly and nothing else mattered. We could have lived on our love and died happy. I think we still do. Nothing can come between us, no matter how big or small.

"That is the kind of love I want for my daughter. An endless love that lasts the test of time; be it good, bad or ugly, not the rash, sentimental infatuation I see these days; here today, gone tomorrow because being in love got too hard or became overbearing or too complicated. Do you know what I mean?"

Agyeman nodded.

"Son, I feel as if you are a part of this family already" Kamil continued, "but custom demands that we deal with such matters properly. Marriage is not just a union of two people, but a coming together of two families. Zhara may be my daughter but I am not the head of my family, only the head of my family can agree to your proposal. What you need to do is ask your family to meet the elders of my family in Yendi and put your proposal to them. They will then consult with the elders of my family in Kano and Medina before making a final decision."

"Thank you." Agyeman said, "I will proceed with the necessary arrangements."

"Good!" Said Kamil, "but first, you must join us for dinner. Kwansima has made her legendary TZ (maize flour dish) with guinea fowl stew and jute leaf soup. After dinner I will give you the name and address of the people you need to see."

Agyeman followed Kamil to the dining room. He knew the whole marriage thing was a complicated affair but he did not expect it to be so difficult.

CHAPTER THIRTY FOUR

The Ashanti people are one of the largest tribes in Ghana. Kumasi, the capital city is renowned for its massive Kejetia Market, which is reputed to be one of the largest markets on the continent, covering over 25 acres in the centre of the city and surrounded by crafts villages where skilled men weave the multi-coloured kente cloth and make the adinkra cloth which is artfully designed with special symbols sacred to the Ashanti people. According to legend, the Golden Stool and a sword descended from heaven. They are kept in obscurity and brought out only for special ceremonies such as the ascension of a new King to the throne.

The King of Ashanti, Otumfuo Nana Osei Tutu, had been deliberating over family issues with his younger sisters at the Palace in Kumasi. When they got to Nana Agyeman's intention to seek Zhara's hand in marriage, the King had no doubt that his nephew had chosen wisely, but his youngest sister, Yaa Asantewa would not hear of it.

Adjusting the richly woven Kente cloth over his shoulder the King listened attentively to his sisters. With a hint of a smile on his lips, he watched his three sisters, all looking magnificent in different shades of Kente cloth and adorned with thick gold anklets and bracelets. The years had been good to them and he was pleased that they were all in remarkably good health.

"I insist that we do what our Prince has instructed," said Nana Pokuwa, the eldest of the sisters. "After all, he is old enough to know what he wants."

Nana Konada agreed with her older sister but she knew her younger sister could be relentless once she decided on something. "What exactly do you have against the girl?" she asked Nana Yaa Asantewa.

"I do not have anything against her," she replied sharply. "I assumed Agyeman was just have a fling, as he had always done. It never occurred to me that he would want to settle down with her. As you know, Ampoma has been betrothed to him since childhood and I strongly believe she will be the perfect wife for him."

"I beg to differ," said Nana Konadu. "Agyeman has never introduced any of his girlfriends to us. When he brought Zhara to see us, I knew instantly that it was not just a casual affair. As you know, I met her at his house in Accra and it was obvious that he was deeply in love with her. She is very well educated and comes from a respectable family. Her father is one of the best lawyers in the country and a special adviser to the President. He is from the Dagbon Royal Family and the nephew of the Tolon Na (Northern King). Her mother, Lady Araba, owns a successful real estate and property development company in Accra. I think they are perfectly suited."

Nana Yaa Asantewa pursed her lips. "I don't think she is right for my son."

"Why is that?" asked the King.

She stood up and wrapped the cloth tightly around her waist. "Ampoma moved into the palace ten years ago to be trained and groomed to become his wife. The northern girl doesn't understand our culture, our heritage or our traditions, so how can she be suitable for an Ashanti Prince? I think it will be a travesty if we sit back and deny Ampoma her right to become a member of the family she has dedicated her life to for so long."

"We understand what you are saying" said Nana Pokuwa, "but he has made his choice. You can't force him to change who he wants to marry."

"How can we allow our prince to marry opepeni (a northerner) when we have a suitable woman for him, right here in the palace?"

"I agree with Pokuwa and Konadu," said the King. "We can find Ampoma another man. There are many bachelors in the family." He turned to Yaa Asantewa. "Unless there are any other objections, I would suggest we make arrangements to meet Zhara's family."

"Well," said Nana Yaa Asantewa. "what do we do about her religion? You do know that she is a Moslem?"

Nana Konadu stared angrily at her sister. "At the end of the day, it is up to Nana Agyeman who he chooses as his wife. I do understand that you want him to marry a woman befitting our culture and royal traditions. But love has no boundaries, and it should not make any difference whether she is from the North, South, East or West or if she is a Moslem or a Christian. Please put your prejudices aside and let's welcome this beautiful young lady into our family."

CHAPTER THIRTY FIVE

Zhara and Agyeman had spent the morning playing tennis at the Golden Tulip club. Having worked up an appetite, they stopped at a chop-bar for the Sunday special, omotuo (rice balls) and palm-nut soup with a calabash of palm wine and chopped sugarcane for dessert.

From there they stopped at Cocoa beach. A full moon rested low over the horizon, reflecting its beam where the sea met the sky. They kicked off their shoes and strolled along the seashore hand in hand, chatting and laughing. Suddenly a large wave rolled onto the shore and dragged them into the sea. Buried knee deep in water they held onto each other, laughing heartily.

It was while they were retreating to dry land that Agyeman's phone buzzed. He ignored it. A few minutes later, it started ringing. He switched it off.

"Honey, it could be important." said Zhara.

"Whoever it is can wait till I get home!" he fumed.

"Why don't you turn on the phone? If it's urgent they will call again. If no-one calls in the next three minutes you can switch it off."

"Do I have to?" he asked, hoping she would say no.

"Yes darling," she said convincingly.

As soon as he switched it back on the phone started ringing.

Fifteen minutes passed and he still hadn't finished talking. As he paced the ground angrily, Zhara wondered who he might be speaking to.

"What?" He said sharply." OK if that's how you … Fine, I'll be there as soon as I can."

He hung up.

"Is something wrong?" Zhara asked softly.

Agyeman pulled her into his arms. "Yes. I need to go to Kumasi as soon as possible."

"But it is almost four o'clock. How do you plan to get there? I hope you are not thinking of driving?"

"You are right," he said thoughtfully. "I'll catch the first flight tomorrow."

"When do you plan on coming back?"

"It's hard to tell, but hopefully Wednesday or Thursday." He caressed her face. "Will you miss me?"

"Maybe," she said, looking cross.

"I know you'll miss me and I will miss you too. He leaned down and stroked her cheek. "I promise to call every day."

"You don't have to."

"Yes I do. I will need to hear your soft soothing voice to get me through the issues I will be facing there."

"What issues?"

"Nothing to worry your pretty head about. I will take care of it. Now where were we?"

"She started to run," catch me if you can.

"You know I can, and I will," he said cheerfully and run after her.

CHAPTER THIRTY SIX

Nana Yaa Asantewa sat quietly in her room. Her eyes were filled with tears. Suddenly Agyeman's words echoed in her head 'Maame, she is the only woman for me. I will marry her whether you liked it or not. ...then I will have to carry on the rest of my life like I did before father died'.

She put her hands on her head, "mewuoooo, mewuooo, mewuooo … (I'm dead! I'm dead! I'm dead!)" she cried, pepefuor no aye me adeieoooo! Eduradee begye me ooo, ye di me ba no ko malam (God save me, the northerners have charmed my son)."

Her sisters rushed to her side.

"Yaa Asantewa, what is it? Please talk to us" said Nana Pokuwa. She quickly removed Nana Yaa Asantewa's hands from her head. "You know you mustn't do that, it's a bad omen!" she said, looking frustrated, "what is the matter?"

"Hmmm, what can I say?" she wailed. "I told Nana Agyeman what happened in the north and now he wants to disown me. He means the world to me. I would rather die than have him out of my life again. Mewuoooo!!! My only son has chosen to disown me, because of a woman! Hmmm, it cannot be, they have charmed him."

Nana Pokuwa had had enough of the moaning and

wailing. As the eldest of the sisters, it fell upon her to put things right and she was determined to put a stop to the upheaval that was tearing her family apart. Tightening the scarf wrapped loosely around her head she asked everyone to sit down.

"That is enough!" she said to Nana Yaa Asantewa. "No one has died. Why are you lamenting? And as for Nana Agyeman being charmed, that is the most ridiculous thing that's ever come out of your mouth. Are you forgetting who we are? We charm people, not the other way round. We are an extremely mighty force with immense powers, never forget that! Our Prince may not like you very much at this very moment, but he could never disown you, never!" she pounded her chest. Don't forget, you may have carried him for nine months but it was I who put you and his father together, so he is very much my son as he is yours. Had it not been for me, he would not be here. But God is great, and he has given us a son we can all be proud of. We need to get to the bottom of this ugly situation, quietly and sensibly. So my sister, please tell us exactly what happened, starting from the beginning."

Nana Yaa Asantewa stopped wailing and took a deep breath. "Hmmm...," she said and paused for a few seconds. "I called my son to tell him about our trip to the north. I told him that when we arrived at Chibye Yili, the family home in Yendi, we were told the head of the family, Alhaji Iddrissu Yahyah, had just left for the mosque. I said we waited and waited, and after about an hour we left and returned to Kumasi."

"What did he say to that?" said Nana Konadu.

"He sounded surprised and disappointed. He asked if we had informed Zhara's uncle that we were coming."

"I said it!" said Nana Pokuwa. "I told you that we should wait a little longer, but you wouldn't listen. It was silly of us to travel all the way there without informing them. I hope you told him that?"

Nana Yaa Asantewa turned up her nose. "Not exactly," she said, wiping her face with a handkerchief. "I told him we had agreed to meet on Thursday, however due to Queen Ama Komfo's memorial service we changed our plans."

"You are right," said Nana Pokuwa, "the Queen's memorial was very important but we should have agreed an alternative date with Zhara's uncle before setting out to Yendi. I insisted that we should send our apologies and set a mutually convenient date, but you wouldn't listen. The fact that we are royals doesn't mean we can always do as we please."

Nana Yaa Asantewa frowned. "Anyway, Agyeman suggested that we arrange a mutually convenient date and I said he should take what happened as a sign that the girl is not right for him. He said if we could not do what he wanted we should let him know and he will do it himself."

Nana Konadu shook her head in despair. "Did you tell him that you vowed not to go back to the north?"

"Not in so many words, but I urged him to do the honourable thing and follow the Ashanti royal tradition, the tradition of his ancestors, by taking a bride who had been carefully chosen for him."

"Yieeee!" Nana Pokuwa laughed. "You never fail to amaze me! How did he respond to that?"

"He said he would marry the woman of his choice, so I told him our bloodlines could not be tainted by an unsuitable bride." She paused for a moment, as if to catch her breath. The words rolled off her tongue like a piece of gristle. "He said I had made it very clear that his wishes did not matter. He said he will marry the woman of his choice whether I liked it or not. He said he would carry on the rest of his life without me, like he did before his father died." She broke down, screaming "buei! buei! buei!"

"Please say it isn't so." Nana Pokuwa jumped up, "may God forbid! The devil is a liar! Back to sender!"

"He wants me out of his life," Nana Yaa Asantewa sniffed, "he wants to disown me, his biological mother. I carried him for nine months. Giving him to his father when he was two was the hardest thing I have ever had to do in my life. Look how my actions have come back to haunt me! I only did it to please his father, to build a bond between father and son, but I will never live it down. He doesn't love me, he has never known how. He may care about me and appreciate me but we will never experience that special bond a son shares with his mother. You know how I cried every night, from the day I gave him away. I thought I was securing his future with his father, but it has cost me my son. He blames me for everything! My cherished son wants to hurt me by disowning me and throwing away his royal heritage so he can marry a Dagomba girl!"

"We cannot lose our Prince," said Nana Konadu. "We need to resolve this matter very quickly."

"What am I going to do?" said Nana Yaa Asantewa. Tears were streaming down her face.

Nana Pokuwa pulled her into her arms and rocked her gently. "We have to do what he wants. I will call the people in the north and arrange another meeting. Please cheer up. This is meant to be a happy time for all of us. Let's go to the north and make our Prince proud!

CHAPTER THIRTY SEVEN

Agyeman, his mother, her two sisters and two of his uncles arrived at Chibye Yili, Zhara's family home in Yendi, the traditional capital of the Dagbon Kingdom on the morning of April 27 to ask for Zhara's hand in marriage.

They were welcomed by Alhaji Iddrissu, and treated to kulikuli (groundnut biscuits) and cornmeal porridge.

After the pleasantries, the serious matter of marriage was discussed and Alhaji Iddrissu promised to get back to them after he had consulted with their elders in Kano and Medina.

★★★★

A few days later Alhaji Iddrissu informed Nana Pokuwa that the elders of his family had agreed to their proposal. A meeting was scheduled for 20th June between Agyeman's family and Zhara's family to discuss the requirements for the engagement and traditional wedding.

★★★★

The formal engagement took place on 31st August, Zhara birthday.

Very early that morning young men arrived from Nima, Tamale, Yendi, Kano and Medina to join Kamil and the rest of his family in prayers. After a recital of the Quran a cow was slaughtered and given as alms to the poor.

Accompanied by his family and friends, Agyeman presented the dowry to Zhara. It contained a Quran, lace cloth, Kente cloth, Adinkra cloth, wax print fabrics, jewellery, crockery and a sealed envelope containing an undisclosed amount of money. The gifts were meant to honour Zhara and please her. The money was a token of Agyeman's willingness to accept the responsibility of taking good care of Zhara and bearing all her expenses.

A large crowd of friends, family and well-wishers cheered and congratulated the happy couple.

Music, eating, drinking and dancing followed. It went on until the early hours of the morning.

The date of the wedding was announced. It was to be held on 9th December, the anniversary of Zhara and Agyeman's first meeting in London.

CHAPTER THIRTY EIGHT

Zhara arrived at Agyeman's house just before noon on Saturday 10th September. They had agreed to meet for lunch at 1 o'clock but seeing as it was his birthday she decided to arrive early and surprise him.

Clutching a birthday cake and a present she pressed the bell. When he hadn't answered after a few minutes she wondered if he was sleeping. She knew he was in because the watchman had said so.

She waited another few minutes and was about to leave when he suddenly opened the door.

"Happy Birthday!" she said excitedly."

"Thank you." He kissed her on the lips. You look ravishing, I hope you've not been waiting too long..."

"I have," she huffed, "but since it's your birthday, I'll forgive you."

He steered her into the living room. "The cake smells divine. Did Kwansima bake it?"

"Now I am really cross," she pouted petulantly. "No she did not. I baked it myself. Your step-mum gave me the recipe. Remember?"

"Oh yes."

"I followed the instructions to the letter, but I doubt if

it will taste as good as the one she baked for my birthday. Are we still up for lunch at 1?" she asked, placing the cake and present on the centre table. She hadn't realised he was right behind her.

He kissed the area just below her earlobe. "Can we stay in? I would really like to sleep with my ravishing beauty," he said, meaning every word.

"How can you even think of sleeping at ten o'clock in the morning?"

"I would like to go shopping, but after a little siesta. Would you care to join me?"

"You are something else!" she laughed. "If you don't have any plans, could we look at soft furnishing for our new home?" She hoped he would say yes. The villa that was being built for them at McCarthy Hill was almost complete. It was an engagement present from her parents. Even though she'd agreed to move in with Agyeman after the wedding, she hoped to move in sooner.

"That sounds like a good idea," he said blowing featherlike kisses around her neck and shoulders. He seemed to know just how to make her lose all her inhibitions. She shifted uneasily.

"Why don't you open your present while I grab a plate from the kitchen?"

"No, don't go." He picked up the present and unwrapped it. "Wow!" He looked thrilled. "Thank you so much." He gave her a squeeze.

"Why don't you try it on?" she egged him.

He put the imperious fine-brushed rose gold 18 carat

Tag Heuer Grand Carrera watch on his wrist. "I like it very much, thanks!" he said gratefully.

Zhara's phone rang.

"Hello?"

"Zhara, it's been a long time. How are you?"

"I'm fine, Lawal. Sorry for not returning your calls, it's been manic here."

Agyeman pressed his lips into a hard line and observed her suspiciously.

"I heard about your engagement. It must be serious then. Why him and not me? You barely know the guy."

"It is very serious and..." She did not like the look on Agyeman's face.

"Lawal, I have to go." She switched off the phone. "Are you OK?" she asked Agyeman.

"Why is he calling you when he knows you are engaged?" The anger beneath the quiet delivery was unsettling.

"Don't you trust me?" She looked hurt.

"Of course I do, and I really don't mind who you speak to but..." He hesitated. "I've seen how he looks at you and there is no doubt that he fancies you. Hearing you speak to a man who clearly wants you stirs up all kinds of emotions in me. I hate that feeling."

"I understand," she said softly. "but what you need to know is that there is only one man in my life, and that man is you. I have no room in my heart for anyone else. Lawal is a good friend, and that is all he will ever be."

Agyeman squeezed her hand gently.

★★★★

After several hours of shopping they stopped at Country Kitchen for a late lunch. Zhara was beaming with joy because she had been able to find all the curtains and soft furnishings she needed for the villa.

They returned to Agyeman's house at eight o'clock. The phone was ringing, the answer machine was flashing, and the rain had just started. Zhara decided it was time to leave.

"Please share a slice of cake with me before you go," said Agyeman, as if he was able to read her mind.

"OK," she said even though she didn't like the idea.

He placed two side plates on the dining table and pulled a chair out for her. Then he cut a slice of cake for her and a slice for himself.

"Mmm, this is delicious. I love it!" he said and grabbed a bottle of Don Perignon from the fridge and two champagne glasses. He uncorked the champagne and filled the glasses.

Zhara observed him suspiciously while she ate her cake. It was very good, she thought. She was debating whether to have a drink or not but it seemed he had already worked out what she had on her mind.

"Please, just one glass" he pleaded. "It is my birthday. And in case you are worried about driving, I could take you home or ask the driver to take you home."

He was getting annoyingly good at reading her mind.

Anita Baker was singing Been So Long when the heavens opened up. As the storm raged the lights went off.

Thunder roared and lightning lit up the skyline. Zhara waited for the generator to kick in. She hated the dark.

"Are you OK honey?" he asked, looking concerned.

"Yes, I'm fine" she said, but she didn't mean it. Much as she loved him, the thought of spending the night with him filled her with dread. She thought about her parents and hoped they were having a fabulous time in South Africa.

Even though Agyeman wanted the weather to improve, he could not hide his elation at the prospect of spending the night with Zhara. He'd suggested it on a number of occasions but she'd turned him down and her determination not to sleep with him until they were married never seemed to waver. He took her in his arms. Invoked by a rush of passion he caressed her face and the warm flesh around her neck and shoulders. He felt the soft texture of the dress as his hands wandered down. "You are so beautiful." He whispered. For someone who had once thought he wasn't cut out for marriage, it was nothing short of a miracle that he was in a monogamous relationship and hadn't had sex for ninth months. He was not sure how he managed to withstand the temptation, but as he held her in his arms, he wasn't sure he could last another minute.

The rain wasn't letting up. Strong winds crushed down trees and electric poles. Agyeman felt her warm breath on his chest. They were standing by the dining table in complete darkness. The sound of the wind and rain drowned out Anita Baker's Sweet Love. He touched her face. "Honey, are you OK?"

She breathed voicelessly.

His hands moved down her neck and around her collarbone. She closed her eyes as the surge of electricity travelled down her spine. He cupped her chin in his hands and kissed her lips.

"It's too dangerous to be out on the streets. I can't let you go home. Let's go to bed."

"What do you have in mind?" Her voice was barely audible.

"We're engaged to be married, does it matter?"

"Yes, it does."

"OK, I won't do anything you don't want me to."

"Thank you. I would like to have a shower."

"Sure. Come with me." She followed him up the stairs. He had tried on many occasions to get her to the bedroom, but she'd always found an excuse not to. It felt strange, but she knew there was no way out and she just had to trust him.

The top floor was light and airy with a large landing and two rooms. He guided her to one of the rooms, his bedroom. It was massive with bold patterns and gold accents. Full-height glass doors opened onto a balcony. A brown leather super king bed beautifully laid with Burberry silk sheets and a purple velvet throw stood at the far side of the room. There was a matching dressing table with two sofas and a coffee table. Above the bed was a mirrored ceiling.

He opened one of the two adjoining doors in the room. "The bathroom is through there" he said. It led to a marble tiled en suite with a large bath and shower.

"Can I stay and scrub your back?"

Her insides uncoiled and melted. "No, thanks" she said shyly. "I will be just fine."

She emerged from the bathroom feeling fully refreshed. The lights had been dimmed and scented candles placed strategically around the room. A bottle of Bollinger peeped out of the ice bucket on the coffee table. Beside it were two glasses and a box of truffles. She could have sworn that the single red rose in the crystal vase on the dressing table had not been there when she entered the room.

With a towel wrapped around her body she sat at the edge of the bed and creamed her body. She was taking in every detail of the room when she heard Agyeman's voice. He must be close, she thought. Wondering who he could be speaking to, she slipped on his dressing gown and moved stealthily towards the second door. Hesitating briefly, she wondered what he kept in there.

She turned the knob and peeped in. Agyeman had his back to her. The magnitude of the walk-in closet intrigued her. The furnishing was dark wood with lines of suits, shirts, trousers, ties and shoes. He was thanking the person at the other end of the phone for a present. She gathered it was one of his friends. Closing the door behind her, she returned to the bedroom.

She was singing along with Ella Fitzgerald when Agyeman entered the room. His heart melted when he saw her in his gown.

"Can I get in the gown with you?" He had a naughty grin on his face.

"Most definitely not!" She tried to avoid his heated eyes.

"Can I cream your back?"

"Nope, already done."

"Can I anoint your feet with frankincense? Please?" he pleaded.

She sighed loudly and rolls her eyes. "OK, if you must!"

He took the bottle of aromatic oil from the dressing table. Taking her feet in his hands, he skilfully kneaded the muscles and joints.

"I must say, you are very good at this. Have you considered taking it up professionally?"

"My masseur services are reserved for my future bride, the love of my life." He kissed her feet, leaving her breathless. When he finished he popped the cork, handed her a glass of chilled champagne and disappeared into the bathroom.

"What am I going to do with you?" he said when he found her curled up in a corner of the bed. Smiling salaciously he reached for her. "Have I told you how beautiful your dimples are?"

"Yes, many times."

He kissed her ravenously. Her head spun.

"Mmm," he groaned as a million braids brushed against his cheek. "Your hair smells divine." He kissed her hair, massaged her scalp and pulled back her dressing gown. The thought of making love to her over and over again gave him immense pleasure. He felt as if he was about to explode.

"You are just what I need. I can see in your eyes that you want this as much as I do. Let me take you where you've never been. I want to show you how sweet making love feels."

Lying on her back she stared at the candle light through the mirrored ceiling. His breath was trailing beneath her, quickening hers. She loved him with all her heart, but she knew she couldn't give him what he wanted. Not yet, not until they are man and wife.

He felt her resistance. Glancing at her with dark, haunted eyes, he whispered, "I love you. Please let me show you how gratifying love can be." His eyes penetrated hers and remained on her. She looked away, gripped by all sorts of emotions. His lips were moist and tempting. She found that very distracting. The tip of his tongue peeped out of his beautiful sculptured lips. Her heart fluttered.

He pulled her to him, squeezing the breath out of her. "Why do you do these things to me? Before I met you the longest I was without a woman was a week. I have never lasted more than a couple of weeks in any relationship. I had to move on and never got to know anyone, not like I know you. But you've changed all that. I am helpless around you. I can't be with anyone but you. You make me do things I've never done before. I want you so much, it hurts. Why are you scared? You look so afraid and yet your body is crying out to me. If I had my way I would let whatever is holding you back set you free so you can experience true love."

Her heart was in her mouth. She knew he was right. There was no way she could go through with what his spellbinding eyes were pleading for. Her body was weak but her mind was strong and determined.

"I want you, Zhara. I need to feel you. We will be married soon, please let me make love to you." He looked vulnerable, sexy, desirable and intoxicating.

She looked longingly into his eyes and smiled. "Whenever I think of our honeymoon, I know it will be perfect. Experiencing lovemaking with you is what I yearn for. I can find out for myself what all the fuss is about. You have been very patient with me and I appreciate that a lot, but I am not ready yet. I would like to be fully committed when I give myself to you."

He cupped her face in his hands. "I've never wanted anything as much as I want this, you and me together. You may be smart, savvy, worldly and shrewd in the boardroom, and I love your strength and determination, however, what I love most about you is your shyness, inexperience and naivety." His voice was deadly quiet. "I aim to uphold your integrity. After all, I've waited nine months, three more shouldn't be a problem. I'll wait until you're ready." He kissed her gently on her lips. "Let's sleep, my princess."

She turned around so that her back was facing him. She did not want him to see the tears in her eyes. "Good night, my prince. I love you." The depth of feeling she had for him was more than she'd ever imagined possible.

He wrapped his arms tightly around her waist. "I love you more."

CHAPTER THIRTY NINE

Surrounded by coral reefs and white sandy beaches, Kukuwa and François repeated their vows. Zhara was maid of honour at the fairytale wedding in the Seychelles Islands.

Among the guests were Olympia and Akatapori, Ngozi and Tunde, Chelsea and her new boyfriend, Pandora and Balotelli and Amira and Conrad.

It was Zhara and Agyeman's first trip abroad and she loved every minute they spent together. Looking lovingly into his eyes she had no doubt that she would spend the rest of her life with him. Plans for their wedding had been finalised, and she longed to become his wife. Their marital home had been completed and decorated just as they wanted. She decided to move in as soon as they returned to Accra.

It was with heavy hearts that Zhara's parents took in the news that she was planning to move to McCarthy Hill. They had expected her to move into the villa with Agyeman after the wedding, so deciding to move in before him concerned them greatly. They tried as hard as they could to persuade her to remain with them until after the wedding, but it was clear her mind was made up. Seeing how elated she was about the move, they gave in.

Nestling high up in the hills between palms and pines, the villa looked spectacular. Built with stone and glass, it offered spectacular views of the city. Surrounded by a green canopy, tropical gardens and an outdoor pool the external façade led to a sleek interior with a tricolor of dove-coloured walls, vibrant accents and lavish furnishings. Granite, marble, dark wood and rich textures from around the world were combined harmoniously to create a stylish contemporary home.

Zhara moved into the villa on 9th October. With round the clock security, Awuni in the boys-quarters and her parents, friends and Agyeman visiting nearly every day she was beginning to feel glad that she had taken the very bold step of moving in alone.

It was the first week in November. Zhara had met most of her neighbours and seemed to be settling in very well.

She left work around 4 pm on Friday, stopped at the butchers and picked up some groceries from the supermarket. She pulled into the driveway around 7:30 pm. The villa looked stunning in the moonlight. She thought of Agyeman and decided to call him before she went to bed.

Awuni raced towards her and took out the shopping bags. After cooking dinner she served him and sent him away. She checked that all the external doors were locked and headed upstairs for a long soak in the bath.

She called Agyeman at 9 pm. His line was busy. She

called her parents and invited them over for dinner the following day. She tried Agyeman again. The line was still engaged. She got into bed and was halfway through Maya Angelou's I Know Why the Caged Bird Sings when she fell soundly asleep.

Her eyes sprang open when she heard the phone ringing. A sharp pain tore through her head. It felt as if she'd been struck a heavy blow. She couldn't get up. Her heart was pounding as if it was about to burst through her ribs. She tried to move her legs but couldn't.

Suddenly, she saw a face. It was fading away in the darkness. She thought she'd seen the face before but it was dark and she couldn't be sure. She screamed, but there was no sound. Weighed down by an invisible force, she could neither move nor cry out for help.

Rattled by her predicament she tried to rationalise her thoughts. She wasn't dreaming; her brain was still functioning and she was wide-awake. A part of her wanted to regress back to childhood so she could hide under the covers until the ghosts went away. The room felt hot and the silence was sinister.

Wishing she'd listened to her parents, she began to pray. Shaking like a leaf, she watched and listened, hoping that whatever was lurking in the shadows would go away. Instinctively she knew her childhood horrors were back to haunt her, only this time her parents could not save her.

A loud bang shattered the silence. It shook her to the core. Seconds later she heard a creak, then heavy footsteps, one at a time. Someone or something was coming up the stairs. A few steps from her bedroom it stopped. No! she thought, transfixed to the bed, unable to move nor scream.

She was distracted by a rustling sound. It was coming from outside. All of a sudden the footsteps started again. The loud thuds were heading towards her room. She closed her eyes and prayed. The room temperature dropped instantly. A cold breeze moved around her. The sweat oozing from her body turned cold against her skin. Her heart was beating loudly. She continued to pray. Her body was shivering from fear and cold. Even as she repeated the Lord's Prayer she felt as if she was being stifled but she carried on regardless.

Suddenly a bright light flashed across the room. She passed out.

CHAPTER FORTY

Araba and Kamil took turns to sit by Zhara's side. They'd been waiting 24 hours.

With sad anxious eyes Agyeman watched the medics attend to Zhara. He'd found her unconscious and rushed her to the hospital.

Zhara slipped in and out of consciousness. Her head and throat hurt. Her nose felt as if it had been doused in acid. She recognised some of the voices around her, but couldn't make out what they were saying. Someone was sitting by her side, holding her hand and praying. The soothing touch felt like her mother. Sometimes there were several faces in the shadows around her. Other times there was one or two.

Where was she, she asked herself. She tried to move her legs but couldn't. Her hands felt stiff at the joints. There was a foul taste in her mouth and her body ached. Her head felt odd, as if she was not quite present. She lay still for a while.

Suddenly she could see and hear clearly. Agyeman was standing by her bed. He looked dishevelled. A man in a white coat, possibly a doctor, was speaking to her parents. A young nurse was taking her temperature. She listened.

"The concussion is consistent with a fall or a blow to her head" the doctor was saying. "I recommend that she sees a specialist as soon as possible. It is essential that we find out what happened. Thankfully, she is responding well to treatment. It's a good thing the young man brought her here as soon as he found her. I hate to think what could have happened."

The nurse whispered something to the doctor. He moved swiftly towards Zhara and smiled.

"Good evening Zhara, I am Dr Fishtail. You've been in our care following your admission yesterday." He checked her pulse and reflexes and talked through what he was doing.

"How is she doing?" asked Araba.

"She's coming around slowly, but she needs plenty of rest." He rubbed her shoulder. "Don't worry, she is in good hands."

The doctor turned his attention to Zhara. "How are you feeling?"

She blinked rapidly. "My head and throat hurt," she muttered.

The sound of her voice made Agyeman's heart leap. Her parents hugged each other and gave thanks to God.

The doctor nodded sympathetically. In the fifteen years he'd worked at the hospital he had never come across such a mysterious case.

"Your parents and your fiancé are dying to speak to you" he told her. "Let me leave you with them for a little while. I'll be back shortly."

Araba hugged her daughter fondly. Kamil cupped Zhara's face in his hands and looked tenderly into her eyes. "Please come back home, I would rather die than see you helpless like this."

Zhara felt the lump in her throat and nodded.

Relieved that his daughter was finally out of danger, Kamil wiped the tears from his eyes.

As she stared blankly at the white walls, Agyeman took her hand and kissed it softly.

"What happened?" she asked. "How did I end up here?"

"I saw your missed calls but when I called there was no answer. Figuring you might have fallen asleep I decided to surprise you. I let myself in with my keys. When I opened the bedroom door you were hunched over on the bed, a bible in one hand and a rosary in the other. Blood was oozing out of the side of your mouth. I carried you to the car and brought you here. Then I called your mum and dad."

"Daddy, what happened?" she cried. "Why does my head hurt so much?"

"Sweetheart, I wish I knew." He looked tormented. "No one knows what could have happened to you. At first we thought it might have been a burglar or some sort of intruder, but all the doors and windows were locked and there was no sign of a forced entry. Nothing has been touched in the house and it appears you were the only person in the house. The only reasonable explanation is that you fell, but we can't be certain. I am forced to believe this could be linked to the mysterious events that happened many years ago."

"Honey, I think this could be a recurrence of the nightmares and all the other stuff" said Araba.

Zahra blinked rapidly and swallowed. "I wish I had taken Chido with me to the villa. How long have I been here?"

"Since midnight yesterday."

She seemed confused. "What day is it today?"

"Saturday."

Zhara tried to summon her memory, but it made the headache worse.

Dr Fishtail returned with the nurse. "How are you feeling?" he asked with a warm smile.

"My head hurts" said Zhara. The nurse began examining the wound on Zhara's head.

"Is she going to be OK?" Kamil asked the doctor.

"She seems distressed" he replied sympathetically. "But that is common with head injuries. They can be dreadful, but she is doing fine. It may take her a while to remember everything. I would recommend that she sees one of our senior therapists. He is the best in the business."

"Haba! A shrink? Is that necessary?" asked Kamil.

"I'm afraid so. My suspicions are that there is more to this than meets the eye. Think about it." He checked his watch. "It's getting late and Zhara needs to rest. Let's talk some more tomorrow."

Kamil and Araba kissed Zhara and wished her goodnight. Agyeman hugged Zhara and squeezed her hand. "I'll be back in the morning" he murmured.

CHAPTER FORTY ONE

The immaculately dressed receptionist smiled pleasantly as Zhara approached the front desk. "Good afternoon Madam, how may I help you?"

Zhara returned the smile. "I have a four o'clock appointment with Dr Mensah."

"Oh yes, Miss Al-Jamal. Please come with me."

Zhara followed the elderly lady to an office along the corridor. It was rather large, with rose white walls and rich coffee-brown furniture. Two evenly-spaced tub chairs were placed a remarkable distance from the doctor's leather chair and desk.

"Please take a seat," said the lady. "Dr Mensah will be with you shortly."

Zhara sat at the edge of the tub chair closest to the door.

"Can I offer you a drink?" the lady asked with a megawatt smile. "Guava, or maybe pineapple juice?"

Zhara did not want a drink, but she seemed unable to find the words.

"Perhaps you prefer herbal tea?" the woman continued. "Would you like peppermint or chamomile and vanilla?"

Zahra eased into the chair. "You are very kind. Chamomile and vanilla please."

She was debating whether to stay or leave when a tall handsome man in a dark brown linen suit opened the door.

"Ah Miss Al-Jamal," he said, proffering a hand. "I am glad you made it."

Zahra shook his hand. He was not what she had expected.

"May I call you Zahra?"

"Sure" she muttered.

The doctor took a few strides towards the desk and turned. "Zh-aa-ra" He said, with a pensive glare. "You do have a lovely name." Without taking his eyes off her, he crossed his legs and leaned against the desk.

Zhara was wondering what she'd let herself in for when she heard a tap on the door.

"Do come in Cynthia" the doctor said with a charming smile.

Cynthia placed a steaming cup of tea on the side table next to Zhara.

"Thank you" said Zhara.

Cynthia smiled politely, retrieved a file from the doctor's desk and left the room.

Enticed by the refreshing smell from the porcelain cup, Zhara took a sip.

Dr Mensah was seated and observing Zhara from steel-rimmed glasses. "Dr Fishtail explained what happened to you" he began. "I believe the physical wounds have been treated successfully. My role here is to help you with the mental and psychological healing." He paused as if to gather his thoughts. "Is there anything you'd like to know?"

Zhara shook her head. She wasn't convinced she needed a shrink but didn't have the courage to say so. She figured she was in too deep and might as well finish the session.

Dr Mensah flipped through a notepad on his desk. "Your heath record is very impressive, so with your cooperation my work should be relatively easy. Today's session is mainly to get to know and understand you better. If you don't mind, we will begin with your childhood. When I have a better understanding of the situation I may delve a bit deeper into your family and the relationships you've had. Hopefully, we can work well together and achieve our aim in a matter of weeks; it all depends on you and how much you want this. Do you have any questions?"

Zhara shook her head.

Dr Mensah sensed her anxiety. "I can't promise that we will find all the answers, but I will do my best to shed some light on what might have caused this incident. Our sessions may get harrowing at times, but I want to assure you that whatever is discussed here will remain strictly confidential."

Zhara stared blankly at the painting of a wooded pathway on the wall. Had it not been for her parents, she pondered, she would never have agreed to see the shrink.

Now she had to sit before a total stranger and discuss her deepest, darkest secrets. Harrowing as it sounded, she couldn't object without giving it a try. Folding her arms, she shrugged and resigned herself to what lay ahead.

"I know you must be dreading this" said Dr Mensah. "Just relax, you will be fine." The conviction in his voice made Zhara feel slightly more optimistic.

"Let's begin with the incident that led to your admission. What do you remembered about that night?"

Zhara told him everything she could.

"So this face you saw, can you describe it?"

"Not exactly. Every time I try to picture it, I end up with an excruciating headache. I think I may have seen it before."

"Where?"

"In the nightmares I used to have many years ago."

Dr Mensah drew his brows together in thoughtful consideration.

"Tell me about your childhood. Were there any unpleasant occurrences?"

Zhara sipped tea while reflecting on the question.

"My first trip to the dentist was a painful experience. I was about seven or eight. My mum had taken me to her office at Kimberley Avenue when the toothache started. Seeing the pain I was in, she took me to the nearest dentist in the area, a market-street quack."

"I am not too fond of dentists. Was it really that bad?"

"Oh yes it was, and very quick, thankfully! He sat me down on a wooden stool, and asked me to show him which tooth was causing the pain. I did. He put a plastic apron around my neck, pulled out an instrument that looked like pliers, said 'open wiiiiiiide' and yanked out my tooth. He held the decayed tooth like a trophy in one hand and gave me salted water to gargle and told me to stop eating black and white and condensed milk toffee."

"Did you?"

"Not entirely, but I switched from sweets to fruit."

"Good, they are better for your health. Have you seen a dentist since?"

"Yes, at a dental surgery in Cape Coast and in London where they examine your teeth, talk you through the procedure and use proper dentistry equipment."

Dr Mensah leaned into his chair. "Have you experienced any other unpleasant episodes?"

"Yes. Many."

He nodded, urging her to continue.

"I had been in kindergarten for a few months and was enjoying it very much until the headmaster decided to shave my hair off."

"What!" Dr Mensah looked troubled. "Why did he pick on you?"

"I have no idea. Everyone was running and screaming. All I remember is the headmaster grabbing hold of my hand and shaving my hair from my forehead down to the nape of my neck with a razor."

"What did you do?"

"As soon as he let go of my arm I ran as fast as my tiny legs could carry me. Luckily my house was a few yards down the road from the school. I was so petrified that I lost control of my bowels. As I passed through the gate to my house I saw my father standing on the veranda. I was so relieved to see him. He scooped me up in his arms and I clung to him sobbing. I later learned that my father had marched up to the school but there was no-one there. The head teacher had been taken to the asylum."

"That must have been an awful experience. What do you think your father would have done if he had seen the headmaster?"

"It's hard to say. My father is very protective of his family and he is known to have a volatile temper."

"So it could have turned ugly?"

"Yes, very."

"Does that happen often?"

"What?" Zhara looked puzzled.

Dr Mensah removed his glasses. "Does your father lose his temper often?"

"Only when he has reason to, like when we were burgled and when my neighbour's dog nearly bit me."

"That is understandable. How did he react then?"

"After we got burgled he threw a few warning shots. He continues to fire a few rounds of bullets before he goes to bed every night. As for the dog who tried to bite me, it scarpered so fast when it saw my father running towards him with an AK47, I've never seen it again."

"He sounds frightening. Has he ever lost his temper with you?"

"Once."

"Really? You must have been an exceptional child. What did you do?"

"I can't even remember what I did. I was about nine or ten but I am sure whatever I did must have been bad because it was the first and only time he used the barazim on me."

"What is that?"

"It's a kind of whip."

"Did it hurt?"

Zhara grinned mischievously. "No, it didn't."

"How come?"

"Well, when I realised I was about to be whipped, I dashed into my room, loaded my backside with cloth and rushed back to him, hoping he wouldn't detect my enlarged bottom. It was big anyway, so I didn't think he would notice the extra layers. After two or three smacks he let me go. After dinner that evening he explained why he'd had to discipline me, but seeing how distraught he was made me wish I'd never done what I did and I was determined not to ever put myself in such a difficult situation again."

"Did he ever find out about your padded bottom?"

Zhara laughed. "Yes he did. You can never get anything past my mum. She knew my secret right from the start but she didn't reveal it until a year later. Dad laughed his head off."

"What about your mum, does she fall prey to his temper?"

Zhara puzzled over the question.

"She does, and at times I think she winds him up purposefully. Her passion matches his strong will, so when they disagree, sparks fly, and when they make up, their love for each other is so strong, it's overwhelming."

"Do the arguments get heated?"

"Yes, at times. The worst was when I was five. They came home very late at night. They'd both had a few drinks. She accused him of flirting with some woman, and he said he was only being nice, but she wasn't buying it. Some unpleasant stuff was thrown around. They assumed I was asleep, but I wasn't. I heard everything. What I heard caused me a lot of pain and made me very sad for many years."

"What was said that you were not meant to hear?" Asked Dr Mensah.

"After Mum accused Dad of flirting he accused her of still seeing her ex-boyfriend. She denied it. Then he asked if she was sure I was his child and not Dr Lane's."

"What did she say to that?"

"I don't know. I was in such shock. I couldn't bear to hear another word. I wept with my head buried in the pillow, so they wouldn't hear me and come to my room. Funny enough when I woke up the next morning, it was as if nothing had happened. They were back in love and calling each other 'darling' and 'DD'. It was as if I had imagined what happened the previous night."

"Did you ever tell them what you heard?"

"Not for a few years. I loved my father too much to bring it up. What helped was burying myself in books. I also found solace in food. Sweets, chocolates and pastries became my three best friends, I would hide them under my pillow, and when the nasty thoughts surfaced I would devour them away. They filled the void and gave me a momentary feeling of pleasure but the pain never went away. As time passed my hips got wider and my face got rounder. My mum was beside herself with worry that her perfect little girl was becoming obese. She put me on a diet but the weight wasn't shifting because the reason for my overeating had not been addressed. I still remember the look in her eyes when she found a bar of chocolate under my pillow.

"Was your father upset about your weight too?"

"Initially he wasn't. He said it was puppy fat and nothing to worry about, but when he realised a few years later that the weight wasn't shifting he decided to do something about it."

"And what was that?"

Zhara observed Dr Mensah as he scribbled on his notepad. He seemed nothing like what she'd expected him to be. Her stereotype of a highly-respected physiologist was an old, balding, boring and intense man, not the smartly-dressed, handsome professional in his late twenties with a soothing voice and an expression that made him look like he really cared.

She realised he was observing her, waiting for her to continue. She inhaled. "He got me a personal trainer who showed me fun ways of getting fit like kickboxing and yoga, which I thoroughly enjoyed. The weight started to fall off and I was so relieved when they stopped calling me names."

"You were called names?" He looked surprised.

"Yes," her voice trembled.

"People can be very mean." He held his jaw thoughtfully. "Why didn't you speak to your parents about what you overheard?"

"I did, when I turned sixteen." Her body tensed up. "I couldn't keep it to myself any more."

"You poor girl" He blinked rapidly. "And?"

"They were devastated that I had carried that burden for so long. Mum explained that she did go out with Dr Lane, but that was before she met my father. She swore that she had never ever cheated on my father. Dad apologised. It was the first time I'd ever seen him cry. He was extremely sad that what he said in a drunken outburst had caused eleven years of anguish. He held me in his arms and assured me that I was his flesh and blood, through and through. He said he loved me more than life itself. I clung to him and cried. When Mum joined in, Dad had to put his foot down. He just couldn't bear to see his two favourite girls looking sad and miserable. He took us out for a meal to cheer us up."

"How did that feel?" asked Dr Mensah.

"It felt cathartic, purifying, liberating, cleansing, releasing and invigorating. It was the happiest day of my life. I have never doubted my father's love, but his reassurance gave closure to the matter. Regardless of whether I am his biologically or not, I will always love and adore him. I couldn't have wished for a better father."

Dr Mensah looked pleased. "I am glad we've ended

our first session on a high note. How did you find it?"

"Scary at the beginning, but I'm glad I came."

"Good. Can we meet again in a few days?"

Zhara nodded.

CHAPTER FORTY TWO

Dr Mensah welcomed Zhara with a smile. "Do take a seat. You look well. How is the head?"

"Much better, thanks."

"Dr Fishtail informed me that you moved back in with your parents."

"Yes. My father wouldn't have it any other way."

"I think he may have a point there. Are you sleeping well?"

"Much better, thanks."

Dr Mensah removed his glasses and placed both hands on the desk. "I think we've made good progress. In our session today I would like to dwell on any incidents of abuse - sexually, emotionally or psychologically. Does anything spring to mind?"

Zhara took a deep breath. "Yes." There was a long silence.

"Would you like to talk about it?" His voice was soft and compassionate.

Gazing at the ceiling, she inhaled, then slowly exhaled. "It was during the summer holidays. I was eight. We'd been catching grasshoppers, me and my cousin, Afua. Then I went to the bathroom to wash my hands. I was turning off the tap when her stepbrother grabbed me from behind and tried to put me on his lap. He was seventeen. I kicked and screamed but he wouldn't let me go. He unzipped his shorts and sat on the toilet, he smiled smugly and raised me up and tried to sit me on his erect manhood. I fought tooth and nail until I finally wriggled out of his hands and ran away."

"Did you mention this to anyone?"

"No."

"Why not?"

"His mother passed away when he was a child and I knew if I so much as breathed a word of what he'd done he would be on the next bus to the village. Much as I hated him for what he tried to do to me, I couldn't bear to ruin his life."

Dr Mensah looked perplexed. "You thought about your cousin's welfare, at that age, despite what he did to you?"

Zhara nodded. "He wasn't all bad, but I had to let him know that what he did was unacceptable. The next time I saw him, I warned him that if he dared to touch me again I would tell my father. That alone put the fear of God in him, but I wasn't done yet. I told him I would not hesitate to tell his father and stepmother what he did to me. He never touched me again."

"You are remarkable. Were there any other inappropriate encounters?"

Zhara nodded. "There were many suggestive remarks, by so-called friends and uncles. Nothing serious. When I passed my Ordinary Level exams, my dad gave me money to go shopping. I asked the driver to take me to a boutique in Malata. After buying a few dresses I saw a shoe that I really liked but they didn't have my size. The owner of the boutique, an elderly Alhaji [one who has completed one of the five Pillars of Islam] said he had a new delivery of size six shoes at his office. He even offered to give me a lift there but I told him I came with a car so if he gave me the directions I would go there myself. When he insisted on taking me there I got in his car and asked the driver to follow us. I was surprised when we arrived at a hotel, but I assumed his office was there. He ushered me into a suite on a third floor and brought out a box full of shoes. I picked three pairs and tried them on. They fitted like a glove. I was so happy. I reached out for my purse.

"That was when I felt his arms around my waist. He said I didn't have to pay for the shoes. I insisted. He grabbed me. Overcome by the feeling of déjà vu I lunged for the door. He was quicker and stronger than I thought. He pinned me down, but I fought back and overpowered him. I still don't know where the strength came from but I got into the car unscathed."

"Was that your last encounter with the Alhaji?" asked Dr Mensah.

"No it wasn't. My best friend, Kukuwa arrived from Switzerland that weekend. She attended school there. When I told her what the Alhaji had done to me, she came up with a plan. It was meant to teach him a lesson. We went to the boutique on the last Friday during Ramadan and were in time for Zuhr [noon prayer]. As he came up from his bended knees we shouted Allahu Akbar [Allah the greatest]. He just stood there, glaring at us. We left with a feeling of triumph and hoped he would get the message that Allah sees everything. Our intention was to make him stop molesting young innocent girls."

"Do you think you achieved it?"

"I doubt it, but at least we tried. Doing what we did felt great at the time, but we were young and not so wise at sixteen. On reflection we should have let Allah deal with him in His own way. In Romans 12:19 the bible says Dearly beloved, avenge not yourselves, but rather give place unto wrath: for it is written, Vengeance is mine; I will repay, saith the Lord."

"What you say is true, but at sixteen you were a child and acted as such. In Corinthians 13:11 the bible says When I was a child, I spoke like a child, I thought like a child, I reasoned like a child. When I became a man, I put aside childish things. You have done just that." He observed her with affection. "Zhara, I am astounded by your intellect. You amaze me with your knowledge of both the bible and the Quran. What inspired you to study both religions?"

"My father is a moslem." Her face lit up. "He taught me everything I know about Islam; Arabic, performing ablution, praying five times a day, reading the Quran and fasting. It was hard going at first, learning a new language, but I soon mastered the prayers. By the age of nine I could recite all the prayers. I also learnt a lot from my father's philanthropy, his kindness and his desire to promote the welfare of the less fortunate. Watching him invite a hungry person off the street to share his meal or give away his possessions to those he believes need them more than he does inspired me to study the Quran. When he donates generously to worthwhile causes and gives Sadaqah (alms to the poor) after Friday prayers, kills a cow after Ramadan and shares it among his neighbours or pays for the tuition of orphaned and underprivileged children I am touched by his love for mankind and yearn to know everything about Islam, his way of life." She paused. There was a distant look in her eye. "Sometimes I wish he wasn't so generous."

"Why is that?" Asked Dr Mensah.

"Because I have seen people lie to him about their circumstances just to take advantage of his kindness. Businessmen come to him with made-up proposals and forged documents, hoping to pull the wool over his eyes and dupe him. It is disheartening to see how greed and selfishness makes people lie, cheat and stab others in the back in the pursuit of wealth and power."

Dr Mensah had a niggling thought. "I would like to take you back to the encounter with the Alhaji. Your reaction, when he pinned you down, was very powerful, which gives me the impression that something may have happened prior to that. It is what made you react the way you did. Could something else have happened that might have affected you emotionally or psychologically?"

Zhara looked dazed.

"Perhaps the only way you've been able to deal with it

is by blocking those painful memories out of your mind" he went on. "It is a natural reaction."

He could see her muscles tightening.

"Would you like a drink?" asked the doctor.

"Water, please."

He lifted the phone. "Cynthia, could you bring Zhara water please.

Cynthia appeared instantly with a glass of water and left the room.

Zhara took a deep breath and drank the water. Her eyes watered as she recalled what happened with the beast. "You're right." Her voice trailed off.

"You can let it out" he said softly. His voice was kind and soothing. "Denial is what we do to cope, it is also what makes us feel so alone. It's OK. You will feel better for it."

She hugged herself and focused on the light blue carpet. The memories started flooding back. "I was crossing the road to go home after church, when I heard someone calling my name. I turned around. The Sergeant Major was waving at me to come over. He lived right beside the church. At first I didn't want to go because it was getting to lunchtime and my mum was cooking fufu and palm nut soup, and I was getting hungry. I knew I wasn't supposed to talk to strangers, but he was very well known in the neighbourhood and my parents knew him, so I didn't consider him a stranger. As I walked towards him he told me he had a package for Auntie Rose, my next door neighbour, and asked if I wouldn't mind taking it to her. She was my mum's friend, so I said yes. He was well known in the neighbourhood for his military skills and all the things he'd done in war. I followed him to his front door but refused to go in. I was watching people coming out of Kaneshie Presbyterian church in their beautiful frocks when the Sergeant Major's wife emerged from the small white bungalow. She was in her early twenties. When she suggested I wait for her husband in the sitting room I followed her in, hoping he would be quick with whatever he was doing. While I was waiting she nipped into the kitchen and brought out a bottle of Fanta and a box of biscuits. I politely declined because I was getting a bit anxious and I didn't want to ruin my appetite.

"She sat with me for a while, then said she was going to fetch her husband. I was staring blankly at the black and white TV, humming Rock of Ages when I heard heavy footsteps. I jumped up, intending to take the package and head home. It was the Sergeant Major, standing by the door completely naked. I knew instantly that there was no package, it was just a ploy to get me into his house. I thought of screaming, but I knew I was trapped and it would only make things worse.

"He moved towards me, fat greasy cheeks wobbling on either side of his ugly podgy face. I moved a few inches back. He advanced towards me, very slowly, arms resting on the shelf of the protruding belly. His grubby claws explored the repulsive body. It was as if he was analysing the texture and density of the thin weeds of hair and unsightly moles all over it. His hands wandered up to his chest. Then it went back down, all the way down and disappeared under his stomach. Suddenly, he grabbed his manhood. Come, my beautiful one, come to me, touch me, he coaxed."

Zhara took a sip of water and stared blankly at the walls. "He must have noticed that I was weeping and shaking all over because he stopped and said, don't be scared, I won't hurt you, please don't cry, it won't hurt. His thick chapped lips twitched into an ugly smile. The demonic eyes gleamed as he licked his lips. It is OK, he said, please touch it, I have longed for this day for a long time, to be touched by the prettiest girl in the neighbourhood. Do you know how you haunt me with those luscious hips and angelic smile? You are so pure and innocent, not like the others. Come, come, come. Feel this, touch it, touch me."

Zhara felt the tears fall involuntarily from her eyes. She continued. "For a moment he seemed to be spaced out as he stroked and pleasured himself. I averted my eyes from his unsightly bits and moved backwards slowly until I was out of his reach. Then I looked down at the concrete floor and was confronted by the most repulsive verruca and yeast infected in-grown toenails. With my hymn book firmly placed under my armpit and my fingers knotted tightly I wracked my brains for a way out of the house before he pounced on me. You see, the only apparent exit was the main door but with him in the way I ruled that out. The thought of getting any closer than I already was to the ogre made me want to throw up. I raised my eye slightly so I could monitor his movement. Thankfully he was still in a trancelike state and totally absorbed in what he was doing to himself. Suddenly a ray of sunlight beamed through the room. It was coming from the door behind me. I moved towards it with quick backward strides. As soon as my heel touched the door I turned around and fled. I found myself at the back of the house. From there I kept running until I reached the main road. I continued running. I was as free as a bird in the warm summer breeze. Taking long purifying breaths I carried on until I reached home."

"How old were you?" Asked Dr Mensah.

"I was ten."

"That was a lucky escape. I am inclined to think his wife knew what he was up to. Did you tell anyone?"

"I tried to erase it from my mind. Thinking about what happened makes me feel dirty. You are the only person I've told. Much as I wanted to tell my parents when it happened, I couldn't. I was scared my father would shoot the pervert. Even though I would have liked to see his brains blown out, I did not want my father to become a killer. He was not worth my father breaking the Lord's commandment."

"Is he still living there?"

"I have no idea. We left the area the following year. My friend, Tamali, still lives there. She told me that a number of children had complained about a paedophile who offers them soft drinks and money, molests them and warns them not to breathe a word, else their whole family will be vanish. She also mentioned a Catholic Priest who had been molesting young boys in his church since he arrived from Europe. It is so sad when you hear what some children have to endure at the hands of their abusers. I hope to set up a foundation for abused children in a year or so. I can't wait to see all the paedophiles from our schools, churches and the community shamed and thrown into prison."

"Do you think that experience may have affected you?"

"Certainly. It has made me wary of the male sex and less trusting of people in general. I feel safe with my immediate family and close friends and tend not to socialise much."

"How do you feel about sharing your dark secret with me?" he smiled.

She returned the smile. "I think you are a genius. You have offloaded a great deal of hidden pain and anguish. I am glad to be rid of the burden. Thank you."

He cocked his head coyly. "I am delighted with your progress. You make me love what I do. Thank you." She was growing on him. "Same time next week?"

She nodded.

CHAPTER FORTY THREE

It was a humid November day. Agyeman picked Zhara up from work at 1:30 pm. After lunch at La Palm Beach Club he dropped her off at the clinic.

Dr Mensah was in the office when she arrived. He seemed very pleased to see her. The white linen pants and turquoise short-sleeved shirt gave him a boyish charm. "You look well" he said, skimming over the figure-hugging burgundy dress.

"You don't look too bad yourself." His dark hair had been cropped. It suited him. She liked his boyish charm. She was thinking that he looked far too handsome for a shrink, when one of Dr Mensah's assistants, a young pretty girl, popped her head through the door.

"Would you like a drink, Miss?"

"Water please. Thank you." Zhara eased into the chair, ready for her third session.

"We seem to have uncovered a lot in a relatively short time" said Dr Mensah. He scribbled something on the notepad, then sat back and removed his glasses. "I would like to take you back to the incident that brought you here." He paused, hazel eyes focused on her. Sunlight poured in through the bay window, radiating his mocha complexion. "Was this your first out-of-the-ordinary experience?"

"No, there have been many."

Dr Mensah's assistant tapped on the door, placed a glass of water on the coffee table and left the room.

"Would you like to tell me what happened?" He seemed totally absorbed in what was going on in Zhara's mind.

She puzzled over the question. "Of course." She took a sip of water. It was chilled and refreshing. She took another sip and felt it travel down, cooling her insides. "I had a maid when I was eight. She came from a village called Mowure in the Central region. She was called Esi. Even though she was in her teens she was about the same height as me. We played together. I liked her a lot. She'd been with us about a year when we heard her screaming early one morning. My parents rushed to the maid's quarters to see what was going on there. They found Esi rolling around on the floor in her bedroom. She was foaming from the mouth. My father quickly called my uncle. He is a doctor. Uncle Kwamena managed to calm her down. She was dripping with sweat and shook all over. He tried speaking to her but she couldn't speak, not for a while. Suddenly she slumped against the wall and started talking. She said she was a witch and had been sent to kill me. Apparently there was a bright light surrounding me, which made it impossible for her to get to me. She said it was too powerful and each time she tried she was pushed back. In her latest attempt, the previous night, she had tried to take me to a forest in her village so she could meet with the witches and find a solution to her predicament. She said it was done spiritually, so that even though it looked like I was sleeping, my soul was not in my body and if her plan had worked I would be dead by the morning. But none of the witches could touch me so she had to return my soul to my body. The angel protecting me had warned her that she would die, unless she confessed what she had tried to do to me and leave my house. She was crying hysterically and begging me and my parents for forgiveness, saying it was the work of the devil. She was sent back to the village."

"Interesting" said the doctor. "Do you have nightmares?"

"Yes, all the time."

"When did they start?"

"From as early as I can remember, possibly three or four years old."

"You must have a very good memory."

"I remember some things vividly but others not so well, it depends on what it is."

"How early can you remember?" He had a hint of a glow in his hazel eyes.

Zhara stared at the crystals on the ceiling pendant. "When I was very young, between a year and eighteen months, my mum would often bath me in the kitchen sink. I still remember it so clearly. She was shocked when I told her. She never thought I would remember. Apparently it was my grandmother's idea. You see, I loved to play in water. The bath-tub was too big for me to play in and the basins were not deep enough, but the kitchen sink was perfect. It was sturdy and smooth and deep enough for her to immerse me in. She would sing to me while I played."

"You can remember all that?"

Zhara nodded. "And I remember some of the songs too. Some things are hard to forget. It may also interest you to know that I have some psychic abilities."

"Really?" His lips curled into a half-smile.

"I can sometimes sense when something very bad is about to happen and there have been moments when I have been able to see through pretentious smiles. I used to see a lot of weird things when I was young, things that are hard to explain and certainly out of this world."

"It may be that you have supernatural powers, or the gift of insight. This is when you can see and sense things that others don't. Do you recall what your nightmares were about?"

"Yes. They were usually the same. I would be fast asleep, then wake up, feeling as if something sinister is at work. I would try to scream for help but the words wouldn't come out. I would become frustrated while struggling to be heard. I would wake up shaking, sweating, crying and screaming. My parents couldn't bear to leave me alone in my room at night, so I slept with them.

"My mum told me about something that happened when I was four. She said I woke up screaming and shaking. They'd become used to my nocturnal activities, but she said this was different. It was more than a night fright. She said I clung to her arm with my head buried in her chest and my eyes firmly closed. I was petrified of something in the room and kept pointing at it and saying it was coming to get me. What worried her was that neither she nor my dad could see anything besides us in the room.

"I kept screaming hysterically, so they took me out of the house just to calm me down. Dad drove around the city for about an hour. My mum sat me on her lap in the back of the car. My head was buried in her chest. I was too scared to look up. At around 4 am he stopped at my aunt's house. Dad carried me over his shoulder with my eyes firmly shut. Apparently, as soon as we entered my aunt's house I opened my eyes and stopped crying. My cousin watched me while they prayed. By the time they had finished praying I was sound asleep. I have no recollection of this."

Dr Mensah screwed up his eyes. "You remember things that happened much earlier but not this?" He crossed his arms.

Zhara nodded.

He scribbled on his notepad. "Were there any other inexplicable events?"

"A few." She took a sip of the drink. "On one occasion I went to bed with my parents, mum on one side of me and dad on the other. When they woke up, I was nowhere to be found. What they found bizarre was that the front door was still locked and the latch was firmly in place. In any case it was way off the ground and I could never reach it. After looking everywhere in despair, they decided to do a house to house search of the neighbourhood. My parents were heading out with a search party of friends and relatives when they spotted me with an elderly lady. They raced towards me. The woman was holding my hand. My mother held me in her arms and wept while the lady explained how she had found me about a mile away wandering along the streets at 4:30 am, barefoot. She told them that even though I looked content she couldn't believe that a child could be left roaming about at that time of day.

"The woman said when she asked where I lived I told her I could show her my house from the Presbyterian Church. She was new to the area so she asked for directions until they reached the church, then I pointed at my house, which was just round the corner from the street facing the church. The woman said she had intended to tell off my parents, but seeing how torn they were and on hearing how I disappeared, her anger turned to sadness and disbelief. My mum said I stood there barefoot in my white cotton lace-trimmed nightgown, smiling angelically, as if nothing unusual had happened. My dad said when they asked how I managed to get out of the house, I kept saying I wanted to play, but couldn't answer them. They thanked the lady and just hugged me."

"Astonishing" said Dr Mensah. "How old were you?"

"I was six. The following year the most eerie thing happened. I got home from school around 3 pm, changed, grabbed my dolly and hopped across the road to play with my friend. The gate was open so I entered the house and was heading to the front door when I noticed something in the middle of the garden. It was a white figure with a human structure but no face. I felt as if I'd frozen on the spot. I screamed but no sound was coming out of my mouth. There was a frightening silence all around me. I clenched my fists as a cold breeze swirled around me. The air was filled with a strange flowery smell as a horde of beautiful butterflies circled around the white figure. I tried to run but I couldn't move.

"Then in the twinkle of an eye everything suddenly vanished - the figure, the smell, the chill and the butterflies. The sunshine returned, and with it, dogs howling. I ran as fast as my little legs could carry me back home. I wasn't aware of the long high-pitched mindless screaming of pure terror coming from my mouth, not until my father scooped me in his arms and began reciting scriptures in the Quran. He said I looked terrified when I ran into the house, like I'd seen a ghost. He said I was shivering frantically, my skin felt as cold as ice and there were goose bumps all over my hands. With my breath coming in little hiccoughs I kept pointing at my friend's house and saying I saw it."

"He must have been beside himself with worry."

"He was, and still is. That is why he didn't want me to move into the villa without Agyeman, my fiancé. Funnily enough, that was my motive for living alone. I yearned for a glimpse of freedom, the chance to prove to myself that my childhood mysteries were over and I could survive on my own, if I had to."

"I see" said Dr Mensah. "Was that your only unusual sighting?"

Zhara inhaled deeply. "I wish I could say so." She took a sip of her drink. "The next one started as a dream. I was somewhere out of this world. A radiance of bright white light surrounded me. From a distance I could see a woman in a black cloth. She had a black scarf draped around her head. She was heading towards me. At first I couldn't see her face. As she got closer I could have sworn she was my grandmother, my father's mother, but there was something different about her. I wasn't sure what it was but it made me want to run from her. I didn't quite understand what was happening, I adored my grandmother and yet something was holding me back from running to her and hugging her like I always did. She was smiling at me, with her arms spread out wide to embrace me. 'Come my child,' she called. Her wrists were strong and supple, like the neck of a powerful mare, beckoning as she called. She turned her palms upwards in her quest to hold me but I moved back and away from her. When she saw how frightened I looked she coaxed me to go to her. 'My beloved,' she cried with pained eyes, 'it's me, your dearest Mma, don't be scared, please come to me'. I moved a few steps back.

"The image changed abruptly. It wasn't my grandmother anymore. A strange old lady was staring at me. I tried to run but the ground was slipping from beneath me. I couldn't breathe.

Suddenly I was awake. I could hear myself screaming

'Jesus!' My mum was sitting beside me, on my bed. She had tears in her eyes. My dad was looking down on me. Mum threw her arms around me. 'Thank God!" she sobbed. "We thought we'd lost you." I asked her what she meant by that. She said she heard me screaming and ran to my room. When she turned on the light I appeared to be asleep. She was about to kiss me goodnight when she realised I wasn't breathing. She screamed for my father. He checked my pulse. There was no beat. Suddenly I screamed 'Jesus'. They were totally perplexed and overjoyed. It was about 1 am.

"My dad decided to give thanks to Allah. It was while he was praying that we heard a wailing sound. As the noise got louder my mum decided to go outside and find out who was making so much noise in the middle of the night. When she opened the front door she found my father's sister sitting on the veranda. She was dressed in black and holding her head. She'd come to tell my father that his mum had passed away."

Dr Mensah sat back, deep in thought. "How did your grandmother die?"

"Peacefully in her bed."

"Were you close?"

"I adored her. She was sweet, gentle and kind. I believe an evil force was trying to use her to get to me."

"Why do you think that?"

"Because my grandmother would never harm me. It just doesn't make sense."

"Some things can never be explained."

"I know, and what happened on the day she was buried is still impossible to explain.

"What happened?"

"My parents travelled to the north for the funeral, but I couldn't go with them because I had my common entrance exam that week. I went to bed feeling fine. When I woke up I felt a sharp pain on my upper right thigh. It looked scalded, like a hot iron had been placed on it. The top layer of skin was burnt, leaving a large round wound. My nanny was beside herself when I showed it to her. We went to the hospital to have it treated. Even the nurses could not believe that it just appeared while I was sleeping. It sounded ridiculous, but it was the truth."

"How old were you?"

"I was ten."

"How did you feel, knowing people doubted what you knew to be the truth?"

"I felt nothing. I had no judgement, no expectation. The people that brought me into this world believed me, that is what mattered."

"And the wound, was it painful?"

"Yes, especially when the nurse tried to clean it. I still have the scar on my thigh."

"I want to take you back to the dream about your grandmother" said Dr Mensah. What do you think it meant?"

"My grandmother would not want to take me away from her beloved son, so I can only assume that it was some sort of revelation about her death."

Dr Mensah looked at her thoughtfully. "You called out to Jesus in your dream, and woke up from your unconscious state, that is remarkable."

Zhara smiled. "I must have screamed so loud in my dream that I woke myself up."

"Perhaps," said the doctor. "but it could also be that your faith brought you back to life. Have you thought about that?"

"I have, but I have also given up the need to know why things happen. I just trust in the Lord and accept what is."

"It is profoundly clear that you have faith. Where do you get your inspiration from?"

"My parents mainly. I've lived with Christianity and Islam all my life and believe God and Allah are one and the same. The goodness and pure devotion of my maternal grandmother, Maame Akua, an epitome of wisdom and a devout Christian, inspires me a lot. She took care of me when I was born. My mum was in hospital then. I think those first few months with her helped shape my life. I have learnt a lot from her, particularly Obra nye woara abo, which means life is what you make it. Attending a Catholic and Methodist school and learning about Islam makes me believe that there is only one God and He is beyond any religion."

"That is interesting" said the doctor.

"Having read the Bible and the Quran I know there isn't much difference in what they teach us, yet religion has done more to separate us than bring us together. Coming from a home where Eid, the Hajj, Christmas and

Easter are celebrated with equal regard I find it hard to understand why people torture and kill each other in the name of religion."

"I totally agree" Dr Mensah said with a smile. "Many acts of injustice have been committed over the years in the name of Christianity and civilisation." He sighed deeply. "Now back to the scary dreams. Were there any more?"

"The last one I can recall happened when I was twelve. I was home from secondary school and looking forward to the long vacation. My friend from primary school, Tina, invited me and a few friends for a sleepover at her house at Dzorwulu. Tina's mum, a nurse and her father, a doctor were working the night shift and not expected back until the morning.

"We talked about our experiences at boarding school, boys etc. A few of the girls were puffing away, trying to be cool and coughing their lungs out. Some of us watched a movie with popcorn. We all fell asleep around midnight in the living room.

"I was woken up by a strange sound, a loud hooting call, like an owl. The noise stopped when I shot up. I lay back down and pretended to be sleeping. The girls were breathing softly around me. It was pitch-black except for a peculiar pillar of moonlight filtering through the window. I scanned the room and listened. My heart was pounding. After convincing myself that I might have imagined the hooting sound, I closed my eyes and went back to sleep.

"Within a few seconds I heard the owl cry again, only this time it was much closer and as clear as a bell. I rolled gently to my side. That was when I saw it. It had the figure of a woman, a tall woman, old and hunched over with long grey hair. She was standing by the window in a long flowing gown. I closed one eye and pretended to be asleep. Her face was screwed up and fierce red eyes stared angrily in my direction. Standing a few yards from me, she raised both hands and moved towards me. I felt breathless and my mouth dried up. I prayed silently, in my head. A slow, evil grimace spread across her face and she inched closer. I lost control and screamed. Instantly she dissolved into a ball of steam and vanished.

"Tina and two other girls woke up. They asked why I was screaming. I told them I had a bad dream and I wanted to go home. I rang my parents to come and get me and got dressed. It was about 2:30 am. As soon as my father arrived I jumped into the car."

"Why didn't you tell your friends what you saw?"

"I didn't see any point in frightening them."

"Did you tell anyone?"

"No, never."

Dr Mensah tried not to get attached to his patients, but he was becoming very fond of Zhara. She'd been through a lot and seemed resolved to get to the bottom of her predicament. He was determined to do everything in his power to heal her mind and soul.

"Same time next week?" He uplifted her with his smile.

"Certainly!" She felt as if a huge burden had been lifted off her shoulders. Seeing a shrink isn't that bad after all, she thought.

CHAPTER FORTY FOUR

Sunlight beamed on the city of Accra as Zhara drove to the clinic. She watched children playing happily in Kwame Nkrumah Park and listened to the birds chirping merrily as they glided above the trees. The day had started well and held a lot of promise.

She was flipping through a Cosmopolitan magazine while waiting in the reception area when she heard the deep soothing voice.

"Good afternoon Zhara, do come in."

Rising to her feet she smiled and followed the doctor to his office.

"How are you feeling today?"

"Very well. Thank you."

"I thought so. You are healing beautifully. It shows in your eyes."

"Really?"

"Yes." He gave her a reassuring smile. "The eyes are the window to the soul."

"And what sayeth my soul?" She eased into the chair and crossed her arms.

"Many things, all good. I am glad you've found some comfort in our sessions."

"Are you psychic?"

"A little, and my doctorate in psychology helps me understand the human mind." He gazed intently at Zhara. "How is your fiancé?"

"He is very well, thanks."

"Does he know any of what we've talked about?"

"We have discussed some of it. After he proposed I thought it was only fair that I let him know what he was letting himself in for."

"Did it bother him?"

"Not at all, but his threat to strangle those who had tried to harm me was worrying."

"Would he have done that?"

"Maybe, but I didn't tell him who they were."

"Does he share many similarities with your father."

She smiled. "Yes, he does."

"Have you been back to the villa since the incident?"

"Yes."

"Has what happened affected your relationship?"

"It has, in a good way. At least now he knows what to expect. He seems to take it all in his stride though, and doesn't appear to be fazed by any of the craziness. In fact, he continues to be loving, caring and very attentive."

"You have a good man. How are your parents?"

"They are fine."

"And work?"

"Work is good."

"Are you sleeping well?"

"Yes, very well."

Dr Mensah clasped his hands. "Most people are

susceptible to parasomnia or night terrors, especially when they reach adolescence, due to hormones and physiological changes of the body. Changes to the body often affect the mind. However in your case, the night terrors began long before you reached puberty. Some drugs are known to cause or worsen nightmares, but judging from your medical records you've had a clean bill of health except for a few bumps and bruises. Do you drink coffee before going to bed at night?"

"I started drinking coffee when I was in London. I was eighteen. I rarely drink coffee here."

"I ask because caffeine, the stimulant in coffee, tends to keep the system moving at heightened levels. If taken before sleep it can, in some cases, make one susceptible to parasomnia. Also, lack of sleep, for whatever reason, can lead to a perpetual state of REM sleep instead of cycles, thus increasing the chances of nightmares. Not getting enough rest can lead to fatigue which causes physical, mental and emotional stress.

"Based on what we have discussed I can conclude that there is no medical explanation for what happened to you. I am convinced that the unpleasant childhood encounters and what you overheard about your paternity when you were five have definitely contributed in making a bad situation worse. The underlying issue though appears to stem from a spiritual source. There are many religious beliefs concerning dreams, angels, demons and the like, but why they affect some people and not others is beyond me. In your case, the tell-tale signs are all there, but what is unusual and possibly distinct from the parasomnia is the physical injury. The burn on your upper thigh when you were nine, of which you still bear the scar, and what occurred recently are inexplicable. The only possible explanation is that you harmed yourself, but I doubt that, hence I am led to a spiritual solution.

"Many religions agree that when dealing with the unseen, the only recourse is faith and prayers. I would recommend that for peace of mind, body and soul that you seek the help of a holy person with experience in such matters."

Zhara fixed the doctor with an unwavering stare.

"About a year ago one of my patients suffered the most horrendous night terrors and was plagued by images of her dead brother. She hadn't slept for weeks and when she came to see me she looked terrible. Her plight began after her brother was killed in a road accident. After trying to kill herself on many occasions she was referred to me, but after a few sessions with her I was sure there was nothing more I could do for her. Her distraught relatives took her to see Cardinal Abaka, who is well versed in such matters. Her plight was wiped away by prayers. The Cardinal is exceptional, but he can only heal those who have faith. I have witnessed it myself. Would you be willing to give it a try?"

"Yes, I will" she whispered. Having come this far she was determined to do whatever it took to get to the root of the matter.

"Marvellous! I will let him know you'll be calling." He

gave her a piece of paper with the Cardinal's contact details.

"Thank you."

Dr Mensah shook her hand. "Good luck. You deserve nothing but the best. I would love to know how you get on."

CHAPTER FORTY FIVE

Threading their way across the cobbled stones, they proceeded through the imposing colonnades and descended the stairs to Cardinal Abaka's Holy Basilica. It was a beautiful Sunday morning. The air was filled with the sweet smell of frankincense. Bright sunshine poured through the medieval stained glass windows and onto the golden mosaics glowing from the apse.

The Cardinal, a portly middle-aged man, was kneeling before the altar. When he heard the footsteps behind him, he rose and welcomed his guests, looking magnificent in an orange-tinged cassock and skull cap. He extended his hand.

"You must be Zhara." His smile was warm and celestial.

"Yes Cardinal. And this is my mum and my fiancé."

"The Cardinal shook hands with Araba and Agyeman. He led them to the altar and took Zhara's hands in his. "I am glad you came" he said. "The Lord sees and knows everything that is in our hearts." He made the sign of the cross. "His work has already been done. It will be well with you."

Then he asked Zhara to kneel before him. After

sprinkling holy water he gave her a crucifix and a rosary and prayed.

"May the LORD bless you, and keep you;

May the LORD make His countenance shine upon you, and be gracious to you;

May the LORD turn His countenance to you and grant you peace.

I bless you in the name of The Father, The Son and The Holy Ghost. Amen."

Cardinal Abaka continued praying for Zhara and her family. When he had finished, he held Zhara's hand and helped her up. "You are blessed my child, you have nothing to worry about" he told her.

He turned to Araba and smiled. "Mother, wipe away your tears. You should be delighted, your daughter is one in a million. She is blessed with love and purity and surrounded by goodness. Fear not, for she has angels all around her. No person or thing can ever harm her. Keep your faith and be delighted because the Lord is with her, always."

The Cardinal turned to Agyeman. "Young man, you have been blessed with a rare jewel. You must honour and cherish her. She will be your rock."

They thanked the Cardinal and left the church, feeling rejuvenated.

Later that night, while in bed, Zhara read Corinthians chapter 13 verses 1 to 13. She fell asleep at 10 pm. It was a fitful sleep, falling in and out of dreams and tossing and turning.

She shot up suddenly in the middle of the night. For the first time, she was not scared, even though she could feel a presence in the room. As her eyes adjusted to the darkness she saw something standing at the threshold of her bed. There was a peculiar breeze in the room. She could move or cry out, but somehow, she didn't feel the need to.

Removing the rosary Cardinal Abaka had given her from under her pillow, she closed her eyes and repeated the Lord's Prayer over and over again. Images of her childhood flashed through her mind. She was three years old and playing in the rose garden. Her father had just returned from work. She raced into his arms. He kissed her forehead and threw her up in the air. She seemed to love it. Another image appeared. Her mum was sitting by her bedside. She was wiping the sweat off her face after another nightmare. She seemed much older, seven or eight.

The images began to move quickly. Within seconds they'd become chaotic and were crowding in on her. She could hear screams, but couldn't make out the faces. They were coming so fast. She continued praying, eyes shut and rosary firmly in hand. The room was spinning around and there was a sensation of falling. The images went from bright and colourful to monochromatic and dismal. It was very confusing, but she was not scared. The images flashing in her mind's eye seemed to be pushing towards the surface.

She opened her eyes. The image was no longer there. Her eyes moved towards the ceiling. In the far corner of her room a face was being projected in mid-air. It was the spine-chilling face of a woman. It looked as if an invisible hand was holding up the face so Zhara could see it. Even in the darkness the face was illuminated so she could see it clearly. Without knowing why or how she knew it, she could tell instantly that it was the face of her tormentor.

The hideous mask of the woman hovered for a while, then contorted into grotesque movements, crying out in pain until it vanished. A halo of light surrounded her bed. Pure white light zoomed in and swallowed up the room. A large pure white figure with crystalline wings unfurled like a canopy around Zhara. She felt as though she was being showered with love. As the swirling sheets of brilliance encircled her she fell on her knees and gave thanks to God.

In that moment she understood clearly what Cardinal Abaka had said. She felt instinctively that her angel had revealed her tormentor to her. As the joyful tears flowed of their own accord she felt at peace; physically, mentally, psychologically, emotionally and spiritually.

CHAPTER FORTY SIX

A line of luxury cars headed up the steep hill to the beautiful castle deep in the Akwapim mountains. The atmosphere was serene, with a cool breeze and lush tropical hillside views overlooking the Aburi botanical gardens and the golf course.

A valet in a white shirt and black bow-tie opened the door just as the white limousine pulled up. François put an arm around Kukuwa as she stepped out of the car.

"I never knew Ghana was this beautiful," he said, observing the lush green lawns and picturesque hills and valleys. "We could live here forever!"

Kukuwa took her husband's arm possessively. "Yes, honey. I love it here." They'd been married for three months. She was one of Zhara's bridesmaids, two months pregnant and blooming.

Olympia emerged from a black tinted limousine looking stunning in a pale green silk gown and eight-inch Prada pumps. She had been going over her maid of honour speech and couldn't wait to have a dance with the best man, only this time he happened to be her fiancé. She was delighted to be in love again, and this time with a man who loved her for who she was, a man her parents adored.

Samira and Georgiou Callimanopulos, together with their sons, Milo and Stavros, followed their daughter into the castle. They were glad she'd found a good hardworking man. Samira looked ravishing in a diamond-studded lace dress with Chanel open toe heels and a matching purse. Georgiou was wearing a white linen kaftan.

A cavalcade pulled up with the remaining bridesmaids, Tamali, Juliana, Amira, Lydia and Pandora.

Pandora observed the elegantly-dressed guests and dignitaries alighting from their cars. "Damn!" she exclaimed, "I never knew people lived like this in Africa."

Juliana fluttered her lashes. "Yes dear, don't believe the hype!"

"Na wa for oyibo ooo," Ngozi chuckled. "Ignorance de kill them sha-a!"

Zhara and her father arrived in a white Rolls-Royce Phantom. She looked absolutely divine in a white silk gown with an intricate low-cut lace bodice. Her hair was worn in a beehive and adorned with a sapphire, diamond, ruby and pearl tiara. It was a gift from her mother.

Taking his daughter's hand, Kamil whispered in her ear. "You look more beautiful than ever, my princess. I have never felt more proud."

Zhara squeezed his hand. "I love you Daddy."

The maid of honour and the bridesmaids gathered around Zhara. Lydia and Juliana held the 20-foot sheer veil train while the others fussed around her, making sure everything was perfect. Clutching a bouquet of roses, stephanotis and orchids, Zhara stepped forward at the sound of Here comes the Bride and proceeded to the private chapel where Agyeman and his best man, Akatapori, were waiting anxiously.

Surrounded by vermilion and white orchids Kamil walked his daughter up the aisle. Seated in the front row Araba and Maame Akua looked on in awe as a feeling of pleasure seeped through their bodies.

Agyeman's heart skipped a beat when Zhara was presented to him by her father. He hesitated for a moment, spellbound by her beauty. With the top of her head just below his chin, they stood side by side gazing into each other's eyes.

Agyeman's mother and members of the Ashanti royal family watched their Prince repeat the vows.

Among the guests were Agyeman's stepmother, Zhara's housekeeper, members of her household and office staff, and many of their friends and family.

After the ceremony two white doves were released into the air as a symbol of peace and unity. The guests proceeded to the grand hall for a five-course dinner after which music and dancing commenced. It began with the Asafo talking drums. The Royal Ashanti kete drums joined in. Amid the melting pot of people from all corners of the world an atmosphere of laughter, joy and unity prevailed. There was no room for tribalism, racism, sexism or any form of prejudice.

As the sound of Brian McKnight's Love of My Life blasted through the speakers, MC Potosee invited the newlyweds to take their first dance. With arms entwined and passion in their eyes, Zhara and Agyeman slow-danced under the moonlight.

Overwhelmed with emotion, Agyeman pulled his wife into his arms. "First time I looked into your eyes, I saw heaven in your eyes. Everything I did before you wasn't worth my while. It should have been you, you all the time. I'd do anything and everything to please you. You know how much I need you. You're always, always on my mind. You're more than wonderful, more than amazing, the irreplaceable love of my life. You're so incredible, here in these arms tonight. The irreplaceable, love of my life. Always, seems like a reality. Forever, don't seem so far away. All I want to do, all I want to feel, all I want to be is close to you. Every day is my lucky day. All I want to do is love you."

MC Potosee dedicated the next song to the happy couple. It was I Do, by Jahman Levi & Madge. Dancing cheek to cheek, it felt as if the lyrics had been written for them.

The newlyweds cut their four-tiered carrot cake, with passion fruit, buttercream and a cascade of delicate sugar petals. It had been personalised with Zhara and Agyeman's profile. Their initials were entwined in gold petals.

After throwing her bouquet into the crowd, Zhara changed into a white lace summer dress. Agyeman changed from his white tuxedo into a navy Armani suit. A stirring sound of rockets soared into the air. A canopy of sparkling lights dazzled over the ocean. More rockets were fired into the air, exploding into a kaleidoscope of colour.

A glimmering message in red, gold and green read "Congratulations Mr & Mrs Johnson." It was met with a spontaneous applause.

Araba hugged her daughter. "Best wishes, my jewel."

Kamil embraced his daughter. He shook Agyeman's hand firmly. "You must take very good care of her."

Agyeman acknowledges the threat with a smile. "I will not let you down, sir."

Nana Yaa Asantewa hugged her son fondly. Happy tears flooded her eyes. "Son, I've never seen you this happy.' She swallowed. "She brings out the best in you. Be good to her."

He smiled. "I know, maame, I must be a lucky man."

Nana Yaa Asantewa embraced Zhara. "Thank you. I am truly grateful."

Holding hands, the newly-weds thanked their guests and set off on their honeymoon.

CHAPTER FORTY SEVEN

They were picked up from Côte D'Azur airport at 9:45 am and driven to the Fontvieille Harbour in Monaco. The skipper welcomed Zhara and Agyeman aboard the luxury yacht *Azura*. After a tour of the yacht's duplex sun deck, vast main deck with indoor and outdoor entertainment, gym and jacuzzi pool, they were shown to their balcony suite. The room was beautifully decorated with natural palettes of walnut and cream.

After indulging in a spa treatment and massage, Agyeman and Zhara emerged feeling completely refreshed. Beaming with love, they were ushered to the upper deck. The chef greeted them in French. Surrounded by the deepest blue ocean and scenic views they sat down to grilled lobster, kobe beef, French fries and a bottle of Louis Roederer 1990 Cristal.

"Mrs Johnson, please eat up. You haven't touched your drink" Agyeman scolded. He looked temptingly delicious in denim jeans and a white cotton shirt.

"Can I just have the dessert?" she pleaded.

"No my love, eat up and drink. You will need all your energy for our siesta."

"Are we having a siesta?" She asked innocently.

"It's been a long journey, we deserve a little rest before the sightseeing." He gave her a wicked smile.

The aroma of the crème brûlée was enticing. Zhara cracked the golden crust and took a spoonful of the dessert. "Mm, this is absolutely delicious" she said. "Why are you not eating your dessert?"

"Because I plan to have only one dessert and she is sitting in front of me."

A brief smile flickered across Zhara's lips. As soon as she had finished her dessert, he picked her up and carried her to the suite. He lay her on the queen bed and stepped out of his jeans.

She felt incredibly shy, yet unable to take her eye off the finest specimen of man she'd ever seen. His licked his lips as he peeled off the white cotton shirt. Standing before her in his birthday suit - biceps toned, stomach flat, abs ripped, long dark chocolate legs toned and perfectly moulded. Her throbbing heart melted when he gave her his sweet smile and began peeling off her clothes, starting with her wrap dress. She felt funny all over when he kissed her lips. She ran her hands through his short, black neatly-trimmed hair. Her senses were captured by the smell of grapefruit, dry cedar notes and laudanum. She loved his smell and his untouchable confidence.

"I love you, Mrs Johnson," he murmured. He explored her body, strumming her with large skilled fingers. "You are so beautiful, my love. Your skin is soft and smooth... it feels like velvet. You smell so good. You are everything I've ever wanted."

He was killing her very softly with his words. The touch of his lips on her bare skin ignited the muscles in her deepest parts. They tightened deliciously.

"Relax, my love." His breath quickened.

She embraced his masculinity. It was enigmatic, irresistible and impenetrable. Her pulses ignited under his merciless ministrations. Losing her inhibitions, she detonated and cried out as an intensely pleasurable feeling ripped through her body.

He gloried in her heated passion with a gentle plunge. Having waited for a whole year he wanted nothing more than to be buried deep within her soft voluptuous body.

She held on to him, climbing higher and higher, countering his rhythm in perfect symmetry. Lost once more in the void of pleasure, she screamed his name and came apart. Just then he cried out triumphantly and convulsed beside his bride.

Tears rolled down Zhara's cheeks. Her heart sang as she embraced its ruler, delighted she'd saved herself for her true love.

Agyeman smiled contentedly at the speck of blood on the white Egyptian cotton sheets. He had never banked on marrying a virgin. Drawing his bride into his arms he kissed her passionately.

"How was it for you, my princess?"

She rubbed her eyes. "Better than all the romantic books and films put together."

"That good eh?"

"Yes, my prince."

"I love you so much, it frightens me. I never thought I would ever love anyone this much. You make me come alive. I want to be with you forever."

"Me too" she said, overwhelmed by the sincerity in his eyes.

He kissed her lips and smiled salaciously. "I am hungry, my princess."

She sat up. "What would my prince like to eat?"

"You, my princess." He smiled lecherously.

She pouted petulantly. "Didn't you just have your dessert?"

"Yes, but I can never have enough of you."

"You should have warned me that I was marrying a cannibal," she teased.

He smiled his boyish smile. "I never knew I would enjoy you so much. Thank you for making me your first."

CHAPTER FORTY EIGHT

She woke up in his arms. The clock read 3:15 pm. Pulling herself out of his arms, she decided to have a shower.

Agyeman stirred as she bounded into the suite from the bathroom. She had a towel around her waist.

"Can we go shopping? It looks lovely out there."

He sulked. "Do we have to?"

"Yes darling."

Reluctantly he got off the bed and got ready.

They shopped at the Golden Circle, framed by high-end designer shops, before making their way to the Condamine Market. Then, strolling hand in hand along the Promenade des Anglais in Nice, they popped into Hotel Negresco to sample Chef Jean-Denis Rieubland's Michelin star cuisine. The snails in puff pastry with hazelnut oil, egg yolk with white pearls, Carpaccio of Malemort green asparagus and lettuce emulsion starter; fillet of beef cooked with nori seaweed and French Oscietre 'Sturia caviar', puffed potatoes and white port wine bordelaise sauce main; and rum baba flavoured with verbena, strawberry jelly and vanilla mascarpone Chantilly cream was a gastronomic experience.

Later that evening they were driven back to Monaco,

where they watched the world's richest gamblers at the Grand Casino. On the spur of the moment Zhara decided to have a flutter. She played 50 Euros on the slot machine and ended up with 500 Euros. It was getting late so they headed back to the yacht.

Back on the yacht they looked forward to cruising along the French Riviera. They watched the nightlife from the top deck before retiring to the suite. The bed had been beautifully laid with cream silk sheets. Agyeman pulled Zhara into his embrace. She looked intoxicating in a deep red off-the-shoulder long fitted dress. He traced the contours of her hourglass figure and pulled down the dress with expert hands. He kissed her eyes, her nose, her soft succulent lips, her neck, shoulders and her breasts. Caressing the multicoloured beads around her tiny waist, he lowered her onto the bed, parted her hips and sunk into her, dancing rhythmically with every stroke.

As the yacht cruised along the Mediterranean coastline Agyeman propped up on the pillow and watched Zhara sleep. Breathing softly, she seemed serene and childlike. He had to pinch himself to believe that she was all his. It took his breath away.

She opened one eye and wrinkled her face.

"Good morning, my beautiful princess."

She yawned and stretched. "Where are we heading?"

"St Tropez, St Maxine, St Raphael, Cannes, Antibes..."

She nipped into the bathroom, brushed her teeth and stepped into the Jacuzzi. The sweet smell of jasmine and sandalwood filled the air.

Agyeman joined her. Before she could stop him he began bathing her. When he finished he massaged her feet with frankincense oil.

Mirroring his actions, she foamed up the sponge and bathed him. He was amazed at her confidence. Watching her intently, he suppressed a smile when she hesitated between his thighs. Knowing it would take her a while to get used to his body, he helped her out.

"What would you like for breakfast?" Agyeman asked.

"French toast, omelette and a cup of Earl Grey tea" she responded happily. "What about you, your highness?" she teased.

He looked her straight in the eye. "You, if you please, my princess!"

She chuckled. "Now that we've established that you are a cannibal, your wish is my command. Breakfast is served."

He grabbed her from behind, burying his face in her hair as she tried to evade him.

"Your hair smells lovely," he whispered, inhaling her sweetness. "You are my ultimate aphrodisiac, do you know that? The more I have of you, the more I want. I can't have enough of you. And right now I want to make sweet love to you, over and over again."

He tugged at the beads around her waist and devoured her lips. She let out a heartfelt face-splitting, belly-spinning laugh, like a free spirit without a care in the world.

In one swift move he picked her up and carried her onto the bed. He kissed her passionately all over. When he reached her belly button she closed her eyes and surrendered herself to her husband.

Curled up in the arms of the man of her dreams, Zhara was overwhelmed by the intense pleasure seeping through her veins. To love and be loved completely, for better or worse felt like floating above the sun, the moon, the mountains and the rivers and the clouds. She remembered her grandmother's words. Life is full of hidden messages and opportunities. When we listen to what people say without following our instincts we may end up losing the diamond in the stone by simply passing them by. But when we listen to our heart and nothing else, that is when we find our treasure.